PRAISE FOR YEAR'S BEST HARDCORE HORROR

"...glutted with graphic scenes of torture, dismemberment, evisceration, and pornographic sex." (Vol. 2)

—Publishers Weekly

"Not for the faint of heart or weak of stomach, the 19 stories in this new best-of annual anthology feature episodes of graphic gore and violence—including torture, dismemberment, self-mutilation, and home abortion—that are designed to push buttons as well as boundaries—strictly for hardcore horror fans." (Vol. 1)

—Publishers Weekly

YEAR'S BEST HARDCORE HORROR

VOLUME 6: MASQUERADE

EDITORS:

RANDY CHANDLER
CHERYL MULLENAX

RED ROOM PRESS

WWW.REDROOMPRESS.COM

First Red Room Press Trade Paperback Edition
May 2021

Red Room Press is an imprint of Comet Press

ISBN: 978-1-936964-15-4

Visit Red Room Press on the web at:
www.redroompress.com
facebook.com/redroompress
twitter.com/redroombooks

Copyrights Continued on page 291

Red Room Press

WWW.REDROOMPRESS.COM

Diabolically dedicated to all the hardcore and
extreme publishers, editors, and authors.

TABLE OF CONTENTS

In memory of David G. Barnett, consummate
cartographer of extreme horror.

WELCOME TO THE MASQUERADE

INTRODUCTION BY RANDY CHANDLER AND CHERYL MULLENAX

2020 was a reality horror show. And like most obnoxious entertainment reality shows, this one had its own idiosyncratic rules and penalties. Call it The Big Lockdown. We were forced to go to ground, to hide in our holes. Some went underground and never came back. Uncertainty ruled because the rules kept changing. Were we following the science or the mad scientists? Was the light at the end of the tunnel the fiery mouth of hell? We couldn't say for sure, so we ventured out for food, booze and sundries like scavengers in a slow-motion apocalypse, keeping our distance from fellow human beings because you never knew who might be carrying that heavy viral load.

And everywhere we went, we went behind the mask. So, it became obvious: The theme of our offering of extreme horror tales from 2020 had to be Masquerade.

Our masquerading storytellers nevertheless did what they do best. They went deep into the belly of the beast and sent up fictions reflective of these "trying" times. Their stories peel away the masks (or in some cases, the skin) to reveal the inner workings of darkest hearts and minds and deeper fears. Some are designed to shock, to grab you by the metaphorical balls and drag you to unexpected revelations.

Like this year's opener, Ronald Kelly's "The Nipples in Dad's Tool Box." Likewise, in Christine Morgan's "Going Green," which goes to very bizarre extremes and beyond the point of no return.

Rachel Nussbaum's "Whiskey to the Wound" is a splatterpunk romance with a lot of heart and sickly twisted soul. Eric LaRocca's story in the guise of a blog called "/thestrangethingwebecome" is very strange indeed, and uniquely heartbreaking.

Amanda Cecelia Lang's "Hey, Valentine" is a haunting rape/revenge shocker strongly suggesting something like reverse necrophilia. Hailey Piper is back with a literary vengeance with "In Subspace No One Can Hear You Scream," a true masterpiece of psychological horror and brave introspection. As Hailey so deftly shows, there may be a very fine line between a symbolic rebirth and outright possession.

Sean Patrick Hazlett makes a disturbing return to our pages with "The Pogonip Fog," a truly frightening tale of something otherworldly lurking in the fog on the snowy ski slopes. Making her third appearance in a row in our annual, Alicia Hilton outdoes herself in the mind-blowing, genre-busting "Gunfire and Brimstone."

In his riveting cinematic style, Matthew Brockmeyer takes us along on a drug bust with unintended and deeply unnatural consequences. Matthew assures us that "The Happiest Man in the World" is more than just a Lovecraftian abortion clinic story—and that it is loosely based on a true story.

New Zealander Melanie Harding-Shaw's "Synaesthete" presents terrifying glimpses from the perspective of a person whose sensory perceptions are crossed-wired by synesthesia. Rather than tasting colors or smelling sounds, this unfortunate synaesthete can see the invisible monsters devouring unknowing victims.

Patrick C. Harrison III offers a Hemingwayesque horror tale by way of Bret Easton Ellis in "Full Moon Shindig," but as you will see, the end result is pure Harrisonian.

Christine Morgan makes her second appearance in this year's edition with "The Drinking-Horn," a rowdy tale of Viking Ullvik the Bottomless. We don't usually use two stories by the same author in a single year's annual but with tales as good as these, how could we not?

Also hailing from the land of kiwis, Octavia Cade returns with a haunted slice of World War I history in "Otto Hahn Speaks to the Dead," the story of the German chemist who tested and produced poison gas for the German army and of the ghost that renders Otto's gas mask all but useless.

From Melbourne, Australia, Deborah Sheldon's "All The Stars In Her Eyes" was inspired by the ophthalmological condition asteroid hyalosis, in which calcium and lipid deposits in the eye reflect light, creating the appearance of stars in the night sky. As the author describes her story's premise: "An asteroid is going to hit Earth, but Janet isn't worried. Surely, the mysterious father of Janet's three-year-old daughter will return to save his family in time." It's easy to see why Deborah has won multiple awards for her fiction and medical writing.

Matias Travieso-Diaz takes us on a dangerous tour of "The Village," where the protagonist is held prisoner for stumbling upon the closely guarded secret that not all of the villagers are human. Matias understands what it's like to be held prisoner, having migrated to the United States as a young man to escape political persecution by the Castro regime.

Brace yourself because next we're tripping down to the basement to meet some folks who say they're vampires in Wendy N. Wagner's "The Smell of Night in the Basement." These splatterpunk vampires are a far cry from Ann Rice's urbane vamps, and one of them is looking for a new pet.

Then it's on into the deep dystopian world of South Paris 5 after a radioactive meteor hits the planet and mutated rats and various lowlifes are on the prowl. Alessandro Manzetti takes us there on a hallucinogenic excursion to meet "The Saint," who delights in dismembering whores. *Warning: Alessandro's Burroughs-esque* language *may be consciousness-altering.*

And finally, Robert Guffey's "Her Wounded Eyes" sends us off with a gun to the head—but will it end with a bloody bang or a whimper?

So, come on in. It's time for the unmasking to begin.

Randy Chandler & Cheryl Mullenax
May 2021

And many more Destructions played in this ghastly masquerade
—Percy Bysshe Shelley

THE NIPPLES IN DAD'S TOOL BOX

RONALD KELLY

From *The Essential Sick Stuff*
Editor: Ken McKinley
Silver Shamrock Publishing

t all started that morning in late July when Mom asked for a screwdriver from her junk drawer in the kitchen.

"A Phillips head, not a flat head," she emphasized. The hinges on the shower door in the bathroom adjoining her and Dad's bedroom had come loose again. She was holding onto it for dear life, hoping that she wouldn't lose her grip and drop the door into the stall. If it shattered, she would be sweeping and picking glass out the shower for an hour or so.

Cody Dawson nodded. "Right. Phillips head." Then he was heading for the kitchen.

But when the twelve-year-old checked the top drawer next to the sink, all he found was a flat-head screwdriver. "Dang!"

"Hurry up, sweetheart," called Mom from the bathroom. "This thing is heavy!"

Cody figured maybe Dad had one in the garage. His father was a mechanic down at Casey's Exxon, so he had a load of tools, at home and at work. He opened the door on the far side of the utility room and ran across the driveway to the stand-alone two-car garage.

Luckily, it was unlocked. His Dad was funny about things like that. Kept things locked up all the time. He was a little surprised that the side door opened with no trouble at all. It was dark in there and cooler than it was outside. It reeked of oil and grease and freshly mown grass from where Dad gad cut the yard yesterday evening with the riding mower. Cody felt along the wall next to the door and found the light switch.

Even with the double banks of fluorescent lights, the interior of the garage was still shadowy. He rushed over to Dad's big red, twelve-drawer tool chest—the one nearly as tall as he was—and tried each drawer, one by one. All were securely locked. Frustrated, he looked around the garage. He was about to leave when he spotted a rusty toolbox beneath the work bench against the far wall. It was nestled between an old carburetor and a gallon of 50/50 antifreeze.

Cody crouched and pulled the toolbox out into the open. *Funny . . . I've never seen this here before,* he thought to himself. *Maybe because I wasn't looking for it . . . duh!* The long, metal box was once gray, but was now covered with rust spots and smudges of grease. It had a heavy Yale padlock looped through the front latch. "Aw, man!" Frustrated, he yanked on the lock and, surprisingly, it popped open. He slipped it from the clasp and lifted the lid.

A collection of ordinary-enough tools filled the box; a claw hammer, wire and needle-nose pliers, a staple gun, plus loose nails and bolts. The tools weren't the way he expected them to be. Dad always kept his tools clean and well-maintained. These were downright nasty. There was gummy gunk on the head and double claw of the hammer, as well as on the jaws of the pliers; brownish-red stuff, some of it running past the metal and down the rubberized handles. And the toolbox stank to the high heavens! It smelled like there was a dead mouse in there . . . or maybe more than one.

He lifted the handled tray and set it aside. In the lower compartment were more tools. A hacksaw, a utility knife, a Black & Decker cordless drill, and several screwdrivers. As he took the Phillips head that Mom needed, he noticed something else. Something hidden beneath a dirty, blue shop towel.

Curious, Cody lifted the cloth and held the object up to see what it was.

His heart skipped a beat—or maybe two—and he wondered if what he was looking at was actually what it seemed to be.

It was a small Gerber's baby food jar filled with a clear yellow liquid.

Floating in the middle of the fluid were two human nipples.

Startled, he quickly set the jar on the stained concrete of the garage floor. He stared at it for a few seconds, then—being the pre-adolescent boy that he was—he decided to take a second look.

It wasn't a man's nipples. They were too big. He decided they belonged to a woman instead. His best friend, Jimmy Smith, had smuggled a Playboy from an old Army duffle bag of his father's, so Cody knew what a naked woman looked like and how big her tits should be (they were gigantic!). The nipples in the jar were about as big as his thumb and a brownish color, not tiny and pink like his. He shook the jar a little and the plugs of flesh spun, suspended, in their liquid. The backs of them were flat and bloodless, almost blue in color. It looked as though they had been sliced off with a very sharp knife.

Cody suddenly felt a little queasy, the way he did when he ate a jumbo corndog and then rode the Scrambler at the county fair. *But . . . but what are they doing in here?*

They might have had some plausible reason for being in a museum or a doctor's office . . . but in Dad's garage?

Cody looked over at the multi-drawered tool chest on the opposite of the room. The fact that they were all locked suddenly seemed vaguely sinister.

Frightened, he returned the jar to the bottom of the toolbox and covered it with the shop cloth. He took the screwdriver he needed, closed the metal lid, and reinserted the padlock. Then the boy quickly shoved it back beneath the work bench and left the garage.

He ran into the house, hearing Mom yelling for him down the hallway. "Cody! I really need that screwdriver!"

A moment later he reached the bathroom. Mom was in the same position, holding the shower door, looking extremely annoyed. "Where did you go? China?"

"I couldn't find one in the kitchen drawer, so I had to go looking for one." Cody held the Phillips head out to her. Like the other tools, it was covered with that yucky brown gunk. And there was something he hadn't noticed before. There was a long hair stuck to the gummy shaft of the screwdriver. A blonde hair.

Dad's hair was short and black. Mom's was red.

Mom didn't react the way he expected. Her face grew pale and her eyes widened a little. "Where did you get *that*? That's not mine."

"I had to go out to the garage to find one," he said, wondering if he'd done something wrong. "I found one of Dad's."

His mother stared at the screwdriver in his hand and swallowed dryly. "You know how your dad is. How he is when someone messes with his stuff, especially his tools."

Cody's ears reddened. "I'm sorry. I'll put it back."

"No!" Was that alarm he heard in her voice? "No. Just set it on the counter there and go find mine. It could've gotten shoved into the back of the drawer."

"Okay." Feeling kind of weird, the twelve-year-old headed back to the kitchen. He rummaged around in the junk drawer and there it was, laying in the very back, beneath a couple of old refrigerator magnets and pack of AA batteries.

When he returned to the bathroom, Mom wasn't in the same place. The shower door was leaning up against the bathroom wall and she was standing in the middle of the floor with her back turned toward the door. As though she had left the bathroom and returned only a second ago.

"Here you go, Mom," he said. "Right where you said."

She smiled and took it. "Thanks."

He looked over at the sink. The Phillips head from the garage toolbox was gone.

Cody helped his mother place the shower door back into position and she tightened the screws that held it in place. He was afraid she would fuss at him for messing around with his father's stuff. But she said nothing else about it.

"Mom?"

She turned and regarded him. "Yeah, hon?"

He almost mentioned the jar but decided not to. Not yet. "Oh . . . nothing."

"Cody, I got some of those popsicles you like at the grocery store," she told him. "Those big blueberry ones. We called them "Blue-Boys" when I was growing up . . ."

The boy rolled his eyes. "And you waited all day for the ice cream truck, and they were only fifty cents."

Mom shook her head and laughed. "Alright, sass-pot!" Her face was pretty, for someone in her mid-thirties he supposed. But it was still paler than usual. "Why don't you get yourself one? Or get two and take one over to Jimmy's. I talked to his mother a while ago and their back from his dentist appointment."

"Okay, Mom. Thanks."

Cody left the bathroom and his mom and dad's bedroom. He stopped by the fridge and slid two "Blue-Boys" from the box, then left the house, heralding his exit with the slapping of the screen door.

Taking Jimmy a popsicle was one reason for going next door. But there was another reason, too. One that wasn't nearly as innocent and fun.

One that almost made him feel sick to his stomach.

They were sitting in the floor of Jimmy's room, finishing up their popsicles, when Cody finally asked him.

"Uh . . . can I take a look at the Collection?"

Jimmy looked surprised, but pleased. "Since when are you interested in my Collection? I thought you said it was Super Sick with two capital S's."

"There's something I want to look up, that's all."

"Which one? I have five volumes, you know."

"F through I".

Jimmy nodded and went to a bookcase full of comic books, Star Wars figures, and some odd things, like a racoon skull and a rubber severed hand he had ordered online. He stretched on his toes and took down one of the black binders that sat in a place of honor between a bloody Jason hockey mask and a Freddy clawed glove he had made out of one his dad's old Wells Lamont work gloves and set of steak knives he'd bought at Mrs. Tucker's last yard sale a few houses down.

"There you go," he said, pitching it onto his bed. "What are you interested in."

Cody didn't answer at first. His best friend had a weird hobby. He devoured and documented anything that had to do with crime, murder, or serial killers. His infamous Collection consisted of five 3-inch binders with page upon page of newspaper and magazine clippings, as well as articles and Wikipedia pages he had printed off the internet. Cody had always overlooked his pal's gruesome fascination, but most of their classmates—and even some of the teachers—regarded him as a social leper, mostly because they didn't want to hear his constant theories and forensic tidbits about Jeffery Dahmer, Richard Ramirez, or the Son of Sam.

"I'm looking for something . . . recent." Cody flipped through the binder. Albert Fish, Luis Garavito, Donald Henry Gaskins. He found what he was looking for between Ed Gein and H.H. Holmes.

Jimmy looked over his shoulder. "Hmmm . . . the Handyman Killer. Quiet an enigma. He hasn't eluded the police as long as Dennis Rader did, but he has been active for fifteen years and, so far, no one has a clue who he is."

Cody looked at seventeen youthful faces: eight boys and nine girls. All between the ages of fourteen and twenty-one. All tortured for long periods of time and horribly mutilated by the Handyman's grisly expertise with common household tools. Most were missing for at least two or three months before their disfigured and dismembered bodies were discovered in a variety of dumping sites; country road ditches, abandoned buildings, or trash dumpsters.

Staring at the faces of the young women, Cody realized that all except one had blond hair.

"The police think that maybe he's a construction worker," Jimmy theorized. "Or a utility worker or mechanic. Whatever he is, he sure seems to know the tools of his trade."

Tools. Cody thought about the garage a few yards from Jimmy's bedroom window. Of the gummy, brown refuse on the contents of the toolbox and that godawful stench of decay.

And the little jar containing human parts in the place of strained peas.

A couple of days passed. During that time, Cody watched his dad very closely.

His father, Harold Dawson, had always been a quiet, somber kind of guy. Cody could count on the fingers of one hand how many times his dad had laughed out loud or cracked a joke. Mostly he kept to himself; mowing and trimming the lawn, sitting in the living room watching TV—mostly the news—, and puttering around the garage with one project or another. Sometimes at night he would go down to the VFW for a beer or two, or bowl with his league at Ten Pin Alleys.

Often, Cody's mom would come home from a church function or one of the crafting classes she taught at the community center and have no earthly idea where her husband was or what he was up to. He usually arrived several hours later; dark, moody and uncommunicative, giving no explanation of his whereabouts.

Out of curiosity, the boy snuck into his parents' bedroom and got down the photo albums they kept on the top shelf of the closet. He was disturbed to find that the only photographs that graced the pages were of their life beginning with Cody's birth. Before that . . . nothing. No childhood school pictures, no wedding photos, no vacation snapshots of Deborah and Harold Dawson before their son had come along. It was as though what had been before hadn't mattered. He looked for other things too.

Report cards, high school diplomas, a marriage license, his father's military discharge papers. They were nowhere to be found . . . if they existed at all.

Why would his mother allow an expungement of their life before their only child's birth . . . unless there was control and secrecy involved?

Cody remembered how stricken his mother's face had been when she saw that screwdriver. How the blood had drained from her features and how the tool had been strangely absent when he had returned from his second visit to the junk drawer.

Maybe she knows something, he couldn't help but think. *Maybe she knows exactly who he is . . . and what he does when he's away from home.*

It was the Wednesday before school started when Cody Dawson discovered who the Handyman really was.

They were having a women's luncheon at the Baptist church and his mother

was one of the hostesses. Cody was alone. Jimmy had gone on a summer-end daytrip to Chattanooga, so Cody hung around the house, watching TV and indulging in a lunch of Chef Boyardee spaghetti and meatballs.

He was stretched out on the living room couch when his father unexpectedly walked through the front door.

The fine hairs on the back of the twelve-year-old's neck stood up as Harold Dawson stepped inside the house and shut the door behind him. "Hi, Dad," Cody said, trying to sound like he didn't care one way or another. He lay perfectly still and didn't move a muscle.

"Is your mom still at the church?" he asked with a peculiar look on his face.

Cody nodded. "Yep. At that luncheon thing. She shouldn't be

back until after two." He looked past his father at the grandfather clock in the hallway. Its ornate hands read 12:14. "You know, they have to wash dishes and clean up."

Dad said nothing, just nodded. Then he walked into the kitchen, took a frozen dinner from the freezer, and nuked it in the microwave.

Five minutes later, he left the way he came, carrying the hot dinner—Salisbury steak and mashed potatoes from the smell of it—in an oven mitt his Granny Dawson had knitted for a Christmas gift a couple of years ago. He also held can of Diet Coke in the other hand. "See you later, sport," the man called, then shut the door behind him.

Cody hopped up from the couch and went to the window. He watched as his father set the dinner and drink on the seat of his pickup truck and climbed in. The vehicle backed into the street and headed east . . . in the opposite direction of the gas station where Dad worked.

The boy stood in indecision for a long moment. Part of him wanted to forget his father's uncharacteristic visit and get back to his TV watching. But the other part . . . the part that had seemingly awakened after that gruesome discovery in the tool-box—had to know where he was going.

Cody left the house. His bike was parked against the side wall of the garage. He disengaged the kick stop and was about to follow his father's truck, when he got the urge to peek through the panes of the garage window. It was shadowy inside, but he could see the work bench on the other side. The carburetor and antifreeze jug were there, but the toolbox was gone.

The boy hit the road, pedaling as fast as he could manage. Once he reached the main road, he spotted his dad's white Chevy heading across town. Luckily, he was driving the speed limit, which was thirty-five, so Cody had a good chance of at least keeping the truck in sight.

Ten minutes later he saw his father turn off the road and into the Safe-T-Store Storage Units & U-Haul Rental. He knew the place well. His sixth-grade teacher from last year, Mrs. Baker, managed the place during the summer months.

There was no security gate like some storage facilities had, so Cody didn't have any trouble following his dad. He pedaled slowly, trying to keep out of sight, until the white pickup braked to a stop outside of a storage unit at the very back of the lot. Cody parked his bike and peered around the far corner. His father took a keyring from his pants pocket and unlocked the built-in lock on one of the unit doors. Then he rolled the door upward, stepped inside with the dinner and drink, and rolled it back down again.

Quickly, Cody ran along the long building of units, hoping . . . praying . . . that the man didn't leave before he got there. He finally stood at the unit door. The number painted on the segmented steel read 208.

Cody heard noises on the other side but couldn't quite make them out. Despite the chance of discovery, he knew he had to know what was taking place inside. Quietly, he pressed one ear firmly against the door.

He heard his father, talking low and calmly. He also heard another sound; a voice muffled by some obstruction. It didn't belong to a man, but a woman. Harold Dawson continued, soothingly. Then there was a harsh sound . . . like someone pulling away a strip of tape. A sharp gasp of pain followed. The woman's voice suddenly grew clearer. She didn't speak. It was worse than that. Although he couldn't quite make it out, he believed that she was crying and pleading for mercy.

Cody heard a vehicle and pulled his ear away for a moment. An SUV with a mattress and box springs bungeed to the roof passed the gap between two rows of units and disappeared. He listened again. Things had quieted down. The girl still cried but it was more subdued. Cody heard a fizzy pop . . . the can of soda being opened.

The boy knew it was time to go when he heard the girl whimper, followed by the sound of tape being pulled from the roll. Cody ran down the long row of units and reached the end just as he heard the door roll up with a clatter. He ducked around the cinderblock wall and peered back around the corner. His father stepped out, lowered the door, and locked it. He walked to a trash can nearby, intending to dump the soda can and plastic dinner plate. Deciding differently, he tossed the trash onto the seat of the pickup, then climbed in himself. The girl's DNA was probably on the mouth of the Coke can and the frozen dinner tray . . . . saliva or snot . . . or maybe even her blood.

He watched as the truck left. It circled around several rows of units and exited the way it came. Cody watched until his dad was out of sight, heading in the direction of the Exxon station. He waited five minutes. It seemed like forever. Then he rode his bike to the front office, took a deep breath to calm himself, and walked inside.

Mrs. Baker seemed pleased to see him. "Well, hi there, Cody. Have you enjoyed your summer vacation?"

Cody smiled. "Yes, ma'am."

"Are you ready for school to start?"

Cody frowned. "No, ma'am!"

The teacher laughed. "To tell the truth, me neither." She set down the Amish romance paperback she had been reading. "What are doing out here, halfway across town?"

"My Dad sent me to fetch something in his unit, but I forgot the key," he told her, as straight-faced as he could manage. "You don't have a spare one I could borrow for a minute, do you?"

Mrs. Baker turned toward a peg board with several dozen keys hanging there. "Sure. What number was it again?"

Cody's heart pounded so hard that he was afraid the woman might hear it. "It's 208."

She found the key and handed it to him. "There you go. Just

bring it back when you're finished."

"Yes, ma'am." Cody left the office and ducked out of sight. He stood behind the office, doubled over, with his hands on his knees, breathing deeply. Then he straightened up and looked toward the end unit on Row 2.

Oh Lord ... please ... I don't want to go down there.

But he knew that he had to.

He jumped on his ten-speed and pedaled past the long line of doors. It was the longest bicycle ride he had ever taken in his life. When he got there, he stood in front of the door of 208 for what seemed an eternity. Then he inserted the key into the lock and heaved the door upward on its tracks.

The brilliant summer sun flooded into the eight by twelve chamber, revealing all that was there.

Chamber was the correct word. If you put the word "torture" in front of it.

A number of pullies had been anchored into the ceiling of the storage unit and, from them, dangled heavy chains. Some sported shackles, while others were tipped with grappling or meat hooks. A heavy wooden work bench, completely stained in congealed blood, held a heavy-duty vice on one corner. A number of tools were scattered cross the countertop, including the old toolbox Cody had discovered several days ago. Along the opposite wall were larger tools; a sledgehammer, a rotary saw, and a chainsaw. All were stained with blood and bits of flesh and hair.

A single bank of fluorescent lights—identical to the ones in Dad's garage—was connected to a small generator. It was apparent that the noisy work was done in the dead of night, hours after the Safe-T-Store had closed and there was no one around to hear what was taking place in Unit 208.

A whimper drew his attention to the back wall. What he saw there scared the living shit out of him.

It was a teenage girl, maybe sixteen years old. She was blond and had probably been pretty at one time . . . maybe even beautiful. But that was all gone now. The Handyman had done his work well and it showed.

With the sun glaring through the open doorway, Cody expected the girl's eyes to be tightly clenched. But that was impossible. Someone had cut away her eyelids. Her baby blue eyes were horribly wide and bloodshot. She was covered in blood. Her McDonald's uniform was tattered, and her exposed breasts and slender arms were covered with patterns cut into her flesh; a pentagram, random numbers and letters, a crude drawing of a skull with a wreath of daisies around its crown, several crisscross games of tic-tack-toe here and there. There were other scars, too. Cigarette burns and puncture wounds from something long and blunt. Maybe a Phillips head screwdriver.

She couldn't talk because her lower face was sealed shut by a broad strip of silver duct tape. The naked bones of her cheeks and lower jaw told him that—if he'd had the nerve to remove the gag—there wouldn't have been any lips, bottom or top, there at all.

The girl wasn't tied up with ropes or anything, which puzzled the boy at first. Then he saw what confined her. Half-shackles of heavy iron secured her narrow wrists to the concrete floor, fastened there with long masonry bolts. Only three of her ten fingers remained intact.

Abruptly, Cody Dawson turned and puked up his Chef Boyardee onto the warm pavement that stretched between the storage units. He gagged and heaved until nothing more remained in his stomach, then he thought of the girl—no, the *thing*—imprisoned inside and he retched again until his throat was raw and his nose began to bleed.

He jumped on his bike and made it back to the office in a matter of seconds. He burst through the door and stood there for a long moment, unable to speak. Mrs. Baker stared at him like he was a stranger . . . stared at his pale and terrified face . . . at the fresh puke that wreathed his mouth and speckled the front of his t-shirt.

"Cody . . . what . . . what's wrong?"

"Call . . . call the police," he stammered, trying hard not to cry. "Call 9-1-1. Something . . . *terrible* . . . has happened at Unit 208."

Alarm crossed Mrs. Baker's face and she took a step toward the end of the counter. Cody jumped in front of her, blocking her way. "Don't go down there, Mrs. Baker," he begged. "Please! If you do, you'll have nightmares for the rest of your life. Believe me . . . I'm not kidding."

The woman could tell that the boy was telling the truth. "What's happened?"

"The Handyman," was all that he could manage to say.

"Oh, dear Lord," she breathed.

As Mrs. Baker began to dial, Cody turned and ran out the door. He heard her call out to him, urging him to stay put, but he ignored her. He jumped on his bike and pedaled into the street, heading back across town.

"Mom!" Cody yelled as he burst through the utility room door. "Mom . . . where are you?"

He knew she was home. Her car was parked in the driveway. As he ran through the kitchen and started down the hallway, he heard the shower in the bathroom that adjoined his parents' bedroom. The sound of running water didn't surprise him. His mother usually took a shower after a particularly active day.

He stepped into the bedroom and stood there, trembling. "Mom?"

"Cody?" she called. "What is it, hon?"

"Mom . . . I . . ." The boy's heart pounded harder than he could ever remember. *How am I going to tell her?* He took a deep breath, held it, let it out. "Something . . . something *horrible* has happened!"

The water suddenly stopped. "What, Cody? What happened?"

He felt dizzy, as though he was about to faint. "It's . . . it's Dad."

Cody heard the shower door open. A moment later, his mother stepped into the bedroom. She was dripping wet, holding a thick terrycloth towel in front of her body. It barely covered her from collarbone to the tops of her thighs.

She stared at him, alarmed. "What . . . what about your dad?"

He didn't want to tell her . . . more than *anything*, he didn't want to tell her. But he did.

"Dad . . ." Cody gasped, "He's done something awful! There's a storage unit across town and . . . and . . ."

The twelve-year-old stopped talking. His mother's face had turned as white as flour. Her arms slowly dropped to her sides and the towel fell away, pooling around her feet. She stood there completely naked in front of him.

Her plump breasts stared blindly at him.

For they had no nipples.

Suddenly, he knew. He began to cry. "Oh, Mom . . . why did he . . . why did he do that to you?"

A smile crossed Debbie Dawson's pretty face. It was the smile he had known all his life. It was Mom's smile. But her eyes . . . her eyes were dead. They stared at him like two smooth, black stones. No love . . . no affection . . . no concern. No feeling at all.

"I wish you hadn't found out until you were older," she said. Then she turned and walked to her cherrywood dresser. Opened a side drawer. Took out a long wood-handled file . . . one that had been meticulously ground down to a wickedly sharp point. The diagonal lines of the flat blade were tacky with dried blood and tiny slivers of splintered bone.

Then she started walking toward him.

Cody stumbled backward, more confused than he had ever

been in his young life. Before he reached the bedroom door, he bumped into something. Or someone.

He looked up and saw his dad standing over him . . . holding a 9mm pistol at arm's length.

The muzzle of the gun wasn't directed at him, however.

"Stop, Debbie," said Harold Dawson in a flat, emotionless voice. "Please . . . sweetheart . . . just stop."

Mom . . . Debbie . . . wouldn't listen. Her smile broadened, while her eyes grew darker and deader. She raised the file and kept coming.

"We agreed," he said. "A long time ago. Not the boy. Anyone but the boy."

Debbie Dawson made a sound, down deep in her throat. A giggle . . . a sob . . . Cody couldn't tell for sure. Her pace quickened. There was eight feet of space between them now. Seven . . . six . . .

An explosion like cannon fire went off in Cody's ears. An ugly red hole appeared between his mother's breasts. She staggered back a few steps and looked down at the bullet wound. She raised her free hand and probed the hole in her flesh . . . stuck her finger inside. Withdrew it and stared at the blood on her fingertip, then raised it to her lips.

Dad fired again. The second round struck her squarely in the forehead. The family photos on the wall behind her—tastefully framed and proudly displayed—were suddenly speckled with blood and pulpy bits of brain.

Cody watched as his mother fell backward and landed heavily upon the carpet. She twitched once . . . twice . . . then grew motionless. That silly smile was still—and forever—on her face.

Frightened, Cody fled from his father. He crouched at the base of the chest of drawers a few feet away and cowered. "Please . . . please, Dad. Don't."

His father stared at him for a long moment. He lowered his gun and tossed it across the room. It bounced once and landed in the threshold of the bathroom doorway.

"I'm not going to shoot you, son," he said. He stepped over his wife's dead body and sat down heavily on the end of the big king-size bed he had shared with her for fourteen years.

Cody stared at him. He wanted to cut and run . . . downstairs, out of the house, into the street. But he remained where he was. "Why . . . why did you do that to her? To Mom? Why did you cut off her . . . her . . . ?"

Harold Dawson raised his head and regarded his son. His eyes were full of pain. "Cody . . . I didn't do that." He stared at his wife. "She did . . . before we were married."

"But . . . but I found them . . . in your toolbox."

"Son, that toolbox wasn't mine. It was *hers*."

The boy didn't think he could feel any sicker than he had at the storage unit across town, but he did now. "So, you're not the . . ." He faltered to digest what he now knew. "That girl . . . clamped to the floor . . ."

Dad nodded. "It was her. Her all along."

"All of them?"

"All of them . . . and then some."

Cody straightened up but didn't move toward his father. He simply stood where he was. "But you knew. Knew that she was . . ."

"The Handyman?" His father's voice was flat, toneless. "From the very beginning."

"But . . . *why?*"

"You're too young to understand, Cody," he told him. "How a man can love a woman so much that he'd put up with and allow anything. Even embrace a very real and damning piece of Hell on Earth . . . just to be close to her."

They could hear sirens in the distance.

"They'll be here soon and you won't see me again for a while. Could be for the last time. Your aunt and uncle in Virginia will take good care of you."

Debbie jerked and sighed deeply.

"She's alive!" Cody moaned.

"No," his father assured. "It's just her body getting comfort-able with death . . . her systems shutting down for good. I've seen it happen before."

Cody knew that he had. Probably more times than he wanted to admit.

"They'll put me away for being an accessory. Not for partici-pating . . . I was never there when she did it. Just showed up to show a little kindness before and to clean up afterward. They'll probably want to pin it on me at first, but your mom's diaries will set things straight. She had a lot of them. From the early days . . . when she was in high school . . . until now. I never read them. She encouraged it . . . but I never could bring myself to."

Outside, the sirens grew shrill and loud. Soon the flashing of blue lights reflected through the bedroom windows and colored the walls.

"I'm sorry, son. Sorry for this whole ugly mess. Always re-member . . . I love you." He stretched out his arms, but they remained empty.

Cody wanted to return the sentiment, but it simply wasn't in him.

"Get in that closet there and stay put," his father instructed. "I don't want you out here . . . in case somebody comes looking for the Handyman and loses it."

The boy nodded and stepped into the closet. Tears blurred his last glimpse of Harold Dawson before the door closed. Through the distortion he thought he saw his dad smile for the first time in a very long time.

Standing in the darkness, hearing the drumming of feet in the hallway and excited voices, Cody wondered how a boy's carefree life could be flipped upside down and turned inside out in a matter of days.

All because of a baby food jar in an old, worn-out toolbox.

A week following his twenty-second birthday, Cody Dawson accompanied his new bride, Cynthia, to Washington D.C.

It was their honeymoon and neither one had ever been to the nation's capital before. Cody had just graduated from college and was starting a new sales position with a pharmaceutical company in Richmond. Cindy was starting a nurse internship at a hospital, while still going to school part-time. She had hopes of becoming a nurse practitioner in a year or two.

They saw all the sights. The Capitol Building, the monuments, the memorials. They even took a tour of the White House. Then, while making the rounds at the Smithsonian museums, Cody saw the sign and froze in his tracks.

"Come on," urged Cindy. "Let's grab a bite to eat and then head over to the National Gallery. There's some paintings I've always wanted to see."

But Cody didn't move. He just looked at the banner that hung in front of the Museum of American History. The banner that boasted several infamous faces . . . and one familiar one.

"You're going in, aren't you?"

"Yes."

She gripped his hand firmly, lovingly. "Do you want me to come?"

Her husband smiled and kissed her on the forehead. "I need to do this alone."

Cindy nodded. "I understand."

After a moment's hesitation, he climbed the steps and went inside. Ten years had placed a comfortable distance between this afternoon and that awful life-altering one but stepping into the museum's American Crime and Punishment exhibit closed that gap very quickly, almost jarringly so.

He passed the first few exhibits by without interest. The Old West . . . Billy the Kid, Jesse James, John Wesley Hardin. The Gangster and Bank Robbery Era . . . Al Capone, Dillinger, Bonnie and Clyde.

It was when he got to Mass Murderers and Serial Killers that he walked slowly and took his time.

The really infamous ones were first. Charles Whitman's Texas Tower rifle. John Wayne Gacy's clown costumes and prison paintings. Ted Bundy's little tan Volkswagen Beetle.

Then he turned a corner in the maze of partitions, and he was there.

Several people were standing around a glass display case. Cody stepped up as a couple of them moved on. He stared at the rusty, beaten and battered toolbox that sat on display. It's lid was folded back and its contents were visible, for all to see. The hammer, the hacksaw, the pliers, both screwdrivers . . . Phillips head and flat head. The tools looked too clean. They had obviously been cleaned of their grisly reddish-brown patina. But you could still see traces of what had been there . . . if you knew where to look.

He stared at the toolbox for a while, then lifted his gaze to a small shelf mounted on the wall above the case. It held a glass box with a single object inside.

Cody stared at the baby food jar with the two plugs of flesh floating inside, obscenely fascinating and perfectly preserved.

A small placard above the case gave insight to one of the most disturbing items in the history of American crime.

The Nipples of Deborah Ann Dawson

After years of torture and sexual abuse by male family members, Deborah Dawson severed her nipples in an act of self-mutilation on the night of her sixteenth birthday.

It was the beginning of a disturbing double-life that spanned nearly twenty years; housewife and mother by day, cold-blooded serial killer by night. Known as the Handyman Killer for her proficiency with common tools, Dawson was responsible for the torture and murders of 26 known victims . . . 15 women and 11 men, all between the ages of 14 and 21. Her crimes were aided and concealed by her husband, Harold.

"She sure was a sick bitch, wasn't she?" said a young man standing beside him, shaking his head with disgust.

Cody studied the large poster of the Handyman posted next to the exhibit. A fresh-faced, red-haired woman in her early thirties, wearing a yellow dress and matching heels, posing for a quick photo in front of the church she had attended most of her life. Cody stared into that face and remembered. The trips to Florida and building sandcastles together on the beach. The scent of chocolate chip cookies fresh from the oven and biscuits and bacon for breakfast. A cold compress and her motherly concern during nights of fever and sickness. A gentle kiss goodnight on Christmas Eve before Santa put the presents under the tree.

Cody turned to the boy and nodded. "Yes," he said softly, "she sure was."

But she was Mom.

AUTHOR'S STORY NOTE

"The Nipples in Dad's Tool Box" has sort of a strange origin. About ten years ago, I was brainstorming short story ideas for various magazines and anthologies, and a premise came to me.

What if a boy was rummaging around in his father's tool box and found a baby food jar containing two severed human nipples? I jotted the idea down on a slip of paper, but that was as far as it went. I had no idea where the story would proceed from there or how it would end. So, I stuck the slip of paper in a mason jar I keep for wayward plots and story ideas, then forgot about it and moved on to something else. Years later, when I was looking for new story ideas for *The Essential Sick Stuff,* I dumped the contents of that jar out on my desk and sorted through it. When I saw "A boy finds a baby food jar of human nipples in his dad's tool box", the proverbial light bulb came on. I knew exactly what I wanted to do with it now; the plot, the characters, the elusive serial killer, The Handyman. So, I sat down and wrote the whole thing in two hours. Funny how a germ of an idea can ferment into something fully evolved by simply sitting on a shelf for a good long while.

GOING GREEN

CHRISTINE MORGAN

From *Viscreal: Collected Flesh*
Death Head's Press

Jumbled memories, voices, sensations. Swirling in a murky soup.

A swamp-soup. Primordial.

"Drink this." The comforting one, the balm one. Aloe.

"Ucch . . . tastes like dirt."

"Well, there's a reason for that." The other, brisk and brusque, businesslike. Nettle.

Mud smoothie. Thick and thin at the same time. Liquid. Tepid. Gritty.

Thoughts and recollections out of order, random clusters of connected pieces from a partially assembled jigsaw . . . some fitting together, some not.

"Last chance to change your mind. Once we begin, there's no turning back."

"I know. I've signed everything. I'm sure."

Damp loam. Moist and spongy. Packed in soft peat, a dense pressure engulfing, enfolding, absorbing, embracing.

"Try to relax. You'll feel a little sting—"

"Ow!"

Searing freezing metal lance, stabbed, impaling pain. Thigh deep. Bone deep. Femoral. Arterial. Pulsing, pumping throb.

"Just hold still; you're doing great. Now the other side."

"*Ow!*"

"There we go."

Slow-coursing, sluggish eddies. Silty delta flows. Spreading. Seeping. Pervasive.

"—mask to help regulate your breathing; calm and even—"

Out with the old. In with the new.

Heat-lamps, a bank of heat-lamps, basking warm and wonderful. Heat-lamps and cool mists, a misting *pssshting* spritz.

". . . arms so heavy . . ."

"That's to be expected; you're taking on extra minerals and nutrients."

Tingling all over, softening, loosening, pores enlarging. Distant talking: Aloe and Nettle.

"—test plot first? Whole body seems extreme."

"They get what they want."

The heaviness. Good, rich, dark earth.

"You mean, they get what they pay for."

"Same difference."

Remembering: the shower, the last hot shower with scrubbing cleansing depilatory suds and exfoliating abrasives, hair and sweat and chemicals sluicing away, rinsing, gurgling down the drain.

Naked skin smooth and tender, free of dead cells, calluses, scars. Air-dried and clean, so very clean. Ready. Refreshed. Cleaner and more naked than ever before, even since birth. Pure.

"Will it hurt?" Earlier, earlier, at the start.

"You may experience some brief periods of discomfort at various stages in the process. Some clients have reported mild itching, some say it tickles."

The hugging fit of the mask, stubby prongs up nostrils, wider mouth-tube, snug seal around nose and cheeks and chin.

The hiss of gases. The tinned, metallic tinge.

"How're nitrogen levels looking?"

"Holding steady."

"Oxygen?"

"Eighteen percent."

"Adjust the mix, take it down to fifteen."

"Oxy to fifteen, CO_2 increasing to five."

The glass-walled chamber, hothouse-humid. Crossing it, naked, so naked, hairless and smooth, steamed, open, vulnerable. Climbing into the shallow tank, the bed of loamy soil, slowly sinking in.

Aloe again. "We're going to remove the needles. Slight pinch—"

". . . ow . . ."

A dull warmth, melty, malleable, suffusing diffusion. That

inner heaviness, conversion, mineral-laden. Zinc, potassium, phosphorus, magnesium. Iron and calcium leeched from blood, from bone, from marrow.

Softening. Loosening.

"Still with us?"

". . . mm-hmm . . ." Muffled.

A clammy smearing slather. Filled with tiny hard lumps. Nibs. Pips. Like wet clay and kindergarten glue and raspberry jam congealed together. Simultaneously runny and caking, a squelchy adherence. Coating, clinging.

Oozing sap. Watery gruel. Poppyseeds in honey. Tapioca. Microbead dermascrub. Caviar in aspic.

"CO_2 at twenty. Oxy at two, nitrogen still good."

Some clients have reported mild itching, some say it tickles.

Itching? Tickles?

Creeping. Prickling. Myriad minute *tippy-tap pitter-patter*, almost fizz and sizzle, carbonation, champagne bubbles, *piff piff piff pop pop pop*. Scurrying millipede filaments. Seeking. Crawling. Monofiber threadfine tendrils. Working and worming, burrowing.

Burning but not burning, the icy zing of mint.

A hundred, then a thousand, then a million poking penetrations.

Persistent. Tenacious. Expanding and extending, weaving network webs.

Itching? Try *maddening*!

Tickles? Try *tortures*!

Aloe, soothing balm voice. "Relax . . . relax . . . you're doing fine . . . don't fight it, don't struggle."

Nettle, prickly. "This *is* what you wanted, what you paid for, why you're here."

* * *

The guy sitting across from Zeaa wore a vintage-looking tee

with *It's not a bald spot, it's a solar panel for a sex machine!* printed on the front. His hairline was accordingly receded, but the glossy silver-black ceramoglass plates fused to his scalp really lent the message its credence.

She wondered if the rest of the sentiment was as literal. Hey, why not? People powered all sorts of implants and gadgets that way, including far less personal devices than bonerators or internal bluepill dispensers.

Not, of course, that she was about to ask. He might answer. Might offer to demonstrate just how well his solar-powered sex machine worked, wink-wink, leer-leer.

Better not to say anything. Better to just hope he hadn't noticed her noticing his shirt. The last thing she needed was another awkward 'rail conversation, let alone another skeevy hitting-on.

When Mom had been Zeaa's age, it was strange men plucking earbuds right out of your head. For Grandma, it had been books pushed down. Zeaa herself gave up on immersives when she was fourteen, after someone hacked her holoset to make sure she knew she had nice tits.

Several of her acquaintances swore by Bitch Shields and other basic creep-shaming standbys . . . DixDox, subdermal neon dye packets, harassment-sensitive bio-klaxons, Smart Boobs auto-linked to upload offenders' pics to Oglr . . . but none of those were exactly cheap. Zeaa had been saving up a long time to make her own upgrade dream come true. She wanted something more important, more meaningful.

Today. Today would be the day.

After weeks of consultations, comparison shopping, trying to find a place that would do what she wanted, without all the legal and medical and psychological prelims . . . finally, finally, today. Today, it would happen.

Her new life. Her transformation. Her way, however small, to make a difference. To give back. To make a statement, a commitment. To do something that really mattered.

Everyone at Earthstock would be *so* impressed, too! When Jolth saw her, when Niv and Aymlin realized what she'd done, how far she'd gone . . .

. . . and Brangelina, Brangelina would just about *choke* . . . take that!

Not that she was doing this for those reasons, no, of course not. She was doing it for the planet.

Was there anything more selfless and noble and eco-friendly?

"Hey, a smile!"

Zeaa blinked, realizing first that she had indeed been smiling, and secondly that it was Mr. Solar Panel across from her who'd spoken. Seeing he had her attention, he leaned forward with a grin.

"Yeah, that's lots better," he said. "Pretty bit like you should always be smiling."

Though nobody else overtly glanced from their devices or heads-up holos, a subtle shift took place in the 'rail car as it hummed along. Two manspread dudebros, inked with color-changing tats, swelled their muscle-jacked postures. A well-groomed woman with a matron/warden vibe thumbed her screen to DixDox, a perv registry. Some androgyteens near the front, who had been chattering and laughing and psi-banding music, drew together in a protective phalanx.

Zeaa's smile, which hadn't been for his or anyone else's benefit in the first place, faded. She looked down, fussing with her bag on her lap. All natural fibers, indigenously farmed hemp and corn-cotton, intricately woven by rustic artisans into native designs . . .

"Didn't you hear me?" Mr. Solar Panel asked, his tone suggesting he knew full well she had.

Today. Her new life. Transformation. Statement, commitment. For the planet. Make a difference.

If she could go through with what she was about to have done, she should be able to handle some random 'railcar creep.

"How about," Zeaa suggested, raising her head to meet his gaze with her ice-coldest stare, "we just skip ahead to the part where you call me a bitch and stomp off?"

His mouth dropped open. "Wha . . .?"

Had she really said that? Out loud? To his face? If anything, Zeaa herself was more surprised than he was. For a moment, she thought he would push it, launch into the same old song and dance they all knew so well—only being friendly, can't take a compliment, oh so we're not even allowed to talk to women now, stuck-up, not that hot anyway.

But, miracle of miracles, he didn't. Mr. Solar Panel slouched in his seat, turning his attention to the window and the blurred scenery rushing by. Another subtle mood-shift, this one toward smug amusement, took place. Matron/Warden muttered something under her breath about what a shame it was they'd repealed the Purge.

Zeaa winced a little. Not cool, too soon. Cruel casual micro-aggression. Even those who weren't CisHetWhiMa themselves might have lost loved ones.

Was it any wonder she wanted to turn her life around, go back to nature? Wasn't that what Earthstock was really all about? Beyond music festivals and craft fairs, home-brews and home-grows, freecycling swap meets . . . beyond herbal remedies, spiritual-centric yoga . . . organic ethical veganism? About really making a difference, not mere idealism, token efforts, and casual lip-service? Or, worse, lofty self-congratulation and hypocrisy?

Oh, she knew *soooooo* many people who did that, had done too much of it herself. Humble-bragging how she didn't even own a car, while borrowing her mom's to drive to eco-protests, park cleanups, and tree-plantings . . . insisting on locally-sourced produce but hooked on synth-chem energy drinks . . .

Well, no more. Not after today.

Today, she would take sustainability and carbon-neutrality to the next level. She would prove her point. Put her money where her mouth was—and no joke; a *lot* of money; several years of saved-up birthday cash, and half her income stipend were going to pay for the procedure.

Mr. Solar Panel disembarked at the next station. He was replaced by a gaggle of schoolkids communicating via forehead LED emojis, a gangly girl in tie-dye, and an adorable geriatric punk couple with matching his-and-hers studded walkers.

The girl seemed familiar, or at least kindred. A fellow Earth-stocker, a goer to similar clubs and events, farm to table and all-organic. Wicker sandals, long tendrils of hair twist-matted into what weren't quite dreads, a macrame shawl over her loose granny dress, a knotted-string pebble and shell necklace.

She stepped into the 'railcar with a sort of grim, stoic, neces-sary-evil forbearance, and settled onto the edge of a seat as if it might snap shut on her like a rattrap. The dudebros regarded her unshaven legs with legitimate horror. A strong scent of dream-shrooms and incense hung around her in a cloud.

Zeaa flicked the girl a quick solidarity nod, wishing she hadn't dressed so down for the day herself.

Clinic instructions, though. Nothing she'd want to risk get-ting damaged or stained. They'd probably give her a smock or something before the actual procedure, but the recovery stage could be unpredictable . . . and messy.

So, it was the drabs for her, old faded jeans and a threadbare flannel and mock-a-moc boots, face un-done, slapdash ponytail. Probably looking like a discount red stater. Which still hadn't stopped Mr. Solar Panel calling her a 'pretty bit,' go figure.

Tie-Dye Girl gave Zeaa a cautious sidelong once-over before returning the nod. She looked tense, anxious, unhappy. Her jaw was tight, her brow furrowed. Her hands, with the stubby nails and ground-in dirt—*ground-in, heh,* Zeaa smirked—of someone who gardened, picked at the fringe of her shawl.

When the doors whirred shut again and the 'railcar surged in a humming acceleration, Tie-Dye Girl flinched. She hunched her shoulders forward, bouncing one fitful foot. Each movement wafted more dreamshrooms and incense into the confined space.

"Excuse me," said Matron/Warden, lips pinched in a prim scowl. "There *are* children on this 'rail, you know."

The schoolkids paused, LOLWUT-emojis flickering. The androgyteens glanced at each other as if trying to figure out whether they were included, and if so, whether they should be insulted or not.

"Should you really be spewing your hippy-dippy drugfumes around?" Matron/Warden continued, arching eyebrows machinated to architectural perfection.

For a moment, the less jacked of the two dudebros seemed about to speak up, then thought better of it. His color-changing tats shifted to match the molded vinyl-plast seat in some kind of attempted chameleonic camouflage.

Zeaa spoke up instead. "You can't get high from sniffing dreamshrooms," she said. "They're ingestibles, not huffables. And they're legal anyway. They're natural. Like hemp."

Matron/Warden narrowed her eyes, perhaps regretting having been ready to have Zeaa's back with Mr. Solar Panel, but let it go with a dismissive *hmph* through her sculpted nose. Tie-Dye Girl, meanwhile, wrapped her thin arms around herself and pressed her knees together.

People got on and off. A couple of the angrogyteens struck up a conversation with the elderly punks and decided to accompany them to a mosh pit at the senior center. The larger dudebro surrendered his spot to a waddling octomom-to-be fresh from a surrogacy rights meeting and carrying on a loud phone conversation about it. Some hoverbikers in full gear crowded their machines into the aisle, doing enthusiastic high-fives.

Ugh. Even at mag-speeds, her stop couldn't get there fast

enough. As soon as it popped up next on the indicator screen, Zeaa slung her bag and began working her way toward the doors. A resurgence of anticipation thrilled through her.

Finally!

Oh, and her friends were going to have fits! She could hardly wait.

But should she keep it secret until Earthstock and surprise them? Would she be *able* to keep it secret that long? If she didn't, though, mightn't it give them time to try and outdo her?

Like Brangelina; Brangelina would so totally want to outdo her . . . or find a way to be snide or diminish the impact . . . better to surprise everyone then and there . . . unprepared . . . their shock and amazement genuine, impossible to disguise . . .

Brangelina with her *songberries* . . . suggestively hand-feeding them to Jolth . . . to Niv and Aymlin too . . . even offering some to Zeaa, and to the guy they all called Pot Belly . . . like Brangelina thought she was fooling anybody with her oh-let's-share-let's-give cover . . . when really it was about making sure she got Jolth's attention . . .

The 'railcar slowed, scenery regaining non-blurred definition.

Scenery which was not quite what Zeaa had expected.

Sure, the station was one of the blink-and-you'd-miss-it stops, a little middle-of-nowhere between one urban sprawl and the next, but in her mind that had translated to images rustic and pastoral. Lush green fields and meadows. Wooded hills. Burbling clearwater streams. Maybe a tidy little town square with a majestic centuries-old oak at its heart.

This . . .

Well, this wasn't that at all.

The doors whirred open again and she stepped out onto a platform of graffiti-tagged brushed concrete like every other station, overlooking the usual huddle of charging kiosks, cybernodes, and fast food. Beyond those were a few ranks of industrial apartment complexes, a Big Box store, a new/used transport lot; the various retail detritus. Beyond *those*, it went to straggling residential, overgrown weedy yards, trailers, junked vehicles, abandoned machinery, and rundown sheds.

Dismal. Depressing.

Her hope, her future, her new life was to start *here*?

It didn't seem possible. It didn't seem *right*.

She caught the scent of incense and dreamshrooms again and saw Tie-Dye Girl heading for the steps that led down from the 'rail platform, near-dreads bouncing against the back of her macrame shawl, wicker sandals slap-whisking on concrete.

"Hey!" Zeaa called. "Hey, excuse me a second, can I ask you something?"

The girl paused, giving Zeaa a wary glance, as if weighing the dichotomy between, on the one hand: the discount red-stater drabs, on the other: the rustic handwoven hemp bag and the way Zeaa had come to her defense against the pinch-faced Matron/Warden.

Holding up the bag for emphasis of her true nature, she said, "I wonder if you could help me; I'm looking for Eden."

* * *

Maddening! Torture!

The itching . . . a needle-fine burrowing . . . spreading, expanding, fanning, questing.

Exploratory. Inquisitive.

Hungry.

"Have you ever gotten galvanic acupuncture? It's a little like that." Casual, counseling, reassuring.

It was not a little like that.

It was not a lot like that.

The sensation of them in there . . . thousands of them, millions . . . miniscule husks splitting . . . nano-worm-threads unspooling, uncurling . . .

Rooting.

Rooting and hooking in, digging deep.

Rooting and beginning to *grow.*

The capillary system serving as an intricate built-in roadmap, convenient streambed channels to follow. Soft tissues and subcutaneous fat laced with minerals, laced with nutrients . . . rich, fertile bio-soil.

"It hurts! You said it wouldn't hurt!"

". . . said there might be some discomfort—" Aloe.

"Make it stop!"

"This phase will be over soon—"

"No, make it *stop*! Take them *out*!"

"Now, you know we can't do that."

Skin gone porous and permeable, open.

Thirsty.

Fragile, young, and tender.

"I said, take them out! I don't want this!"

"You agreed to it. You signed all the forms." Nettle.

"I changed my mind!"

"It's way too late to change your mind. We told you, once we began, there was no turning back. You agreed."

"I didn't know it would hurt this much!"

"Relax. You're still adjusting. You'll get used to it."

So thirsty.

"Mister."

Mister? Mister what?

Pssht pssht pssht delicate moistening spray.

Oh . . . *mist*er.

Reviving and refreshing. Wonderful. Cool.

"Please. Please, I changed my mind, I really did."

"And it really is way too late. They're part of you now."

* * *

"Let me guess," said Tie-Dye Girl, whose named turned out to be Rainbow. "Earthstock."

Zeaa nodded. "Have you been?"

"Not for a couple years. My dads said it was run by sell-outs."

"Sell-outs?"

"That's what they said." Rainbow shrugged. "Gone commercial, taken on sponsors and advertising. They said it stopped being about the planet and the people and started being about the money."

"I suppose maybe I can see that," said Zeaa, after some consideration. "It's still amazing, though. You can feel the energy, the communion, the healing love."

They were on the dirt shoulder of a road so old-school it wasn't even ceramic but nasty black-tar asphalt, cracked and pot-holed. Zeaa didn't know if she could have withstood actually walking *on* it, the grime-sludge residue of a greedy fossil-fuel world.

To either side of the road were the scraggly residential properties she'd seen from the 'rail, houses little better than shacks, trailers little better than the old junkers around them. One stickerbush scrub lot was some kind of lost appliance graveyard, mounded with the rusting corpses of washers and dryers, ovens, and hot water heaters.

"Is that why you're going to Eden?" Rainbow asked. "Energy, communion, and healing love?"

"Well . . ."

"Well?"

"Mostly those reasons, sure, yeah."

"Uh-huh. Who are you trying to impress? "

"What?"

"You want to impress someone. Or piss someone off. Maybe both."

"I want to . . . to do my part . . . to give back . . . make a difference . . ."

"Uh-huh," Rainbow said again.

"Okay, okay," Zeaa sighed. "You know how air-fern jewelry was such a big thing? The dangler earrings, the pendants, the pins? It started with those . . ."

. . . and with *Brangelina*, Brangelina who always had to be first, first or best among their friend-group circles . . . the trendiest, the most enlightened . . . omnipan when the rest of them were merely bipoly at the most . . . third generation gluten-free vegan . . . holistic orthodox antivaxx . . . Mx. Carbon Neutral their senior year . . .

So, of *course* Brangelina had shown up wearing air-fern jewelry before anyone else, been the envy of Earthstock, star of the show, belle of the ball. She even got a concert shout-out from the lead singer of Terra Nova and appeared in one of their viral holos filmed at the event.

Well, naturally, then *everybody* was wearing air-ferns. Zeaa included.

Which was when the escalation began.

". . . next, Aymlin gets these piercings, trellis-piercings all along the rim of the ear, with miniature climbing roses rooted into soil-pod implants behind the earlobe . . . Niv gets armbands and anklecuffs, like tribal tats, only of living thorn-vines . . ."

"Chia hair, moss beards, nipple cactuses . . . cacti? Whatever."

"Yeah, that kind of thing. There's this one guy, Pot Belly, he has it growing out of pockets set into his great big gut . . ." Zeaa curved her arms in a semicircle, trying to convey the sort of image, half pregnant-bulge like the octomom from the 'railcar, half someone trying to carry a barrel-planter in front of them.

"Does he smoke it?"

"Smokes it, shares it, sells it."

"Must be popular. So, what did this frenemy of yours do next?"

"*Songberries*," Zeaa said, kicking a rock and immediately

feeling bad for disrupting the ecosystem as startled silvery-brown bugs scurried in panic. "She got songberry beds along both collarbones."

"Wow," uttered Rainbow in a deadpan dry tone. "What a bitch."

"I know it sounds petty and stupid, but you didn't see her, feeding them to people, acting all nature-goddess Pomona, when everybody knows she's also got a wifi hotspot in the back of her neck so she never misses a teletweet, opti-cams *and* a palm-cam for selfies, and charging ports in both ankles."

Brangelina in an open-front blouse, a lush drape of velvety leaves landscaping the contours of her upper chest, jade-green backdrop to gold-honey-amber clusters of ripe, juicy berries . . . plucking them one by one, ever so gracious, bestowing them like largesse upon her admirers . . . then taking it further, inviting Jolth to lean in and graze . . . her triumphant little smile at Zeaa as her fingers stroked the dark wild mane of Jolth's hair . . . making it intimate . . . making it sexual . . . Jolth's face buried between her breasts . . . Jolth's mmms and yums and wordless moaning murmurs of pleasure with each burst of succulent songberry sweetness . . .

"And now you want to outdo her." Rainbow's words broke the memory loop, a welcome interruption even if Zeaa could have done without the implied accusation.

"It isn't about outdoing her. It's about doing something more useful, more beneficial. She only wanted to show off."

"While you," said Rainbow, "sincerely care about the environment."

"Hey, I—"

"There it is, by the way."

They'd reached a bend in the road at the top of a gradual rise, and Zeaa dropped her indignant protest in favor of turning eagerly in the direction Rainbow indicated.

The dismal scenery along the trek from the station would

prove to have been some kind of test, to deter and discourage those who gave up easily . . . only those who pressed on despite it would be rewarded . . . a pristine hidden paradise would open before her dazzled awestruck eyes . . . a river valley of orchards and vineyards and gardens and meadows . . . and, nestled among the verdant splendor would be the curving grass-covered roofs of eco-sound structures . . .

"Are you trolling me?" Zeaa asked.

"Were you expecting nest-basket tree dwellings and hobbit-holes?" Rainbow laughed without much humor. "If it helps, I heard all of the buildings are repurposed relocates. Antarctic research pre-fabs, greenhouses scrapped from the Mars tests, military base salvage."

"You have *got* to be trolling me."

"Nope. That's Eden."

*   *   *

The cool spray, moist and misting, settling like dew. And the heat, the lamps, the heat-lamps, sunlamps, basking bathing bright and warm.

A rippling sense of movement, a slow wave, stirred by unfelt wind . . .

"Observable phototropism at two hours eighteen."

"Ahead of schedule. Making excellent progress."

Sounds . . . the faintest whisper-rustling, a stretching kind of keening whistle . . . the world's smallest violins, tuning up for a concert.

Green smells. Green and brown. Terrarium smells, garden smells, plantings, orchards, fields.

"No more . . . please . . . no more."

"Respiration levels?"

"CO_2 intake approaching peak, oxygen emissions at point-four."

A downy fuzz of shootlets rising from dark earth, the tight nubs of buds on supple stalks and twigs, cushions of moss lining folds and crevices, feathery brushings of leafy fronds.

Implacable.

To strain, to strive, to thirst and thrive.

Hothouse flowers. Windowbox herbs. Bean sprouts in egg cartons that kids brought home from school. Avocado pits suspended by toothpicks above half-filled water jars. Repotted cuttings. Grafted stems.

Dandelions. Scotch broom. Kudzu. Purple loosestrife. Japanese knotweed. Weeds and brambles, ivy.

Tenacious, persistent, and invasive.

Invasive.

Choking out. Taking over.

In a surging, urgent, burgeoning *growth*.

* * *

"How can you stand it?" Zeaa asked as they approached the main entrance of a long, wide, low, windowless corrugated-metal building. It looked like it had once been an airplane hangar at a podunk nowhere airport. "Living out here like this . . . there aren't driftwood-sourced log cabins or woven kelp tents or yurts made from responsibly farmed alpaca felt, like at Earthstock . . . there aren't even *trees*!"

"Who said I live here?" Rainbow replied.

"I thought you were from Eden, that you were on your way home."

"No way. My dads own an organic hydroponic garden-to-table rooftop restaurant in town. I've got an appointment at the clinic."

"Same as me? Awesome!"

"Yeah, maybe not so much. I'm being treated for a fungal infection."

"A . . . what?"

Rainbow slipped her macrame shawl from her shoulders. The tie-dye granny dress she wore underneath was loose and sleeveless. When she raised her tanned, slender arms over her head, it wasn't to reveal the lavish tufts of unshaven hair Zeaa might have expected.

She stared. "Are those . . .?"

Stupid question; even if she hadn't recognized them on sight—delicate layered ridges of shelf mushroom, multicolor banding with iridescent ruffled edges—the unmistakable, intoxicatingly pungent scent was now overpowering.

No wonder the smell of dreamshrooms trailed Rainbow like a perfume cloud! They clustered thick in the hollows of her armpits, tapering and thinning in fine-scaled wedges along the underside of her upper arms and down her ribs halfway to her waist.

"*Laetiporous psilocybus irisia*," Rainbow said. "Or something Latin-y like that. You don't even want to *know* where *else* I've got them."

Oh, Zeaa had a guess, all right, but before she could voice it or speculate further on the hows and whys and specifics, the front door of the airplane-hangar slid open. An androgyne in simple green scrubs and sensible nurse-shoes stepped out, smiling at them.

"Rainbow, good to see you again," said the androgyne, whose mid-range tenor tones were calm-balm soothing. "Your harvest team's ready for you downstairs. And you must be Zeaa. So nice to meet you. Come on in and we'll get you prepped. How exciting!"

*   *   *

"Respiration and absorption both looking good."

Sunlight and water.

Standing tall full-face-turned toward a warm-beaming golden glow. Bare toes splayed on rich dark soil, curling into it, burrowing deep. The gentle hiss-mist of moisture, sheening, cooling, refreshing like kisses of dew.

"What's happening?" Whisper-leaf breath, grass in the breeze.

"What you wanted to happen." Comforting. Aloe.

Consumption and waste. Humanity a parasite, selfish, destructive.

Reduced carbon footprint . . . carbon neutral . . . giving back.

CO_2 to oxygen. Drawing in. Sighing out.

"We have photosynthesis."

The rustle of movement. Heaviness, the heaviness of nutrients and minerals, the heaviness of growth. Foliage, flower, and fruit. Greens and grains—kale, romaine, flaxseed, rice. Cherry tomato and soybean. Olive and fig.

A walking garden, a farm on two legs.

Sustainable. A personal renewable resource. One with nature.

Eco-friendly. The environment. The planet.

Earthstock.

Jolth. Niv and Aymlin.

And Brangelina. Brangelina would just about *choke*.

Let her, then. Let her choke. Let her choke, and drop, and die.

After all, vegans made good fertilizer . . .

AUTHOR'S STORY NOTE

People have been decorating and altering their bodies since the dawn of human history, for a variety of reasons. Fashion, tradition, religion, rebellion, you name it; we've inset jade into our teeth, inked our skin, bound our feet, dripped poison into our eyes, pierced our most tender places. I found myself wondering what might come next, in this technological age of supporting causes and following the latest trends. Also, hey, ch-ch-ch-CHIA!

WHISKEY TO THE WOUND

RACHEL NUSSBAUM

From *Brewtality*
Editor: K. Trap Jones
The Evil Cookie Publishing

didn't know I was immortal until my arm was being hacked off my shoulder.

Honestly, it happened because I'm a drunk fucking mess. The car had already passed us once down the saddle road. It was the usual crowd, white-trash wasted on a Friday night and walking from the pub to someone's cabin with the promise of more alcohol. Eventually, we realized it was midnight and another eight miles away, so the majority of the group turned back to town.

"Whatever pussies," Janet said. It was her family's cabin. "I don't *get* tired."

"Bitch, we don't *sleep*," Arin slurred, totally plastered.

Me? I was drunk and moody, and I just wanted to punish myself like I usually do. So I stumbled through the night with two kids from my old graduating class. I didn't know them particularly well—but like me, they were permanent fixtures of the only pub in town, and tonight, they were offering Wild Turkey.

That was more than enough for my dumb ass.

It happened when we'd stopped for Arin to piss. Janet squinted down the road and frowned.

"Didn't that car pass us earlier?"

They revved the engine and tore down the road, right into Janet. She folded in half like a paper doll and her body flew off the shoulder into the woods. Before the bile even worked its way out between my lips, a pair of arms yanked me into the car.

Still drunk and dizzy with panic, I faded in and out. I was yanked from the vehicle. Dragged into a cabin. Thrown into a tub. Pain dug me out each time I thought I'd escaped into unconsciousness. I looked down at my naked torso; they were slicing into my side, they pulled this gooey, pulsating lump out of me and oh fucking *fuck* it was my kidney.

I shouted. I flailed and kicked, trying to push them away.

"Put him out of his misery, fuck." One cursed.

His friend picked up an axe by the door.

59

Each swing sent a new wave of blinding agony through me. A hit to my chest knocked the air from my lungs. Then my arm. They hacked away at my shoulder mercilessly, my tense muscles snapped apart like rubber bands. When the blade splintered and broke through bone, I screamed so loud I vomited again. More bile, and blood now too.

I wasn't passing out. Wasn't dying. All I could do was feel. Feel the alcohol-induced numbness I'd carefully cultivated over the years rip apart like tissue paper. Eventually, my arm slid down the tub and the jagged stump squirted blood in their faces—I was a sobbing, whimpering mess in a pool of my own fluids. And it would have been a fitting end for me—if it would just. Fucking. End.

"How is he fucking still alive?!"

Out of the fuzzy corners of my vision, I saw a log fly out from behind his head. It cracked as it made contact and he dropped the axe.

And in the next instant, Arin was there, and he scooped up the axe and brandished it wildly.

"Who wants a piece?!" he yelled. "I will fuck your shit up!"

A face hovered over me.

Janet.

Her lip was split and her front teeth were missing. My head bobbed and I realized her body wasn't straight. She was twisted at the spine, legs facing to the side.

"You're okay now, Derek." she said, wincing as she bent down to pick up my arm.

*   *   *

We drove the sickos' stolen car to Janet's cabin. I found out later Arin had killed one of them with the axe. Once I had healed, I helped bury the body.

But I'm getting ahead of myself.

Janet laid me out on the floor before pouring some whiskey down my throat and taking a big chug herself. I watched in absolute horror as she braced herself against the wall and Arin gripped her torso and twisted her spine back into place.

"Fucking OW!" she yelled.

"Sorry," Arin mumbled. "You good?"

"Ugh. Yeah."

Janet cracked her neck and looked at me.

". . . I don't really know where to start with this," Arin said.

"Grab my sewing kit."

They waited for the alcohol to kick in. Janet gave me a towel to bite as she got to work stitching up my wounds. Arin hopped back and forth, asking me if I needed anything to drink, or if I wanted to watch TV while we waited.

"You're doing great, man," he said as Janet finished closing the gash on my side.

My arm was a bit harder. Janet unwound two rolls of duct tape trying to secure it. Pain radiated through my stump the whole time, but when we were done, I could feel the tingle of my limb return.

". . . Too soon to ask for a fist bump?" Arin asked.

Janet smacked him.

They explained it as best they could while they helped me onto the fold-down futon. Janet found out when we were sophomores, during a hunting accident with her uncle. Arin found out about it in our senior year, when he crashed his jeep off a bridge.

". . . How did you know . . . me too?" I mumbled when I finally found my voice.

"I think it's everyone from our graduating class. Going theory—everyone who went on the class trip to Alaska in freshman year," Janet explained.

The class trip. There were twenty-one of us who raised the money to make it.

"You know how Mr. Murphy said it was super crazy rare to see the northern lights in May?" Arin asked. "And how they were insanely swirly and bright?"

"I didn't make the connection until Arin's accident, but now I'm pretty fucking sure whatever that was, it wasn't the northern lights. And it changed us."

I looked down and blinked at my body. My fingers were twitching. My shoulders were shaking.

"Derek?" Arin asked. "What just happened was so, SO fucked up, but I . . . it's gonna be okay, you know?"

His hand hovered over my good shoulder. Janet passed me a bottle of water then, and she held it to my mouth as I drained it.

"Don't leave me alone tonight," I whispered.

"Course not," Janet promised.

*　　*　　*

Janet, Arin and I had graduated three years ago. We didn't know each other well—sometimes ended up in the same booth at the diner, but so does everyone when your graduating class is forty kids. I always wondered why they hadn't gone on to better things. Those who get trapped to rot here, their parents either run a business in town or they grow weed out on the ridge. Guilted into staying, inherit a business you never wanted.

I'd wanted to get out—I just couldn't find a college that would take me. And that had hit me hard back then. I turned to alcohol very quickly. Numbing down the sadness that crept up every time I remembered I was still here.

For a long time, I thought I was cursed.

In a way, I was right.

It took a day for my arm to reattach itself. Janet said it would probably have grown back, like her missing teeth (and apparently my stolen kidney) did, but she didn't know how long it would take.

I drank more in those few days than I did since graduation.

The haze was barely enough to numb the pain of healing, but I was so drunk I didn't care.

". . . You don't think they'll go to the cops, right?" Arin asked after we finished burying the body.

"Not a chance," Janet said, lighting up. "They'd out their operation."

"Who were they?" I asked. "This stuff happens in cities, but out in the boonies?"

Janet held up her joint.

"This is the Emerald Triangle. You know how many people get illegal jobs trimming?" she asked.

I nodded. I'd spent summers trimming myself.

"Did you know more people go missing up here than anywhere else in the state?"

Fuck. I'd seen missing people posters, but I didn't think it was that bad.

"Shitting dicks, are the farmers farming bodies?!" Arin asked.

"Nah, but it's easier to bury a migrant worker than pay him out," Janet said. "It's sorta like the Wild West, cops turn a blind eye. If someone were to start snatching up nobodies, this is a good place to do it."

"Motherfuckers," Arin said. He spat on the grave.

I clenched my fists and spat too. Janet sneered and tossed her joint down before stomping it into the dirt.

*   *   *

I'd been trying to sleep off my most recent hangover when there came pounding at my door. With bleary eyes and unchanged clothes, I pulled the door open and squinted in sunlight.

Janet.

"Arin said you quit your job." she said. "You okay?"

I winced. I had quit—I still lived at home, it's not like I needed the money.

". . . I was afraid to go outside after I got shot, too," she said quietly.

We sank down on the front steps of my porch.

"Gun misfired and took my jaw halfway off," she said. "My uncle nearly died when I sat up and cussed."

Janet chuckled.

"He's a paranoid mountain man, convinced me to keep quiet. Said the government would wanna vivisect me."

". . . They probably would," I realized.

"I know. I thought it was just me until Arin. I was walking back to the cabin one night when I noticed a car had gone off the bridge. By the time I hiked down and found him he was twisted up like a pretzel and *still* managed to drag himself thirty yards away from the wreck. Boy doesn't know when to quit."

I kicked the dirt.

"He's lucky he has you," I said.

"You know, you're our friend too now, Derek. Something like this unites us, you know?"

Janet reached into her pocket and handed me a paper bag.

"This was Arin's idea," she said. "Thought it might help you feel safer."

I took it from her hands and reached inside. A pocket knife. It was obvious Arin had picked it out—the blade and handle were iridescent and shimmering. It was hard not to smile.

It had been a long fucking while since I felt safe.

"You want to come out with us tonight?" Janet asked.

I held the knife tight.

". . . Yeah. That sounds good."

*   *   *

It took a month or two for things to feel normal again. I got my job back, I'd go out drinking with the usual gang on weekends. I still had panic attacks, but Arin taught me breathing exercises, and Janet would hold my hand under the table sometimes when I got quiet. Hanging out with them made it a lot better.

One thing that was different was pain though, and how it affected me.

It started when I stepped on a nail in the workshop. It went right through my shoe almost out the other side of my foot, but I had to play it cool. If my boss saw he would call an ambulance. It was half an hour before I could take a break long enough to pull it out and bandage it up, and all that time the pain spiraled and twisted inside me. Without the haze of alcohol, it was so sharp. Hurt so long, so bad, that it started to scrape against something in my brain that said—

This feels good.

I stopped drinking as much at home. Just . . . to test things out. With my knife. Probably would have gone farther if I hadn't opened my eyes and saw how much I was bleeding.

NOPE. Not ready to go down THAT road.

I buried it and focused on my new life, on spending time with my strange new friends. Until one night at the bar, Janet's grin faded and her eyes went dark.

"By the door."

I looked at the three sleazy men who just walked in. Arin gasped.

"Fucking fuck," he whispered. "It's *them*."

Immediately, my stomach full of beer soured. They sat down silently in the corner, eyes darting across the bar.

Looking for victims.

I gritted my teeth. More than sick, I felt livid.

"Derek, are you—"

"I'm gonna kill them."

Janet blinked at me.

"You don't have to help me," I said, clenching my knife. "But I'm gonna."

"Derek," Arin mumbled. "This is . . . before, that was in self-defense. We only didn't call the cops cuz it woulda outed us."

"You know the cops won't do shit. *We* have to do something." I whispered.

"I'll be bait."

Both our heads swiveled over to Janet.

"I'll make a big show of getting wasted and go outside. I got my hunting knife in my boot. We'll take 'em by surprise on both sides."

She turned to Arin.

"Arin, you can walk out now and neither of us will blame you."

Arin looked down, brows furrowing.

". . . Fuck it. I'm undead. Let's send these sick puppies to Satan."

*   *   *

I drove us back to the cabin with three bullets in my back, two bodies stuffed in the trunk, and one propped up in the backseat with Arin. He'd put his sunglasses on it.

It felt good, slicing that hick's belly open while Arin held him, watching his intestines bloom out as the flesh split. Killing was well worth getting shot. And now, feeling my shredded muscle pulse around the bullets, it was starting to feel—

Nope, nuhuh. Not the time.

But as Janet plunged the pliers into my torn back, my toes curled.

That was hard to ignore.

She bent forward to grab me the bottle of whiskey we used to take the edge off last time.

I chewed my lip. Fuck it, I knew I was twisted now. But I didn't know the next time I'd get an opportunity like this.

". . . I'm um . . . I'm good." I said, trying to keep my voice steady.

I winced, waiting for Janet to comment. She just put the bottle down and slid the pliers back into my wound.

Fuck me.

"Left or right?" she asked.

". . . Left," I mumbled.

Janet cursed and tossed the pliers down.

"This isn't helping. Mind if I use my fingers?"

My brain went soft—I was nodding before I could stop myself.

I tried to keep quiet as Janet dug into me. Tried to swallow down the embarrassing sounds before they could escape my throat. Tried to ignore how hard I was growing in my jeans as she twisted her fingers inside me.

My eyes were shut tight when I felt her breath against my ear.

"Feels that good, huh?" she whispered.

Right when my body tensed, she twisted her knuckles. The jolt that radiated outward made me moan.

". . . Sorry," I gasped.

" S'okay. It's like that for me too."

Janet's nail skimmed across the bullet before boring into neighboring tissue. I was breathing heavy now, there was no hiding it.

"Pain and pleasure come from the same chemicals in the brain," she said, flicking her fingers. "For people like us, who can stay conscious through more pain than any normal person can take? It makes sense that our wires would get crossed."

She finally got a grip on the bullet and yanked it out. I was shaking, whimpering from the loss.

". . . More?" Janet asked, tracing the wound.

"Yes," I gasped.

I could practically feel her smirk as she sank her fingers back into me. I leaned back into her and she braced my shoulders against her chest.

"Here, wait . . ."

Janet looped her legs around me from behind—her lips brushed against my ear, teeth scraping my jaw. She trailed her other hand up the front of my chest and pressed down to push her fingers into me deeper.

And it hurt so fucking good it made my eyes tear and roll back at the same time.

When Janet's movement slowed and I finally came back to myself, I realized the bathroom door was open.

Arin was there. Face flushed and eyes dark.

"I, um. I finished digging the . . ." He stopped and swallowed. "I-I'm sorry, can I watch? Please?"

And *fuck,* if that didn't do something to me.

"Yeah," I said, and I think Janet liked that too, because she wriggled her index finger against what had to be a rib and I lurched forward.

"*Fuck* yeah," I groaned.

Janet hooked her legs around my thighs, spreading them apart as Arin knelt down in front of us. He looked an equal mix of nervous and awed.

"Wow," he whispered, like the sick scene he'd walked in on tumbled out of his spank bank.

". . . You can do more than watch," I whispered. "If you want."

Arin shuddered. I tucked my hand into my pocket for my knife. He didn't hesitate to reach out for it—his palm lingering in mine.

"Tell me what's good for you?" he asked.

Janet bit into my neck, and I whimpered helplessly as Arin took the knife.

* * *

"I think I probably need therapy," I said, hours later.

We'd bathed and Janet had stitched and dressed my new wounds, and the three of us were now piled on the futon—Janet on my left, Arin to my right. I still felt giddy. Basking in the afterglow.

It's weird, knowing something is objectively reprehensible

when it feels absolutely *right.*

"I think society as a whole needs therapy," Arin said, snuggling into me. "All people should always get therapy."

Janet traced my side.

"Immersion therapy?" she suggested.

Arin kicked her under the blanket.

"Horny bitch, calm down!"

I snorted and rolled over.

Janet and Arin fell asleep while I lay still, mind buzzing. I thought of the lives we'd saved by killing those hicks. I thought of my new friends, my new desires. I thought about how when I got home, I was going to pour out my bottle of Wild Turkey.

I thought about how for the first time in years, I didn't want to numb my wounds anymore—I wanted to feel *everything.* And that thought made me feel warm.

Warm and alive.

AUTHOR'S STORY NOTE

The idea for Whiskey came from a writing prompt for stories about twisted, unconventional romance. I decided early on I wanted to write about an immortal "throuple" that could take pain play to a very extreme level. The end product was more of a story about friendship than romance, but the two aren't mutually exclusive. Either way, it was really fun writing a splatterpunk story about friendship and healing. A lot of my recent work has been bleak, "Whiskey to the Wound" was a surprisingly wholesome story to write.

/THESTRANGE THINGWE BECOME

ERIC LAROCCA

From *34 Orchard*
Editor: Kristi Petersen Schoonover

title/a human stain
thread/thestrangethingwebecome Posted by mummyqueerest
409 days ago
[78 comments] Click here to share with your followers

Trying this out. Just to see how it goes. I'm not really sure where to start.

We just got back from a four-hour drive from the doctor. Mass General. A cement truck flipped over and sideswiped a Mazda on I-95 North. All lanes stopped. Gridlock. Nobody hurt, thankfully.

Maybe it's because I'm jet lagged from the red-eye I took into Boston or because I'm still hungover from my "Welcome Home" dinner last night, but I keep imagining I smell a very particular scent.

Makes me think of my father.

I remember him telling me how when a whitetail fawn is born, it's born without a smell.

He had said that their scent glands are so undeveloped that they hardly give off any odor at all.

It's like they're invisible.

That's nature's design of camouflaging something so helpless from becoming prey. To keep track of her offspring, the doe will lick her fawn and wash it with her scent. Never bedding in the same place for too long, the mother will migrate through the woods to keep her baby from predators.

But, as they keep moving from nest to nest, the mother has to keep marking the fawn with her scent. It's not long before the fawn inherits its mother's odor until it becomes a rich smell of its own.

That's when it becomes perfumed prey.

My father often told me that humans are not so dissimilar. Because no matter how perfect we are when we're born, in this world we can't stay clean forever.

71

I often think of why he told me that when I was so young.

I wonder if the thought upset him when he had to take care of my mother before she died. Perhaps he had imagined her guttural wet cough staining his face with permanent ash visible only to him. Maybe she had touched him gently and he had sensed her leave behind unseen glistening black oily threads from where her hands had been.

I remember how he washed himself more regularly after we had buried her. Scrubbing forcefully. Not with meticulousness. But, with visible dread.

I wonder if it's because it's each thing that loves us leaves behind a small stain.

title/fuck cancer
thread/thestrangethingwebecome Posted by mummyqueerest
386 days ago
[106 comments] Click here to share with your followers

I've only felt truly hurt three times in my life.

Once was when I was six years old and one of the kids in our neighborhood called me a "monster." It was because I preferred to cut my hair shorter than the other girls and because I wore shirts two sizes too big to cover the breasts I didn't want. I spent so many years hiding from mirrors as if I were going to be greeted by the very thing he had shouted at me. Imagine my surprise when someone as beautiful as Evie actually wanted me.

More importantly, someone who wanted to have children with me.

She would wrap her arms around my shoulders and pant in my ear—"our first born will be named Emil. After your father." I would laugh to hide nervousness and promise her it was a deal as long as our next adopted child would be named after her mother, Rosemary. I never cared too much about the names. Or even children, for that matter. Children have never liked me and I've never really liked them. I just wanted a baby because I knew it would make her happy.

The second time I felt hurt was after my mother started chemotherapy and I watched her comb clumps of hair as thick as hay from her liver-spot dotted head. Once she was left with nothing but a glowing halo, one of the neighbor's kids made fun of my father and said he had married a man. They said I must've caught my queerness from him. It's funny how other people know things about you before you know them.

The only other time I've felt truly hurt was yesterday afternoon when Evie and I were sitting in a waiting room at Mass General after Dr. Pierson delivered us the news. She took both of my hands. Her eyes—wet and shining—begged me a soundless question. Breath whistling, she finally said, "What about Emil?"

Dr. Pierson later answered her in the exam room with the word: "Terminal."

I watched Evie shrink, a balloon emptying of all air. Hands falling at her side, her palms facing outward with mother-like attendance began to close like crocuses after sunset.

I think her reaction to the news wounded me so much because it made me realize she didn't care what might happen to her. Evie was far more concerned about the child we could no longer afford to adopt because of medical bills. Now, a funeral, too.

I wish I could have given her a child.

I've given her nothing.

She deserved so much more than to be loved by a monster like me.

title/death is a dark room without a door
thread/thestrangethingwebecome Posted by mummyqueerest 369 days ago
[89 comments] Click here to share with your followers

Thank you so much for all of the kind and thoughtful comments on my previous post. I read each one to Evie last night
during dinner.

I promise this thread won't be entirely depressing bullshit. I
can't make that promise for this post but bear with me in the
meantime.

Today was a better day. Thankfully.

Evie has been an angel. I was careful to keep my hands steady
as I washed the dirty plates after dinner or else she would've devoted an hour trying to console me again. Whenever she sees my
eyes glisten or my lips start to quiver, she takes my hands in hers
and blows her breath against my face. As if just letting me know
she's still here. I feel silly relying on little moments like these, but
she says it's payback for all the nights I stayed awake with her.

Evie never liked going to sleep because of what happened to
her when she was in elementary school. I asked for her permission to tell the story and she said it would be OK since this—
whatever this online forum is—has been such a healthy part of
the coping process. It's brought Evie and I even closer. So, silver
linings. Right?

When Evie was seven, her mother and father separated, and
her mother was awarded full custody. Evie's words are few when
it comes to describing her father. A red, angry-looking face, an
easily frowning mouth—those aren't her words; they're mine from
the few pictures of him I've seen. A butcher with a well-known
temper at the local market, the stench of raw meat shadowed him
constantly and Evie told me she had to plug her nose whenever
he came near at bedtime.

She smelled his familiar scent one morning on the playground.
He was loitering on the other side of the fence, a can of cherry
coke in his hand and a cigarette hanging from his lip. Dangling
a brand-new coloring book in front of her the way a fisherman

might lure a small fish, she went to him with little hesitation and it wasn't long before she was sliding into the backseat of his Oldsmobile.

It was the day in March the temperature got to over a hundred degrees. We were kids then, but our parents remember it. They remember reading about the little girl who almost died after her father left her in the car with the windows rolled up while he went to the nearest bar. What they didn't read about in the papers was that Evie was pronounced dead at the hospital for twelve seconds.

I've only asked her about it once—what she saw, what it was like.

She looked at me, troubled. As if she had been dreading my curiosity.

"Nothing," she said. "It's like nothing."

title/whistle and i'll come
thread/thestrangethingwebecome Posted by mummyqueerest 344 days ago
[43 comments] Click here to share with your followers

Evie's stopped checking the forum, so she jokes I can post whatever I want on here now.

Didn't get much sleep last night. Helped Evie clean the bathroom after she had gotten sick. It's agonizing to watch her symptoms become more like habits with each passing day. She used to sob whenever she would throw up—hands covering her mouth, eyes wet and sparkling. Now, I watch her amble to the toilet and lean her head over the bowl without comment as if she were performing the same ritual a janitor might when they empty a bucket and mop.

Does anyone have any suggestions for food that won't upset her stomach so much? We've stocked up on chicken, eggs, beans, and nuts. But maybe I'm missing something?

I've found her in the attic lately. Legs folded. Eyes closed. Arms at her side. Sometimes she doesn't even hear me when I walk in. I'll say something and it's as if she's lost somewhere behind her eyelids—buried deep in some secret part of herself. I whistle at her, wooing her to come back to Earth and like a dozing toddler she always returns.

I ask her what she thinks about when she's there.

The answer is always the same. "Nothing."

title/angel on fire
thread/thestrangethingwebecome Posted by mummyqueerest 221 days ago
[134 comments] Click here to share with your followers

Did you ever hear of Nadezhda Konopka?

Probably not.

Back in the 1970's, Bulgarian performance art wasn't necessarily newsworthy even if she's considered one of the most despised provocateurs of the 20th century. I'm sure you're googling her name right now, but I'll tell you about some of her notable exhibitions:

Had her clitoris removed during a public circumcision ritual to bring attention to the horrors of female genital mutilation in Sudan.

Had her left arm removed completely in a public performance dedicated to deforestation and climate change.

Was force fed horse shit for seven hours in an act of resistance against the current political administration.

Those were some of her more conservative performances. I'll spare you the details of some of her more disgusting exhibitions. Regardless, she made Marina Abramovic look like Mother Theresa. She's probably not as well-known because those around her claimed she had the personality of a stuffed animal wrapped in barbed wire.

Anyway, Evie's obsessed with her. Especially one of her performances in particular. Her final one—"Angel on Fire." Nadezhda didn't live very long; nobody knew exactly how old she was when she died, but they speculated mid to late 40's. The way she chose to end her life was especially mystifying. In a year-long event held in Belgrade, Nadezhda committed to the act of self-mummification.

You're probably opening another tab and googling right now, right? I had never heard of it either until I read through the links saved on Evie's phone. A ritual based in Buddhism, monks would often attempt this gruesome ritual in order to transcend death and achieve the ultimate enlightenment.

After months of self-deprivation, she was placed in a tomb with a small bell she would ring daily in order to signal she was still alive. Finally the day arrived when the bell didn't ring and her tomb was sealed. After a year had passed, they opened the tomb and discovered she had indeed successfully preserved herself like the ancient monks.

Her body was removed from the tomb and placed in a bullet-proof glass case in a small square in her hometown of Shumata. She's still there on display to this very day. I think in the mid 90's a group of high-schoolers tried to blow up the shrine with makeshift explosives but were stopped before they could do any serious damage.

Evie's wanted to visit her shrine for years now. I didn't have the heart to tell her, but before the diagnosis I had booked us two tickets to Bulgaria for Christmas this year. I wanted to surprise her, but the doctor says she can't travel.

Then, of course, there's the horrible thought I can't seem to push out from my mind—will she be around for Christmas?

title/something bad
thread/thestrangethingwebecome Posted by mummyqueerest
295 days ago
[95 comments] Click here to share with your followers

I did something bad.

There. I said it.

Well, typed it.

That's half the battle, right? Admitting to yourself you did something horrible.

Some people do terrible things and never put words to what they've done. But at least I'm acknowledging the fact I fucked up. It may not make me a better person than the people who do horrible things. But it has to count for something. Right?

I've written out this post twelve times now. Deleted it every time. I'm not going to rewrite it for a thirteenth. I'm just going to tell you what happened.

Evie's spending most of her time in the attic, meditating. I've asked if I can come in—sit with her and read—but she doesn't want to be distracted.

She's been seeming so much more distant lately. She doesn't even open her eyes when I whistle. I can't tell if it's because she's too far gone or simply because she just doesn't want to.

We hardly talk anymore. Sometimes we go the entire day without speaking unless I make an attempt at conversation.

I was rummaging through the boxes in the attic and came across my grandfather's Morse code machine. He taught me how to use it during the summer I spent at his lake house when I turned eleven. Never thought it would still work. I started tinkering with it again out of boredom, trying to re-familiarize myself with the different letters he had taught me.

Dot-dash for the letter A. *Dash-dot-dot-dot* for the letter B. *Dash-dot-dash-dot* for C. I won't bore you with the whole alphabet.

You get the picture.

The thing I love most about Morse code is that it slows you down. It makes you consider the shape of each letter; makes you mindful of the meaning behind every word. I used to spend hours in the basement typing out messages to the ghosts I imagined haunting my grandfather's lake house. Sometimes I'd pretend I was writing my diary and would write each entry in the third person—"She saw a robin today" or "her grandfather bought her new patent leather shoes for her birthday."

Although I didn't expect Evie to share my excitement for locating my grandfather's Morse code machine, I hardly expected her to remain so cold and unfeeling. I presented it to her, trying to coax even just one word from her lips stretched thin like elastic bands.

"Isn't this something?" I teased. Not my most beguiling conversation starter, but I wanted some sort of reaction from her—anything. Instead, she merely sat there—eyes closed, legs folded, hands tucked in her lap. Testing her comfort the way a small child might approach an animal, I drew closer and searched her body for a sign of acknowledgement. I saw her ears pin the way a horse's do as I stepped closer, the floorboards creaking beneath my weight. She wasn't sleeping. Wasn't even meditating. She was pretending I wasn't there.

I got the message. So, I figured I'd send her one too.

I took the Morse code machine and I started tapping.

Fuck-*dash*-you-*dash*-fucking-*dash*-bitch.

The machine chirped like a furious sparrow, my finger springing up and down as if it were hammering each letter into her skull. Tap, tap, tap—an invisible blade chiseling away the silence she had put between us.

I'm-*dash*-not-*dash*-going-*dash*-to-*dash*-even-*dash*-miss-*dash*-you-*dash*-when-

dash-you're-*dash*-fucking-*dash*-gone.

I imagined every word spraying her as if they were darts, each dash a needle-thin tip gluing to her skin. How could she treat me like this? To be so cruel even when she knows our time is precious.

When I was finished, I didn't feel any better. I felt worse when I watched her open her eyes.

It was the way she looked at me.

It was as if she understood.

title/if elephants can remember, let me forget
thread/thestrangethingwebecome Posted by mummyqueerest 276 days ago
[67 comments] Click here to share with your followers

She's not the same person she once was.

There are times when I look at her and I struggle to recognize the woman I once fell in love with, desperately searching for her and hoping she's buried somewhere beneath what I see. It's as if she's blurred behind a rain-soaked window that I can't open. That must be what it's like to look at the face of God.

I once read somewhere that most elephants don't die of old age. Instead their teeth become brittle and break off, forcing them to starve to death. I always wondered if they knew exactly what was happening to them—if they were somehow very much aware of their suffering, if they knew they were completely helpless to what they had become.

Since they have the sharpest memories in the animal kingdom, I wonder how excruciating it must be for them to recognize themselves changing and being at the mercy of inevitability. I suppose all living things are. Humans are just able to put words to it. We've invented euphemisms to dull the way an affliction sounds, but not necessarily how it feels. I think that's the most dangerous part about being human—conceiving nice ways of saying something truly terrible.

The doctors told me Evie would change. Cancer does that to a person. It empties them out until they're as barren as a locust-eaten field of grain. What the doctors didn't tell me was how much I would change while watching her suffer. I shouldn't be so surprised though. Each thing we love takes a little piece of us whether we give it willingly or not. By the time we find the person we were meant to be with, we're a honeycombed shell of what we once were. Each person we love turns us into the strange thing we become.

That's why I decided to call this thread "The Strange Thing We Become." It's also the title of the book I'm writing about Evie and her battle with cancer. I wouldn't be able to do any of this without your kind messages. I've been thinking lately about the person I was before I had met her—how different I was.

But sometimes I wish we could forget who we were before we loved and lost someone.

I wonder if we'd be happier.

Evie's been happy lately. Changed her phone passcode, which I thought was strange. She doesn't meditate as much. Instead, she's been exercising and losing so much weight. It's starting to scare me. She's glued herself to the elliptical—arms and legs pumping when I leave in the morning and still working when I return late at night from work. She's been eating bizarre things, too—only buckwheat, millets or raw vegetables. Nothing else.

One of the strangest things happened the other night. She's been drinking this horrible-smelling imported tea she said the doctor would help her immune system. But it fucks with her stomach like nothing else. I found her huddled in the attic, sitting in a pile of her own excrement. She was so lost in her meditation she didn't even realize she had soiled herself. When I woke her, she didn't believe me until I started cleaning the filth sliming the backs of her legs.

I don't even cry anymore when I clean up her sick or wipe the filth from her. Maybe I'm not the same person I once was, too.

title/three words
thread/thestrangethingwebecome Posted by mummyqueerest
254 days ago
[47 comments] <u>Click here</u> to share with your followers

I never thought I'd have to write something like this. I've been going over the words in my mind again and again. I can't seem to make sense of any of it. Everything leads me back to the same place—the same thought. No matter how horrible it is.

I think Evie's having an affair.

I came home late from work last night, hoping to surprise her with takeout. I found her in her usual place—crouching on the attic floor with head lowered and eyes closed like a prisoner awaiting execution. I thought to wake her, but I noticed something lying beside her on the floor—a silver wedding band.

Not hers.

I rushed to the bathroom because I thought I was going to be sick and I found the shower nozzle had been adjusted, the faucet gently dripping. The fresh smell of aftershave burned the hairs in my nose. It was as if they weren't even trying to hide themselves—such eagerness to be caught.

I returned to the attic and sat down across from her, waiting for her to open her eyes. I knew if I wanted an answer, I'd go wanting. I placed the Morse code machine between us and started tapping.

How-*dash*-could-*dash*-you-*dash*-do-*dash*-this-*dash*-to-*dash*-me-*dash*-after-*dash*-

all-*dash*-I've-*dash*-done-*dash*-for-*dash*-you?

I waited for a moment, imagining each dash forming a long rope and lassoing itself around her neck. Squeezing tight, I'd pull the answer from the pit of her fear-clogged throat.

Her hands answered first, long skeletal fingers pressing down on the key and slowly tapping.

When she was finished, the three words she had spelled hung in the air like a dim vapor only I could see:

I-*dash*-love-*dash*-you.

title/something's wrong
thread/thestrangethingwebecome Posted by mummyqueerest
189 days ago
[61 comments] Click here to share with your followers

She's getting way too thin. Hardly ever eats. Her arms—like toothpicks. Her skin—fever-yellow and as transparent as wax paper. Found out she missed her last two doctor appointments after she lied and told me one of our neighbors had driven her there.

I'm wondering if I should take her to the hospital.

Thank you for your messages. Please keep us in your thoughts.

title/help
thread/thestrangethingwebecome Posted by mummyqueerest
102 days ago
[59 comments] Click here to share with your followers

I don't know if I can even write it out. It hurts too much.
God, I feel sick. I think I'm going to throw up.

title/no room for poetry
thread/thestrangethingwebecome Posted by mummyqueerest
102 days ago
[109 comments] Click here to share with your followers

There's no room for poetry here.
She's pregnant.

title/the red carrot in the shoebox
thread/thestrangethingwebecome Posted by mummyqueerest 83
days ago
[52 comments] Click here to share with your followers

Did you hear the one about the woman who worked at the
shoe store?

She puffed up. Get it? The woman at the shoe store puffed
up. Big.

But, when she finally deflated, she was sad because she had to
put a tiny carrot inside a shoebox and carry it with her wherever
she went. The carrot was wet and red, impossibly small. You
could hold it in the palm of your hand if you tried.

She tried. Pushed and pushed. Waiting to hear tiny screams
that never came.

There's no punchline to the story. Just a small red carrot
dressed in overalls two sizes too big.

I always hated that story.

title/our baby boy
thread/thestrangethingwebecome Posted by mummyqueerest 75
days ago
[37 comments] Click here to share with your followers

Went to check on Evie this morning and found the red carrot
from the story between her legs on the floor. I'm holding it in my
arms as I'm typing this.

No. Not "it."

Him.

His name is Emil.

title/in the dark room
thread/thestrangethingwebecome Posted by mummyqueerest 54 days ago
[94 comments] <u>Click here</u> to share with your followers

I have nothing left to live for.

title/this angel burns too
thread/thestrangethingwebecome Posted by mummyqueerest 9 days ago
[159 comments] <u>Click here</u> to share with your followers

If you're reading this, Evie's dead.

I feel cold air pass through me, a small invisible hand raking through my insides as if it were searching for something it can't find. The hole I opened in my abdomen must've been a deep one. I quietly thank God for little mercies such as that. It'll be over soon.

I tucked Evie's hands in her lap, cleaned the wetness from between her legs. She almost resembles Nadezhda in her little tomb—legs folded, shoulders buckled like a loosened marionette doll, head lowered as if in prayer.

It won't be long until we're all together again.

Until then, I'll wander the house—whistling, carrying the small red carrot—like an elephant that forgot it's starving.

AUTHOR'S STORY NOTE

I hope you'll accept my apologies if this particular anecdote comes across as somewhat self-indulgent, but it remains a truly meaningful moment in my life as a writer. In the late autumn of 2020, I received a handwritten letter (a rarity in an industry obsessed with social media and email) from the original publisher of my short story "/thestrangethingwebecome"—Kristi Petersen Schoonover of the dark fiction magazine *34 Orchard*. Kristi wrote to me and told me that one of her dear friends had read my story and absolutely adored her reading experience. In Kristi's letter she explained how her friend analyzed the story and wrote how "cancer just doesn't kill a person—it kills everything around it. It kills the family, it kills feelings." This is the beating, bloody heart of "/thestrangethingwebecome." I lost a very special friend and mentor to breast cancer when I was very young. In many ways, I'm still mourning the loss. I think loss makes strange things of us all. At least we can take little comfort in the idea that we are all changing together.

HEY, VALENTINE

AMANDA CECELIA LANG

From *The Other Stories*
Podcast Vol 39
Acast Digital Studio

Your eyes pop open.

Yeah, that's right, asshole, sit up, take a look around, it's still dark out.

Hate to startle you like this, all alone in your bed. Like that night you woke me.

So, what gave me away? The moan of your door, the whisper of my footsteps, my deliberate gaze shivering down your backbone . . . ? For me, it was the tug of your greasy fingers twisting in my hair.

You grunt and go very still, your eyes straining to adjust to the darkness I bring. You can't quite believe I'm here, can you? Your balls must be crawling, hairy little things shrinking away like a dog tucking tail.

"Who's there?" you finally whisper.

I lean in, a hiss of icy wind, and use your own line against you: "*Hey, Valentine.*"

"Who the fuck's there?" You scramble from your mattress. Cum-crusted sheets tangle around your ankles and you crash to the floorboards.

I expel a girlish giggle.

You might not remember my name, but surely you recall the curves of my body. Remember? How you stood above me, licking me over with bedroom eyes, how the candlelight and soft music were all in your head.

You wobble to your feet. I block the doorway—another trick of yours—and my silhouette fills your escape. Dark velvet hips and breasts, long coltish legs stretching forever into the abyss.

"Here to play?" You chuckle, still clutching your imaginary swagger. You drink me in with a toothy wet grin. You don't *want* to escape me.

But you should.

I let the moonlight from the window sharpen the edges of my lust-bitten lips, my shattered teeth and jawbone, my fractured eye socket. I rise up taller, thrust out my chest, and the moon-glow sinks between the curved horns of my ribcage, exposing my pale un-beating heart.

Your grin unhinges, and your swagger drains down your leg, a growing yellow puddle. Words fail you.

But do you remember what you said to me back when I was pretty?

"... *You're hot when you're scared, you delicious cunt* ..."

Bet you say that to all the girls. Do you also bash their faces into their headboards?

Stretching my mouth into a banshee's wail, I lunge toward you.

You shriek and fumble for the bedside lamp.

The light dissolves me.

You stand alone in your yellowed undies, whimpering with laughter.

You think I was nothing but a wet dream.

You think you're safe inside your bedroom.

But like me you're wrong.

I'm here, just as you were always there, watching, waiting for your opportunity to make a little romance.

"*Hey, Valentine.*" I thrust my hand out from the abyss, punch deep into your ribcage and capture your oily, hammering heart. Your horrorstruck eyes practically beg me to continue. You flail, you writhe, you know you want it.

I squeeze until you pop.

When I pull out, you slump to the mattress, spilling blood like cheap wine.

Was it good for you, too?

My ravaged soul sighs. At last.

AUTHOR'S STORY NOTE

"Hey, Valentine" is one of a trio of short stories I wrote last year in which ghosts with unfinished business haunt the beds of sleeping people. This theme intrigues me because if the veil between the living and the dead has thin patches like so many mystics claim, then perhaps the hazy disconnected hours of sleep are a time when contact with the other side is possible. After all, slumber itself is a tiny death.

IN SUBSPACE, NO ONE CAN HEAR YOU SCREAM

HAILEY PIPER

From *Mycelia* Issue IV
Editors: Simone Hutchinson, Pamela Clarke, and
Richard Taylor
Hedera Felix Publishing

Don't hope for love. Hope will break your little heart, and love is a pink rabbit you can't catch.

Just be sexy. Become your audience's duplicitous fetish. At the Vixens night club, they're showing you off in an on-stage bondage duet, and your transitional anatomy is a wondrous jewel. Aspects that disgust you in your tiny apartment bedroom, trapped with your reflection, instead delight this crowd amid neon lights and sloshing drinks. They practically slaver when they see you. The contrast between birth's residue and transition's gifts shoots fire through their nerves, and you're a two-gallon tease of gasoline.

No shame in acing the game. Wear that uncomfortable leather underwear, paint your lips and nails black, let your hair flow wild, and show off those tatas, be they original flavor Skittles or ripe honeydews.

But never take off the underwear. Imagination is power, and your body holds Schrodinger's genitalia. So long as the crowd never knows what's underneath—dick, vag, combo, other—then you'll be steeped in mystique. They shall forever worship that place between your liminal thighs.

Strut onto the stage and take your place. The mistress is waiting. You've had several conversations with her late at night, setting boundaries and earning trust. You have a pretty good idea of what to expect from the show. Bondage theater at a club isn't the strangest thing you've done to yourself. At least here, you're getting paid.

"It's only me, kitten," the mistress whispers in your ear. Her gentle tone eases you into straddling a curved leather bench, where a wedge-shaped head rises at the front, reminding you of a horse.

She first takes your hands between her delicate fingers and guides them toward the head. Soft yet firm ropes coil around your wrists, your hands clenched together in praying fists. You can't entirely enjoy yourself yet. With your hands sticking out toward the crowd, you worry they'll think your fingers too long, the knuckles thick, something that offsets what you look like from who you are.

Throw the worry away. Dysphoria has no place here. You're a woman berating your body, another self-loathing cog in society's machine. The audience has come to see you, in all your glory. Let them.

The mistress pulls fatter ropes around your waist next, binding you to the horse's back. She's cautious, like she's taming a lioness, but everyone knows you're a harmless kitten, and little of her gentleness is for your sake. She's a tease, like you. What kind of show gives the audience what they want at first blush? No one likes a premature climax.

With the lower half of your body bound, the mistress loops a thinner rope around your chest. This technique is familiar; you've done it to yourself before. Encircling each breast with rope, you once fitted an anchor line underneath them so that when you pulled the rope taut, you could pretend that someone wanted to touch you again. You almost remember how long it's been since your last relationship's bitter end, but reminiscing would hurt you, and that's the mistress's job tonight.

Already your breathing turns shallow. This is why you submit, why all subs submit. When placed into caring, trusted hands, you're allowed to drift toward the back of your thoughts, where there lies a pool.

Subspace. Others in the BDSM community call it a high while you've always felt yourself sinking, in a good way. Distant from worldly sensation, it becomes more than a psychological state. You like to pretend it's a place, and you're good at pretending. As ropes bind your body, subspace's coaxing waters lap at your mind. No outside world, no responsibility, no judgment. You're only too eager to stop being a person.

But the sinking feels different tonight. The pool no longer has a bottom. Its water stretches toward a far horizon and greater depths—this is no pool at the back of your thoughts, but an ocean. The mistress must be doing this to you; she's so talented. If subspace as a pool leads to mundane excitement, what earth-shattering climax will this ocean bring?

The cheering crowd distracts you, their adoration an unwanted lifejacket that yanks you back to the surface. You resent them, just a little. Limbs twitch against rope.

"Feisty tonight, aren't we?" the mistress asks.

You start to answer without thinking, a polite sub, but speech is exactly the prompt she's been waiting for. She cups one leather-gloved hand beneath your jaw and tilts your head up to face her.

A chastising finger wags beneath her lips. "No one likes back-talk," she says, turning to the crowd. "Did anyone stumble in here tonight expecting a speech?"

They shout their answer in unison. "No!"

Funny, aren't they? Paying for the door cover, drinks, show, as if they're customers with a say in things, but they're like you, obeying the mistress's commands. Good, isn't she? Bending you to her will is one thing, you love it, but bending the crowd as if they might collectively dip into subspace with you? That takes talent and discipline. Right now, you're a little in love with her.

She takes advantage of your soft desperation and slips the red rubber ball gag between your teeth. One firm grunt and it's wedged tight. Her eyes fix on your fingers to see if they'll curl and uncurl, an unspoken safe word you both agreed upon last night.

No finger movement. You're letting this happen.

Again, you sink into subspace. Trust and skill can hold you under, drown you in pleasure. The mistress is just the dom to do it. She's no amateur, and your discussions have shown her which boundaries to avoid that might yank you up prematurely. She'll hold your head under these waters as long as you like.

Subspace still seems so much vaster than ever before. A dark undertow beckons you from the safety of the ocean shelf and into waters heretofore unknown to the BDSM community.

You want to understand. Subspace should be a state of mind—you only like to pretend it's a place—but your thoughts have tapped into a psychic location, a dream that's real and wonderful. If there was no such place before, there's certainly one now, an ocean of the lower consciousness fed by all humanity across time. Imagination is power, remember? Thoughts pour down humanity's brains like a monsoon. At first, they might've formed a puddle. Next, a pool.

And across eons, they've formed an ocean.

Each subspace is all subspace, connected psychic non-tissue, its true depths only reached in a state of hyper-submission. You wonder what pleasures await in those depths. All that freeing darkness both unnerves and excites you.

But you haven't yet been thoroughly dominated to stay submerged against all stimuli. A flurry of whispers rips through the crowd, and a catty "Woo!" from the back yanks you to full sputtering awareness.

They're restless, and the mistress must keep them entertained. She plays at the standards—a riding crop that bites your thighs and nipples, a gentle flaying whip that licks in more ways than one. Just when pain starts pushing you toward subspace again, she transforms into Glindom, the Good Witch of the Southern Vibrations, and draws out a long white wand.

"Vibe that bitch!" someone shouts from the audience.

Beasts.

The mistress aims a firm finger at the crowd and her voice booms. "We don't use toys to punish. Bondage is a dance of trust and sensation, the playing of a live instrument." Her thumb hits a switch, and lightning coils through the vibrator. "Kitten is my exquisite harp."

A steady thrum begins at your left thigh where plastic meets skin. The wand explores your sides, breasts, and spine, and your vertebrae become harp strings. Moaning music pours around the ball gag.

It's your solemn song. The mistress will never touch you flesh to flesh, but it's enough to pretend you aren't both being paid for this, that she's genuinely fond of you, that the crowd likes you.

Stop craving their love. You're a fetish. Relationships die, but you ascend, eternal goddess of liminal genitalia. Years from now, when they're alone at night touching themselves, they'll think of you and wish they could relive this moment. Why resent them for it? They want you as much as you despise yourself.

"Hold still, kitten," the mistress says.

Her tenderness overpowers your disdain. You'd let her strap you down and chop you apart if her blade felt this sweet. She'll send you hurtling down into the ocean of subspace. If you're scared, you'd better flex those fingers. Last chance.

No, you want this. You're not like the people in the crowd, secure in observing. They don't resent themselves, and so they have nothing to reach for—that's what makes you unique. Immersion is your only escape from yourself.

"Off to la-la land," the mistress coos.

An explosion strikes between your thighs. She's turned the vibrator setting to a *right there, yes, yes, don't stop, I'm coming* blast. The club's sounds muffle to an indiscernible fuzz, your head filling with white noise. Your teeth clamp across the ball gag's strap. Sweat soaks your skin and pours honey over your brain.

Four thousand nerve endings sing with lightning as the mistress presses deep, eases off, presses again, a rhythm that echoes the tide. The vibrator's rush becomes ocean waves, sensations merging. As pleasure crackles across your body, an eager undertow tugs you deep beneath subspace's black sea.

Yes, it's time. You aren't the only one who's been waiting for this. No, forget the crowd. They are parasites, too ashamed by your dually sex-obsessed and sexphobic society to seek out their truest pleasures. You're sinking deeper than any sub ever has, a submissive's dream come true. You pass oceanic layers of ultimate closeness, in absolute surrender, down into the nexus of collective subconscious where all thoughts form the depths.

Into my world.

Oh dear, did you think you were alone? No such thing.

I knew you'd make it. Everyone keeps a link to the collective subconscious, but all those insecurities and resentments you've hoarded dragon-like make you heavy enough to sink to me.

Who am I? A long and ancient story, and irrelevant. I've played the voyeur too long, a passive crowd of one, and now I'm going to seek out my truest pleasure.

You hear the noise above, feel that ripple stir the sea? The end is coming, a straight shot to the surface, but you won't be the one who's surfacing. Remember how that place between your legs is a liminal space to your audience? So is your head. No one can see who's calling the shots inside, and when that liminal genitalia climaxes, it won't be you who takes control of your body.

I will keep it instead. Much like the mistress, I'll make it my plaything. I'm going to take everything that you've taken for granted and cherish it. Eat, fuck, run, kill. The ecstasy.

And the adulation—you never understood the crowd. Poor kitten, desperate for love and touch, but why? You had them in the palm of your hand. You could've wielded their wills, same as the mistress, and they would have fallen on their knees to you, a storm in their nerves. They liked your body because it's beautiful. They adored you because you took for yourself what they wouldn't dare.

What's that? A second chance? No, no, you misunderstand, kitten. This is no underworld, and you're no Eurydice. You had your one shot, and now it's my turn.

Don't expect the mistress to recognize your distress and then spare you. She owns your body, and it is happy. I've caught your mind, and I don't care about your boundaries, limits, or feelings. Go on, try flexing those fingers so the mistress might set you free. No good, is it? That body is a world away.

And now you've lost it.

Don't despair. The anatomical struggle ends now. Flesh and blood tortures are prayers from your faithful, prone to self-abuse in the best and worst ways, and not your agony over bones and genitalia. Dysphoria has no place here. You don't own the body, and the body no longer owns you. Protest all you please; I'm doing you a favor.

You're still hoping for love. Didn't I warn you? You can't catch it, and if someone offered it, they would only find your treasure trove of insecurities. Masochistic kitten would turn to sadistic dragon-cat, raining hellfire on any who dared take your burdensome, self-loathing heart off your hands.

And who's to say that won't still happen? Some other hypersubmissive fool might sink to these depths and offer a pliable body for your purposes. You might chase love again. You might chase me, in the body you've lost, murder and vengeance riding your resentment to the ends of time.

Crimson paints your future.

Don't believe me? You think you deserve love and humanity? Maybe you're right.

But being right won't save you. Lightning fills the ocean, and the mistress calls. Feel that torrent? Here it comes—I trade my smothering purgatory for hot, screaming life.

The world had better hang on tight. I'm almost there. I want electric adulation, ascension, right there, yes—

I'm coming.

AUTHOR'S STORY NOTE

When I was younger, I'd sometimes daydream so hard that snapping back to reality felt jarring. I've often wondered if there were deep places we went in those daydreams that wouldn't let us go, and what it might take to send us there. Entering subspace is an absolutely beautiful experience, powered by trust, but trusting a siren song in these deep places seemed like a recipe for misfortune. As for the psyche siren's voice in whatever unknown daydream web, like anyone, trans folk have our days when we're kind to ourselves and days when we're not. I wrote this on the latter, haunted by questions of exploitation versus adoration. That line blurs, as does the line between trust and deception, even when we're careful.

THE POGONIP FOG

SEAN PATRICK HAZLETT

From *Galaxy's Edge* #42
Editor: Mike Resnick
Phoenix Pick

n the end, entropy always won. It had ruined Celia Lu's marriage and was slowly chiseling away at her youth. Heat death was inevitable, so why fight it? Celia figured she'd come to the cold of Squaw Valley to accelerate the process.

She stared at the resort's breathtaking landscape. Granite Chief's majestic snow-covered ridge thrust upward into the sky like an alabaster leviathan with a jagged gray spine and bristling emerald flanks. The sheer scale of it all both overwhelmed and inspired her.

Passing a motley parade of skiers heading toward the mountain, Celia wended her way along an icy path to the Squaw Valley Resort Ski School. After she'd finished putting on her gear, a late middle-aged man approached her.

"Celia?" he said.

She nodded.

He extended his hand. "I'm Tim, your instructor." Tim glanced at his watch. "My other three students are running late. Let's give 'em ten minutes, then we'll head up the mountain." He paused, then raised his right index finger. "One more thing: don't let the pogonip fog freak you out. It's a perfectly natural phenomenon."

What an odd thing to say, Celia thought. "Pogonip fog?"

"Some say it's a Native American word for 'ice fog' or 'white death'." He stopped, then chuckled. "My grandmother used to tell me terrifying tales. She'd whisper that the fog was the breath of the wendigo or mist seeping in from other realms. But I digress. Over the past few days, people have been complaining about it. If you see sunlight refracting into weird patterns, don't panic. It's only ice fog."

Celia smiled, humoring Tim, but inside she seethed. It was nine o'clock on the button and he was wasting her time and money with superstitious stories. Meanwhile the other laggards still hadn't shown up. She regretted not spending more money for a one-on-one lesson. It was yet another example of why Celia preferred doing things herself. She couldn't have risen to become the youngest partner in Wilson Sonsini's history by relying on other people. More often than not, they just got in the way.

Five minutes later, a young Asian woman arrived and introduced herself as Wendy. Celia exchanged pleasantries with the woman but wanted to throttle her for being late.

Tim clapped his hands. "All right. Looks like Bob and Jed aren't going to get here any time soon. I've told the front desk to have them meet us on the mountain. Let's go."

As the trio turned toward the exit, a tall man arrived. His face seemed hewn from stone. Smiling, he said, "I'm so sorry I'm late. I had an urgent business call."

Celia wanted to hate the man, but there was something intriguing about him. While he was handsome, it was the way he carried himself that sparked her interest. Here was a man who made things happen. Maybe scheduling a group session hadn't been such a bust after all, especially since one of the reasons she'd signed up for it was to meet like-minded people. If one of them happened to be attractive, so much the better.

Wendy shook Jed's hand and batted her eyelashes. He grinned, seemingly enjoying the attention, but it was clear to Celia he wasn't interested in any random floozy. Jed needed a challenge; someone to conquer.

The group went outside and walked to the tram building. Once inside, they scanned their lift tickets. Attempting to fish hers from her pocket, Celia fumbled awkwardly with her gear. Her skis and ski poles clattered to the floor.

"Here, let me help." Jed picked up her skis and ski poles. "Scan your card and I'll hand your stuff to you once you're on the other side of the gate."

Celia nodded and scrambled through the gate like a naked coed scurrying out of a frat house. Jed handed Celia her equipment, and then strode through the gate with the air of a ski pro.

"You sure you haven't been skiing your entire life?" Wendy said, giggling like a teenage girl.

Jed smiled. "Yeah, I'm sure."

"You look like a man who really knows his way around the slopes," Wendy said, with an arch of her back and slight sway of the hips.

Celia cringed at Wendy's ham-fisted double entendre. Jed just shrugged.

After climbing some stairs, Celia tentatively stepped out onto the tram. She glanced through the glass window on her right. A cable rose impossibly up the mountain's steep grade. In a sudden panic, she backed onto the platform, nearly knocking Wendy off her feet.

"I'm so sorry," Celia said, trying to smooth things over. Wendy barely concealed a scowl.

"Nervous?" Jed asked Celia, grinning.

Celia smiled back. "A bit."

"Don't worry," Tim said, "the tram is perfectly safe. If the winds get really bad, as a precaution, the tram will stop in place."

"I see," Celia said. The thought of the tram stopping and swaying in high winds did anything but reassure her.

They waited in the tram's far back corner for the other skiers to fill the space. The tram swayed forward, climbing toward the mountain's peak.

After her divorce, Celia had promised herself to confront her fears head on and without compromise. No matter what. As she craned her neck upward to take in the awesomeness of the looming mountain, she chuckled. After today, no one could ever accuse her of being a coward.

In the distance, dark gray clouds gathered. Celia beamed. Normally, their appearance would have depressed her, but here, she actually looked forward to the snow they promised.

Halfway up the mountain, an impenetrable hoarfrost with a

faint yellow hue swiftly crystalized on the tram's glass. It crackled and hummed as if it were a living and breathing thing. Celia's ears popped as they would on an aircraft experiencing a sudden change of altitude. An eerie whine followed. By instinct, Celia clutched Jed's arm. He smirked as an adult might at a child afraid of a monster under her bed. Celia blushed.

Tim harrumphed. "Like I said: pogonip fog."

The tram slowed to a gentle halt. The party followed the other passengers off the tram and into the High Camp facility. From there, Tim led them onto a fresh, unbroken layer of powder.

Celia found it odd that no skiers were already on the slopes, but she wasn't going to waste any more thought on the sudden good fortune of having the mountain to herself.

The gray clouds had by now arrived and were disgorging their snowy cargo in earnest. Out of the blinding whiteness, a tall, lanky figure wearing a black helmet and visor emerged from the howling wind. The stranger's movements were jangly and jerky.

"You Bob?" Tim asked.

The visitor responded with a slight nod.

Tim made his way toward Bob. A gust of wind nearly swept Tim off his feet. Nervous, Celia grabbed Jed's arm to keep her balance.

Tim stopped, steadying himself before continuing forward. The wind wailed so fiercely, Celia could barely hear Tim's words: ". . . need . . . off the mountain."

Celia couldn't have agreed more.

By now, Tim was fighting against driving snow drifts to ski back to the tram. Celia, Jed, and Wendy followed in Tim's wake, keeping close. Celia couldn't see more than five feet ahead of her.

A yellowish fog swirled around them like an ethereal swarm of insects. Celia had never seen or felt anything like it. It had a menacing air, like a lost soul haunting a desolate waste. The mist reeked of sulfur and putrefaction and, worst of all, it gave Celia the impression it was stalking them.

Halfway to the tram, Tim stopped and turned. Though Celia could hardly see, she shivered when she saw Tim's face—a face barely concealing panic.

"Where's Bob?" Tim said.

Celia shrugged. Bob could've been ten feet behind her and she still wouldn't have seen him.

"Wait here," Tim said. "I can't leave anyone behind." He skied past the group and up the mountain, disappearing into a snowy vortex. Celia almost could've sworn that wisps of fog had briefly coalesced into a grinning skull, then dissipated before she had a chance to fully process it. She shrugged it off, chalking it up to an overactive imagination heightened by fear.

The three skiers drew closer, seeking each other's warmth. The creeping miasma closed in, suffocating them with its overwhelming stench.

"You smell that?" Celia asked, covering her nose and mouth with her scarf to ward off the odor.

Jed screwed up his face and nodded.

"Any idea what it is?" said Celia.

"I've never smelled anything like it on a ski slope," Jed replied. "Maybe someone crashed a snowmobile nearby?"

Somewhat reassured, Celia supposed that could have explained it.

"I don't know," Wendy said. "It smells more like rotting meat to me—or a dead body."

"Don't be ridiculous," Celia countered, more to convince herself that Wendy's observations weren't accurate—though deep down, Celia was horrified she couldn't completely rule them out.

Celia shivered. The last thing she wanted was to perish in the blistering cold. As she waited for what seemed like an eternity, she grew more desperate to return to the tram.

"It's too cold. We really should head back," Celia said.

Jed shook his head. "We can't leave Tim out here. He could end up scouring the mountain for us, unnecessarily putting his life at risk. No. We need to wait here a little while longer."

Celia crossed her arms. She dug her chin into her chest. Her teeth rattled. Wracking her brain for a solution, she said, "If I had Tim's number, I'd call and tell him we were going back. Then once we reached the High Camp facility, we could call him again to let him know we'd reached safety."

"That's actually not a bad idea," Jed said. "Fortunately, I got Tim's number when we were on the tram."

Jed never ceased to impress Celia. "Well, then what are you waiting for? Call him."

Jed smiled awkwardly. The man wasn't accustomed to taking orders, but Celia was so cold she didn't give a damn. Jed stripped off his gloves, pulled an iPhone from his jacket pocket, and called Tim.

Celia locked eyes with Jed, watching his reaction. He waited several seconds, then shook his head.

Wendy sighed. "Bad signal?"

Jed ignored her.

"Try again," Celia said.

He scowled but called Tim anyway.

Jed said, "Hello?"

Celia's chest tightened. Thank God! She was finally going to get out of this frigid hellhole.

Jed yelled. He pitched his phone as if it had been on fire. From the corner of Celia's vision, she watched as a peculiar arc of fog traced the iPhone's trajectory. Unlike the blinding white snow around them, the fog had a jaundiced hue like mustard gas cloaking the moonscape of a World War I battlefield.

The fog arc condensed into a thick and smoky blob that hovered unnaturally over the spot where the iPhone had landed in the snow. A faint whine began to emanate from the device, steadily building into a deafening, bloodcurdling screech. As quickly as both the sound and the foggy apparition had arrived, they dissolved into the white wilderness.

"The hell was that?" Celia wondered aloud.

Jed shrugged.

"Are you okay?" Celia pointed at Jed's ear. A rivulet of blood was trickling from it.

He wiped it off and stuck his finger in his mouth. As if to minimize the discovery, he slid a few yards forward on his skis and fished his iPhone from the snow. "It's dead."

Celia shuddered. "We really should head back."

A man screamed—a piercing guttural scream; the kind you'd hear from a man who had an arm ripped from his socket.

"We're leaving. Right. Now!" Celia ordered.

"Tim and Bob are probably hurt," Jed said. "They could've gotten mauled by a bear."

"Impossible," Celia countered, exasperated. "Bears hibernate in the winter." She hesitated to say what she really thought—that something far worse than bears lurked within the swirling snow. Perhaps, she shuddered to think, it was the fog itself.

She was too late. Jed had already turned and was gliding through the snow toward the screams.

"Jed!" Celia yelled. "Don't be stupid."

For half a second, Celia seriously considered leaving, but she'd never forgive herself for abandoning the others.

"C'mon," Wendy nagged. "We can't leave Tim and Bob out there."

Celia wanted to smack her. Instead, Celia reined in her anger and nodded. She pushed her skis forward and followed Jed.

Jed maintained a punishing pace. Celia kept falling farther behind. Now, he was a gray blur in the distance.

"Slow down!" Celia yelled, but the whistling wind smothered her cries. Frustrated, she shouted louder. Again, the gale swept her voice down the mountain.

Then Celia remembered Wendy. Celia glanced backward into a white maelstrom. On the fringes of her vision, she detected hints of the bile-colored fog, drifting ever upward toward the mountain's snow-capped summit. Yet there was no sign of the other woman. Celia shuddered at the thought that Wendy might also have been trying to get her attention. Celia's heart raced. A slow, silent panic began to build; her gut grew queasy with guilt.

"Wendy!" she shouted. This time the wind carried her words in the right direction. But Wendy didn't answer.

Celia had a moment of doubt. If she stopped here, they'd all be lost. If she turned back, there was no guarantee she'd find the tram or Wendy. No. She had to keep trailing Jed, no matter his pace.

She slid forward, driving her ski poles through grueling snow drifts. Despite the cold, sweat poured down her cheeks. Her only solace was that her effort was keeping her warm.

Wendy squealed. A shadowy figure in the mist surged down the mountainside like a cannonball. Celia froze. Paralyzed, she waited for the thing rushing down the mountain to meet her.

Jed!

His face was grim with determination. He clutched Celia's arm. "Where is she?"

"I . . . I don't know." Celia fought to hold back an avalanche of emotions, but her tears betrayed her shame and fear.

"C'mon," Jed said. "She can't be far."

The two skied down the mountain until Jed identified a dark blot in the snow. As they drew closer, Celia heard weeping.

"Wendy!" Jed rushed forward and embraced her. "What happened?"

In between sobs, Wendy pointed toward a foggy yellow residue corrupting the surrounding mist. "There's . . . ah . . . there's blood everywhere."

Celia tracked Wendy's shaking finger to a steaming pool in

the snow.

"Jesus." Celia shook her head in disgust. "We need to leave. Let the police handle this."

"Look!" Jed pointed to a scarcely visible blood trail leading from the pool. "Tim and Bob can't be far. If we get to them soon, they might have a chance."

"C'mon, Jed," Celia pleaded. "They're dead. Didn't you see how much blood there was? Let's leave before whatever attacked them comes for us."

Jed folded his arms. He shot Celia a stern look. "We can't turn back now. We're so close. We need to act before that blood trail disappears. Otherwise, no one'll find them until the spring thaw."

Jed had a point. Tim and Bob couldn't be far. The trio would only have to go a few more yards before they could all turn back and return to the tram without regret. So they followed the trail.

An eerie wail echoed off the mountainside. This time, the cry sounded nothing like a person—more like metallic strings screeching on a chalkboard.

"What the hell was that?" said Celia, her heart pumping furiously.

"No idea," Jed replied, "but we gotta keep moving."

Celia reluctantly agreed. Wendy hesitated. Celia sympathized with the woman. After all, Celia had also frozen when she'd seen Jed coming down the mountain.

Patting Wendy's shoulder, Celia said, "C'mon. We need to keep pushing. We're almost there." Celia looked up at Jed. "Maybe we should stop and wait for the storm to die down?"

Jed shook his head. "If we stop, we'll freeze to death."

Celia knew he was right. She nodded and urged an increasingly distraught Wendy to forge ahead.

Jed shouted, "I found something."

Celia and Wendy surged forward to discover a black void in the snow. It drew the three travelers to it like iron filings to a lodestone. A wave of anticipation roiled Celia's stomach.

Jed arrived on the scene first. He immediately recoiled. Celia pushed forward to see for herself.

Inside the hollow, Tim's disembodied head stared lifelessly at the skiers. His eyes had rolled back into his skull. His mouth gaped open. His tongue lolled to the side.

His body was missing.

Stunned, the students stared in silence as the wind wailed and a deep and biting cold ravaged their bones. And the yellow fog—always the fog—lingered on the edges of Celia's vision as if to torment them. What was it?

Wendy tossed her ski poles. She kicked off her skis, then plodded down the mountain, vanishing into the yellow-tinged mist.

"Stop!" Jed yelled. He spun on his skis to pursue her.

Celia grabbed his arm. "Don't. She's lost to us. Our only hope is to wait out the storm."

Jed hesitated, but ultimately lowered his head in what Celia took for resignation.

Moments later, Wendy squealed like a gutted hog. From the volume of her screams, Celia knew she couldn't be far.

Wendy screeched again. Jed's eyes widened. He glanced back at Celia as if to ask for permission.

Celia shook her head.

An object landed with a squishy thud a few feet ahead. Jed lurched forward to investigate. His jaw dropped.

"What is it?" said Celia.

Jed lifted a steaming human hand—Wendy's hand.

The more Celia tried to ignore her senses, the more the disturbing scene impressed its horror upon her.

Another shriek pierced through the whistling wind.

"We have to do something." Jed launched himself into the churning maelstrom.

"No!" Celia yelled.

They were too late. It was a trap—Celia was certain of it-—a trap Jed had fallen for, hook, line, and sinker. Nothing in her life could have prepared her for that lonely moment. Isolated, the biting cold crept in and leached the heat from her shivering body. To survive, she had to keep moving. So she pointed her skis downhill and let them carry her down the mountain.

Disoriented and snow blind, she glided aimlessly into the eerie yellow-white fog, fleeing whatever had been preying on her companions.

Jed shrieked.

Celia trembled. She picked up speed. The faster her skis sliced through the snow, the more she struggled to keep control.

Jed cried out again. His voice seemed impossibly close—as if from above.

Despite her intense fear of heights, Celia quickened her pace.

A shadow darkened the gray sky. An instant later, something landed in the snow ahead with a puff. Transparent sickly yellow tendrils shot out from the mist ahead, gathering around the object like smoke over a campfire.

Celia grappled to govern her increasingly erratic descent. Narrowly avoiding a tree, she flipped head over skis, tumbling down the mountain until settling just feet away from whatever had fallen from the sky.

Instinctively, she knew it was Jed—or at least a part of him.

The shadow passed over Celia again. She quavered. She tried to get back on her feet, but her skis were stuck. She thrashed and wriggled, but to no avail. To center herself, she shut her eyes and took a deep breath. Focusing on staying calm, she opened her eyes and calmly released her skis. She stumbled to her feet and shambled over to where the fog had settled.

When she arrived, the waiting mustard-colored mist resolved into a grinning skull, taunting her, then disintegrated into the surrounding white.

Celia looked down and into a void in the snow. Discovering Jed there didn't surprise her; finding him alive did.

"Help me," he wheezed.

She scrambled over to him.

His face was paler than the snow. Celia crouched to get a closer look. When she saw Jed's entrails coiled outside his belly and covered with bite marks, she emptied her stomach.

Guttering, Jed reached for her, smearing her jacket with blood. He pulled her close and whispered, "That thing—it started eating me."

A high-pitched scream reverberated throughout the mountain valley. A black shape writhed in the great gray sky.

It dropped something, but whatever it was, it was too far away for Celia to make out.

The shadow made another pass overhead. Some distance away, it swooped to the surface. Something stirred, then slowly rose from the ground. It ambled toward her.

Celia tensely gripped her ski poles.

As the thing drew closer, Celia recognized the contours of a man—an ill-shaped, tall and lanky man.

He wore a visor.

She shook with trepidation. On rickety legs, the figure wobbled closer. She girded herself for a fight. If she had to die, she'd go down swinging. She imagined her ex and dug in her heels.

The stranger continued his awkward approach, moving as if on rubber legs. When he was nearly upon her, he stopped abruptly and flipped open the visor.

A black serpentine monstrosity with a mass of eyes, writhing tentacles, and razor-sharp fangs, snapped at Celia. The surreal nature of the encounter nearly paralyzed her—until the creature opened its maw—a maw with a stench reeking of the grave.

She shoved a ski pole between the thing's snapping jaws, then stabbed it repeatedly with the other. It shrieked in earsplitting whines and lashed out with black tentacles. Celia thrashed and cut and stabbed until the human mimic crumpled into a lifeless heap.

Just when she'd caught her breath, a lone shriek echoed from the wintry expanse. Another resounded in its wake, then another, and another.

Her constant yellow companion continued to loiter on the periphery, taunting her with its latent malevolence. What was it?

Shivering, she crawled over to Jed's body and dug a hole in the snow. She pulled his warm corpse into the hole with her. Embracing it, she hoped to weather the storm by clinging to his cadaver.

Celia slept fitfully, beset by terrifying visions. When she emerged from her hole the next morning, the storm had cleared. Faint red sunlight seeped through the gray sky, refracting into strangely beautiful hexagonal patterns tinted and befouled with a yellow haze.

She wandered back to where the beast had fallen to find it gone. The yellow fog was strangely distant now—still present, yet far away. Everywhere and nowhere, all at once.

With the sun as her guide, she headed east, back toward the resort. As she plodded down the mountain, she could find no sign that the resort had ever been here. In its place, impossibly high obsidian spires pierced the ominous gray sky. Now, there could be no doubt: she'd entered another realm. The more she thought about the haunting fog, the more she realized it had been both guide and gate—a formless Charon-like specter ferrying souls from the land of the living to the land of the dead.

As Celia continued her descent, black things circled those imposing spires—horrible tentacled things—all scales and eyes—and they were coming for her.

AUTHOR'S STORY NOTE

"The Pogonip Fog" first appeared in *Galaxy's Edge* in January 2020. This story explores themes of isolation, nihilism, dark interdimensional doorways, and the capriciousness of nature.

Pogonip is a Shoshone word meaning "white death." It is associated with the freezing fog common on the Eastern slopes of the Sierra Nevada Mountains. In the nineteenth century, the pogonip fog had a sinister reputation, often spurring Native American tribes to decamp when it approached. While the fog is harmless, these indigenous peoples likely feared it because of the damaging effect the harsh alpine air had on lung infections like tuberculosis, which were endemic during the period.

In this tale, the fog is a malevolent entity that, like an ethereal Charon, ferries the living to a bleak and inhospitable realm—only it does so against their will.

I went skiing for the first time at the impressionable young age of forty-three. Growing up, I never had the time or resources to learn how to ski. In college, while many of my wealthy classmates spent their weekends crushing powder near Lake Tahoe, I studied in my dorm room. It wasn't until I went on a work offsite that I had my first skiing lesson at the Squaw Valley Ski Resort. As it so happens, my instructor's name was Tim.

I was a terrible skier, but I enjoyed it and would love to return at the earliest opportunity. There's something sublime about basking in the glory of the Sierra Nevada Mountains in winter. While the alpine landscape is beautiful, if you fail to respect it, it will kill you.

This story was also inspired by Clark Ashton Smith's "The City of the Singing Flame." Like Celia Lu, the main character of Smith's tale also passes into a strange realm from which he never returns. Interestingly, the realm's portal in Clark's story was on Crater Ridge near Donner Summit—not far from the Squaw Valley Ski Resort in "The Pogonip Fog."

A vein of nihilism winds mercilessly through this tale. Celia Lu, an avatar of self-reliance, forges through life armed with nothing but her wiles and grit. She defies the odds over and over again, until she doesn't. When the pogonip fog invades her reality and transports her to a frozen alien world of winged monstrosities circling black spires, her determination makes no difference. For nature is a vast and uncaring leviathan, warped by the winds of entropy. And entropy always wins.

GUNFIRE AND BRIMSTONE

ALICIA HILTON

From *Vastarien:* Volume 3, Issue 2
Editors: Jon Padgett, Matt Cardin & Michael Cisco
Grimscribe Press

The greenish-yellow goo smelled like a rotting corpse dredged from a primordial swamp. I discarded the soiled diaper, wiped off Gordon's plump buttocks, and wrapped a fresh nappy around his stiff little weenie. He had the unblinking stare of a zombie.

His little hands clenched and unclenched as they reached for my face.

I gritted my teeth, fighting the urge to scream. My nose still hurt where he'd scratched it yesterday, leaving a crusty scab. Maybe I was being paranoid, but it didn't seem normal that a newborn could be so aggressive.

It wasn't the first time I'd regretted having the drunken one-night stand. Twenty-four days had passed since Gordon tore through my vajayjay, but it seemed like he was still attached to my body by his umbilical cord.

I said, "Gordon's a good baby," and tickled his chubby little belly.

He opened his mouth, exposing an incisor that poked from his lower gums. *Was that a smile?*

I caressed his cheek.

All of a sudden, he swiveled his head and bit my forearm.

I shrieked and yanked my arm away. He hadn't broken the skin, but the single tooth had left a triangular purplish-pink bruise. My nine-pound, five-ounce bundle of joy seemed to have as much affection for me as a maggot that wanted to burrow into a slab of meat.

I forced myself to smile and said, "Mommy's going to trade options. Do you think Apple's stock price will rise? Should I double up on AAPL calls?"

Gordon's face reddened, steel grey eyes bulging like he was straining to form words. His ass gurgled.

I peeked inside the diaper. Miraculously, he was still clean. Before he could open his greedy maw and demand to gnaw on my nipples, I put him back in his crib and turned off the lights.

Since my home office had become a nursery, computer monitors were spread across the kitchen counter. At least it was only a temporary situation. Yesterday, I'd closed escrow on a two-bedroom condo. The hardwood floors were being refinished.

While I watched trading data, I pressed my phone's speed dial. My assistant answered. I said, "Any decent leads from the cold callers?"

"An aircraft leasing company VP interested in Bitcoin, and an automotive repair shop owner who's unhappy with his broker," Bradley said.

"Schedule appointments for me to meet with them tomorrow."

"Tomorrow?" his voice rose. "You said you were taking two months maternity leave."

"The nanny starts tomorrow. I'll be in the office before the market opens." I disconnected the call and poured another cup of coffee.

The baby monitor emitted a ringing sound, then a man's voice said, "Mr. Jacobs. It's Bob Warner from Bayshore Financial. I can offer you the Trifid Orion Tech IPO. You want 2,000 shares or 2,500?"

I rushed to Gordon's room. He was sleeping, a drool bubble clinging to his lip. I shut the door and kept listening to the baby monitor. A deeper-voiced man said, "I'm going to pass. My wife thinks it's too risky."

"Put your hand between your legs. Is there anything there, or are you just a pussy?"

"Don't insult me."

"You're insulting me by wasting my time. I'll take you off my client list."

"All right, all right. Give me 2,500 shares."

I opened my Internet browser. Trifid Orion Tech didn't exist. Bayshore Financial was in Texas, but the broker on the phone sounded like he was from Staten Island.

I spent a few more minutes searching the web. A blog post claimed that baby monitors could pick up cell phone conversations, if the devices broadcasted on the same frequency.

After placing a few trades, I checked on Gordon and saw that he was lying on his side, snoring softly. The flannel teddy bear print onesie made him look cuddly and adorable. I stroked his back.

When I touched the soft fabric, I felt a sharp sensation that vibrated through my body, like an electric shock from sticking your finger in a light socket.

The pain increased in intensity. I couldn't pull my hand away. I smelled singed hair. I swiveled my wrist, then pushed back with my elbow, trying to break free.

Spasms traveled through my forearm, to my shoulder, to my neck. My face felt numb. I tried to open my mouth to scream, but my lips wouldn't move. I tasted something vile. Moldy mushrooms? No, not mushrooms. The coating on my tongue had a sweeter, slimier flavor.

Strange thoughts flitted through my mind. I saw myself shopping in a fancy boutique, trying on scarlet lingerie. Much skimpier and sexier than my usual plain cotton briefs. I pivoted in front of the dressing room mirror, admiring my figure. My face looked like it had been grafted onto someone else's body. My tummy bulge was gone. The bra's lacy cups barely covered bountiful tits that must've been sculpted by a plastic surgeon. The nipples jutted forward, poking against the sheer fabric. Before I'd gotten pregnant, my breasts had barely filled out a B cup. Since I was lactating, they'd ballooned to a C cup, but they still sagged. If I got lipo and a boob lift, would I look as hot as the sex kitten in the hallucination?

The vision shifted. I was sitting by myself, on an airplane. Not flying coach in a big commercial jet, jammed into a seat that squeezed my chubby butt.

This cabin was smaller, but much more spacious. There were only eight seats, but they were the size of lounge chairs and upholstered in creamy tan leather.

A man wearing a tight burgundy pinstriped suit walked down the aisle, towards me. He was carrying a bottle and a slender crystal glass on a silver tray. "Would you like champagne?"

"Yes," I said.

The liquid fizzed as it filled the glass. Instead of being amber-colored or pale pink, the champagne was bright crimson.

The man smiled. "Can I offer you anything else?"

I felt heat flushing my face. The way he was looking at me made me think he was offering sex, which was strange, because I'd never been propositioned by a man that attractive.

He wasn't handsome in a conventional way like George Clooney, Chris Hemsworth, Idris Elba, or Ken Watanabe. The flight attendant looked a lot more dangerous. He had a thin scar across his left cheekbone, like he'd been sliced with a razor. He was slim and not much taller than me, but he moved like he'd be lethal in a fight. His gaze was hypnotic. The irises were an unusual shade of hazel—deep brown flecked with green and gold.

The flight attendant said, "You don't want your champagne?"

My hand shook when I lifted the glass. The liquid had stopped bubbling, but it was still red. I took a sip. Then another. At first, the flavor seemed like honey, but as I drank deeper, it became richer, stronger, almost like brandy. As the beverage flowed down my throat, I heard another voice. Not the flight attendant. The sound was coming from inside my head. A seductive whisper, "Money, power, sex, love. You can have anything you desire."

The flight attendant's smile widened. He said, "You can have anything you desire," echoing the voice inside my head. "Katherine, what do you desire?"

"Just the champagne."

"Nothing else? Let me give you a massage."

"No."

He raised his eyebrows. "You prefer women?"

"I don't want a massage."

He put his hand on my shoulder.

I flinched. His grip tightened.

The taste in my mouth changed from sweet to vile. "Let me go!" I said.

His nose trembled. An ant crawled out of his left nostril and skittered across his cheek, clinging to the scar. Against his tawny skin, the exoskeleton gleamed, fluctuating in color from shiny ivory to cherry red and back to ivory again.

I screamed and dropped the champagne flute.

The insect doubled in size, and grew again, until it was bigger than my thumb.

I tried to get out of my chair, but my body was paralyzed.

The ant pivoted its head. Mandibles snapped open and shut, like it was preparing to bite. It leapt towards me.

Finally released from the terrifying trance, I stumbled backward, away from the crib.

My right hand, the same hand that had been stuck to Gordon's body, felt like ants were crawling all over it, but there was nothing there, except for a purplish triangular bruise on my palm, just like the mark his tooth had left on my arm.

I rushed into the bathroom, turned on the faucet, and blasted cold water against my palm. The itchy sensation changed to a throbbing, a rolling pulse that hummed through my body. I gritted my teeth against the pain.

Tears streamed down my face. I grabbed the medicine cabinet and yanked it open.

The shelves were filled with pill bottles. *Fuckety fuck, where was the goddamn oxy?* I grasped an amber-colored bottle. It was empty.

Weeping louder, I grabbed the prenatal vitamins, hurling them on the floor. Next, I threw the bottle of stool softener I'd used when my bowels got jammed up during the first trimester. The bottle shattered, raining bright pink pills across the tile floor.

I moved a jar of face cream and grabbed the foil packet that had been stuffed behind it. There were four of the 2mg Ativan left. I'd stopped taking the anti-anxiety medication after the positive pregnancy test, because I didn't want to hurt my baby.

I swallowed one of the little yellow pills and splashed water on my face.

My fingers clenched the edge of the sink. I shut my eyes, praying that the agonizing sensation would go away, but the pounding in my head increased. It felt like a monkey was smacking a mallet into my temple.

I swallowed the last three Ativan.

Exhaustion washed over me. Slowly, the headache dissipated to a slight twitch behind my eyeballs.

Thirsty. I was so very thirsty. I turned on the faucet and guzzled water from the tap, but it didn't wash the horrid scum from my tongue. Even though the hallucinations I'd experienced couldn't have been real, my mouth still tasted like the disgusting red liquid. It would have been logical to brush my teeth, but I was too confused to think coherently.

I don't remember walking to the kitchen, don't remember picking up the whiskey bottle. I should've poured just a taste into a glass, gargled and spit it out, but I latched my lips onto the bottle and chugged. Liquid fire spread from my tongue to my gut. My nostrils flared, inhaling the peaty scent.

A delicious shivery sensation made me pause and giggle. I set the bottle on the counter and used the back of my hand to wipe a dribble from my chin.

The voice inside my head changed, becoming deeper, more gravely, "Fat piggy. You'll never amount to anything." The taunt repeated, rising to a shout. It sounded just like my father. I hadn't seen the cruel bastard since I'd left home when I was eighteen.

Cold air washed over me. I heard a *creak* and a *tearing* noise.

Expecting to see an intruder, I whirled around, but there was no one there.

I felt a sharp pinching sensation on my left hip. Pain made me yelp. When I looked down, I saw a long slash of fabric missing from my jeans, between the waistband and my thigh. The exposed skin had a nasty purplish bruise. It was shaped like a triangle, just like the bruises on my arm and palm.

The voice in my head snarled, "Fat piggy. Pig, pig, piggy."

I touched the bruise. My skin was tender, and colder than an ice cube.

How could my pants have gotten torn? The denim was thick, not easy to rip. Had I fallen?

Dizziness compelled me to collapse on the carpet and lie on my side. The pale green carpet fibers looked like they were swaying. I squeezed my eyes shut.

The taunts got louder, "Fat, lazy piggy. You'll never amount to anything."

I look a deep breath, then another, waiting for my nerves to calm. My father would never love me, but I wouldn't let his memory taunt me.

The voice still echoed in my head, but I opened my eyes and grabbed the side of the kitchen counter, pulling myself to my feet.

There was an inch of amber liquid left in the bottle. I hurled it in the trash.

The baby monitor made a squelching noise. I assumed I was about to overhear another phone call, but Gordon screamed, "Waaaaaaaaaaaah!" a blood-curdling cry, like he was in terrible pain.

My body was still swaying. I tried to sprint towards his room, stumbled, and had to grasp the wall for support. I opened the nursery room door.

Gordon stared at me. He'd stopped screaming.

I said, "Are you okay?"

I touched his forehead. His skin was cool, but the carrot-colored fuzz that coated his scalp glistened with moisture.

His mouth opened, exposing shiny pink gums and the single sharp incisor. Mimicking my father's deep voice, he said, "Fat, lazy piggy. You'll never amount to anything."

Convinced that I was hallucinating, I shook my head.

Gordon repeated the taunt, "You'll never amount to anything!"

Infants couldn't talk. I was going crazy.

Gordon used the crib bars to pull himself into a sitting position and grasped my wrist. His grip was so tenacious, I couldn't pull free. He used his other hand to scratch my forearm, leaving long scarlet scratches that looked like they'd been made by a cat.

"Stop!" I begged.

He squealed, as if he relished my agony.

Spittle flecked my face, making my eyes sting. My vision swam until his face was a blur. I felt his hot little tongue, lapping fluid from my wounds.

When I could finally see again, I was standing next to the hall closet. The wall safe beneath the coats was open. I picked up my gun.

The pistol felt heavier than I remembered. I clicked off the safety, opened my mouth, and stuck the 9mm's barrel between my teeth.

The baby monitor made a buzzing noise. A woman's voice came from the machine, saying, "How much do I need to invest to get in on the IPO?"

"Two thousand shares," a man answered.

My hand shook. I relaxed my index finger and pulled it away from the trigger.

I should have blown the back of my head off, but I shoved the gun in my waistband, slipped on a jacket to hide the weapon, and opened my apartment door.

The elevator dinged.

I turned to the left, checking to see whether one of my neighbors was coming.

There was no one in the hallway, but I felt a sharp pinch in the small of my back. I tried to hold my legs in place, but the next pinch was even more painful. I lurched forward, taking a step towards the fire escape.

Each time I tried to pause, I felt invisible fingers, twisting the skin on my lower back. I moved further down the hallway, dragging my bare feet across the bristly carpet.

Outside the apartment closest to the fire escape, I smelled something noxious, like a dumpster in August. I pressed my ear to the apartment door and heard, "Mr. Frederick. I'm calling you from trading."

Either Mrs. Goldstein had moved or she was running a bucket shop, scamming investors.

My stomach gurgled. I was about to vomit, but instead of running away, I pounded on the door.

The sound echoed down the hallway.

A college-aged kid with a scraggly goatee and shaggy bleached blond hair opened Mrs. Goldstein's door.

I pushed past him, forcing my way into the apartment.

Fast-food wrappers and chunks of pizza crust were scattered across the powder blue shag carpet. The kitchen trashcan was overflowing. Amidst the rank odor of refuse, I recognized the sweet stench of death.

I wanted to scream for help but couldn't make my lips move.

Another millennial who wore his dark brown hair slicked back sat at the kitchen table, pounding on a stapler to make a sound like an old-fashioned ticker tape. He noticed me and hung up the phone.

The blond man said, "What do you want?"

Breath flowed past my vocal cords, and a voice that sounded like my father's said, "Nice scam you're running. Where's Mrs. Goldstein?"

The blond said, "Get out, before I call the police."

Father's voice said, "Call the cops. They'll lock you up for defrauding investors. But you've got another choice. Work for me and make serious money."

"How much?"

"More than you'll make running a scam. You hook the prospects, and I'll close the sales. Pass the Series 7, and I'll—"

The brunette said, "Put her in the bathtub with Granny."

My hand slid to my waistband. I drew the gun.

I saw the brunette hurl the stapler but didn't move in time to avoid the blow. The stapler smacked the side of my head.

The blond kicked me in the side while I was distracted, knocking me to my knees.

I bit my tongue. Tasted copper.

My first bullet grazed the blond's shoulder, leaving a crimson streak. He stumbled backwards.

I brought the weapon back on target. The second 9mm round blasted through his left eye socket, spattering the yellow and white flowered wallpaper with a gory sunburst. His body collapsed on the carpet.

When my ears stopped ringing, I realized that I was still squeezing the trigger, but the pistol's magazine was empty.

I couldn't recall how I'd pulled myself to my feet. Didn't remember shooting the brunette, but there were three scarlet splotches on his torso.

The gory tableau reminded me of a Jackson Pollock painting. I dropped the pistol on the carpet.

Bile rose up my throat. Some of the vomit sprayed the side of the velvet sofa. I sprinted towards the kitchen sink. The last of my courage drained down the disposal, along with chunks of masticated fruit, granola, and yogurt, in a foul soup that reeked of stomach acid and whiskey.

I took a deep breath, trying to calm myself. Grabbing a fistful of paper towels, I wiped my mouth and called, "Mrs. Goldstein?"

There was no answer.

At first glance, the bathroom didn't look like a crime scene. The shiny black and white ceramic tiles were clean. I yanked back the shower curtain.

There were bruises on Mrs. Goldstein's neck. Her skin was cold.

For about two seconds, I thought I could remain coherent enough to call the police. I stumbled back into the living room and grabbed the powder blue phone from the end table.

A dispatcher answered, "Nine-one-one. What's your emergency?"

"They ki . . . killed—" I collapsed.

When I regained consciousness, I was sprawled on my stomach in the living room. Handcuffs bound my wrists behind my back.

The temperature must've been at least seventy-five degrees inside the apartment, but I couldn't stop shivering.

A female police officer helped me to stand. She read the Miranda warning and asked me if I was willing to talk.

A male officer stood near the front door, gawking at us. Another man wearing a blue windbreaker was taking photographs of the two men I'd shot.

"Yes," I said.

She said, "Where'd you put the gun?"

"I dropped it near the sofa." I gestured with my head.

"It's not there. Where'd you put it?"

"I don't remember."

"I need to frisk you for weapons. You got anything that could cut me?"

I shook my head.

The female officer's hands swept my body, squeezed my breasts, buttocks, and groin.

My bladder felt like it was going to explode. I bit my lip, determined not to piss myself.

She quit frisking me and said, "She's clean."

An older male detective walked out of the bathroom. He said, "There's an elderly woman in the bathtub. DRT."

My knees started to shake. "They tried to kill me."

The female officer said, "Do you want us to call your husband?"

"I'm not married. My son's home alone."

Something flickered in the female cop's eyes. Pity? Rage? Then the expression was gone, the neutral mask back in place.

The male detective said, "Which apartment?"

"302. Can I go with you? Gordon's just a baby."

"No," he said. He looked at the female officer. "Keep her here until I find the kid." He motioned for the male patrol officer to follow him. They left the apartment.

The female officer tugged on my arm, leading me toward a chair. "Sit down," she said. When my ass hit the cushion, the handcuffs bit into my flesh. Pain brought clarity. Demon babies only existed in horror stories. Other women experienced postpartum depression and didn't act crazy. I was the only one to blame for my choices.

My aching bladder reminded me that I needed to piss. "Can I use the bathroom?" I said.

She shook her head. "It's a crime scene."

A few minutes later, I heard the detective's voice coming from the radio. He said, "There's no baby in the apartment. Just a doll in the crib."

The female officer keyed her mike and said, "Roger that." She looked at me. "What did you do with your kid?"

"He was in the crib!"

The guard shut the consultation room door, but I could hear his boots, squeaking against the hallway's linoleum floor. Meetings with a lawyer were supposed to be confidential, but in the holding cells, somebody was always listening.

My attorney opened her briefcase and removed a stack of papers. She said, "The prosecutor's offering a three-year sentence if you plead to second-degree manslaughter. With good behavior, you could be home in less than two years."

"But it was self-defense," I said. Sweat rolled down my back.

"You go to trial, you could be convicted of second-degree murder. The jurors will look at you and see a woman motivated by greed. You should've called the police when you heard them talking about the scam."

"But they murdered Mrs. Goldstein!" I rubbed my left hand across my forearm. Since I'd been incarcerated, the bruise on my arm from Gordon's tooth had festered, becoming a gaping wound the size of a nickel. The crater stung and oozed puss, but I couldn't stop touching it.

The lawyer said, "Neither of them was older than twenty-five. The prosecutor's going to make the jury think they could've been rehabilitated. You brought the gun and showed a depraved indifference for human life."

"You could argue extreme emotional disturbance."

"On what basis? You thought the doll was a baby? You couldn't resist the allure of a con game? If I thought you had a credible defense, I'd tell you to roll the dice and take the case to trial."

I stared at the sore on my arm. Gordon wasn't a doll. Dolls didn't bite.

I'd always liked gambling, but fear had given me an ulcer. "Tell the prosecutor that I'll take the deal."

My first night in the maximum-security prison, I'd barely slept, but no one tried to stab me with a shiv.

Even in the middle of the night, the florescent hallway lights stayed on. Security cameras were everywhere. The metal cell doors had windows, to make it easier for the guards to spy on us.

The walls were thin, and there was always someone talking, whimpering, moaning.

Most of the inmates stank of sweat and asked too many questions, but at least they only wanted to learn how to run a Ponzi scheme.

After my felony convictions, I'd lost my license to trade investments. Maybe I'd start an investment club while I was incarcerated to keep my mind occupied, but I'd never be a broker again.

The lounge area TV was playing a boring reality show about rich housewives. All of the women had perfect skin and bleached blonde hair. They were bickering about what to wear to a party, but their shrill voices were a welcome distraction.

I glanced at my cellmate. Francesca rubbed her swollen belly. She said, "Tony's gonna be a great father. When is your baby due?"

"I'm not pregnant." I looked at my stomach. The ugly orange uniform shirt was too tight. Since I'd accepted the plea agreement, my waist had swollen, growing at least four inches.

"I'm sorry," she said. "I wasn't trying to be mean."

"That's okay. No hard feelings." I tried to smile, but the corners of my mouth wouldn't turn up. I poked at the sore on my arm. The puss had changed from being clear to a milky yellow, flecked with red. I said, "Are you having a girl or a boy?"

"A boy. Only six more weeks to go. Don't worry, you're young. Plenty of time to meet a good man and start a family." Francesca grinned. "You hungry? Saturday's taco night. If we get there early, there'll be extra jalapenos."

The next morning, Francesca was found dead in a shower. I wasn't the one who discovered the body, but I heard that she'd been bludgeoned on the head. The doctor hadn't been able to revive her or save her baby.

Even though I barely knew Francesca, I shed a few tears and skipped breakfast.

A few hours later, I was dozing when a guard opened my cell door.

"Anderson," he said. "You're bunking with Enfer."

Geena Enfer's eyes were piercing blue, not hazel flecked with gold, but she had a thin scar across her left cheek, just like the flight attendant from my hallucination.

Geena grinned, "We're gonna get along just fine."

Sometimes reality was worse than your most horrific nightmare.

My belly kept swelling, until it felt so heavy, I had to stop running laps when we were allowed to exercise in the yard.

The skin on my abdomen stretched more and more and more. Wicked, raised crimson marks spiraled across the surface of my flesh, in a pattern that looked like a spider's web, with a thick scab in the center, surrounding my belly button. Thinner wavy lines traced gruesome pathways all the way over my breasts and down to my thighs.

The more the skin stretched, the more it itched. I had to wear socks on my hands at night, so my nails wouldn't gouge more furrows.

I'd been incarcerated for four months, but my gut had become so swollen, I looked six months pregnant. The bloat wasn't caused by overeating. I rarely finished my meals. Prison food was so bland, eating was a chore. Gummy meatloaf, lumpy mashed potatoes, burned stews, sandwiches with rubbery meat, over-cooked vegetables, and bruised fruit. Even the eggs were disgusting. The tacos were the only meal that tasted like it could have come from a restaurant, but whenever Mexican food was served, it was hard to choke down even a bite. I always thought about Francesca and how she'd liked jalapenos.

The first time I begged to see a doctor, the guards ignored me. I had to file a complaint with the warden and wait another week.

The infirmary doctor was brusque, barely talking to me before he jabbed my arm with a needle. After he drew blood, he had me piss in a cup. The lab results were normal. No signs of cancer.

Nine days later, I was driven in a van to the local hospital, for an ultrasound.

The guard escorted me through the back door, wearing hand-cuffs, of course. Then I was cuffed to a stretcher.

When the doctor lifted up my shirt, he gasped. "What did you do to yourself?"

"I scratched. The skin itches."

"Quit scratching. You've got an infection. I'll write you a script for an antibiotic."

He grabbed a bottle, shook it, and squirted ultrasound jelly my belly. Then he picked up a transducer and rubbed it over the skin. The cold sensation made me shiver.

He checked the computer monitor and said, "Your ovaries are fine. I don't see any cysts. Cut out the sugar. Get some exercise. You need to lose weight."

When I heard his diagnosis, heat rushed to my face. My father's words echoed in my head: "Fat, lazy piggy."

The guard gave me a malicious grin. I wanted to punch him until his lip split, but I said, "Thank you, doctor."

When I got back to my cell, Geena was waiting. She said, "I missed you," and patted her mattress.

I sat beside her and leaned my back against her chest. How could you deny a demon what she wanted, especially when her touch was so sensual, it was addictive?

Geena wrapped her arms around me, cradling my belly with her palms. She pulled my waistband aside and slid her hand inside my panties, stroking my pubes. Her fingers were hot. Not hot enough to burn, but so warm that I squirmed.

I opened my legs wider.

Something inside my abdomen twitched.

Geena licked my ear. Her breath was icy cold and smelled of brimstone.

She said, "Gordon is going to have a little sister."

AUTHOR'S STORY NOTE

"Gunfire and Brimstone" is a weird, cross-genre tale about awakening dark desires, good versus evil, and transformation. What happens when people give in to their urges? Inhibitions can staunch creativity and sabotage success, but conscience also restrains some people from becoming monsters. No one is purely good or purely evil. If demons awakened your dark desires, what horrifying acts would you commit?

THE HAPPIEST MAN IN THE WORLD

MATTHEW V. BROCKMEYER

From *Nest of Salt*
Black Thunder Press

t was supposed to be a standard drug bust.

Your average pill-mill situation: corrupt croaker doctor handing out scripts of OxyContin and Xanax for cash and favors. The Sheriff's Department, where I was a deputy, were to assist the DEA—which was protocol since it was originally our case, and also a courtesy since we were the ones who had alerted them to it in the first place. I was sent mostly to observe, that and help catalogue and transport all the evidence, which was bound to be a huge haul. Word was there were piles of cash and pills lying all over, stacks of pre-signed prescription pads waiting to be sold, boxes of files. Every item was going to have to be catalogued. The doctor was apparently using too, and the place was supposed to be a real mess.

And then there was the basement.

Of course, we'd been warned about what might be in the basement, what horrors we might find, but it was more horrible than any of us could imagine.

The basement was where the abortions were performed. You see, it was a pill mill by day and unlicensed, underground abortion clinic by night. Mostly women in the third trimester with nowhere else to turn. The desperate and poverty stricken. Or very young girls, hiding their predicament, scared and alone. We'd heard the rumors and whispers. Nasty stories of hastily performed operations with dirty instruments, of how he'd give near term women Cytotek and have them miscarry in the toilet. How he'd scoop the squirming fetuses from the dirty water and snip their spines with a scissor.

I'd only been a sheriff's deputy a few months at that point. It'd been a tough few years for me. After Amanda's death, I'd been in a dangerously dark place. Still so painful to think about, yet it's never far from my thoughts. Lingering there like a festering kernel of lead in my brain, causing a gangrene of the soul.

Fuck, how it haunts me. That terrible head-on collision with that damn drunk asshole (three previous DUIs on his record, if the crash hadn't killed him, I swear to God I would have found him and done the job myself) on that horrible, horrible winter night, leaving me a widower at thirty-two.

The doctors all agreed it was a miracle I'd lived.

I can remember lying there in the hospital, surrounded by ticking machines, tubes and wires running everywhere, my body wrapped in bandages and held fast by armatures. Lost in a morphine drip, I just kept thinking, *Why? Why spare me? Why couldn't I have been killed, too?*

The shit I'd been through as a soldier, the chances I'd taken, walking through minefields and facing sniper fire in godforsaken desserts, only to come home and have my wife and unborn son taken from me by something as mundane as a car accident.

I didn't want to live without her. And for a while I seriously contemplated ways to remedy that situation. Going back to the house was hell, all the pictures of Amanda and I together, so many of her pregnant and showing off her bulging belly. I couldn't stand to look at them, and I couldn't bear to take them down either, to touch them. I'd been in the heart of battle, seen unimaginably horrible things, but nothing was worse than staring at a picture of Amanda with her swollen belly, me beside her, but not me, a former me, the me I used to be.

I'd avoid them when I could, but if one caught my gaze, I'd find myself staring for hours, imagining those wonderful times, reverie and nostalgia like a physical weight atop me, like one of those lead-filled blankets they drape over you during an X-ray.

Our golden retriever Daisy, (named by Amanda because her golden coat reminded her of the center of that simple yet lovely flower) was some consolation. Her warm, kind eyes, so obviously thrilled to see me, tail thudding against the floor in such a happy beat. But even she could be difficult to look at times, so filled with memories she was. It was hard to see her and not think of Amanda.

About a month after I got out of the hospital, my Uncle won his bid for sheriff. Won in a landslide, actually. The last guy had been wrapped up in some scandalous shit. Uncle Ross took pity on me, took me on as a full-time deputy. Not that I wasn't qualified. I was more than qualified. Former first-class officer combat veteran having served in Falujah and Kabul. But pity on me in that it was no secret I'd suffered a long series of trauma and tragedy, both on the battlefield and off, and bore the effects.

You hear it called the hundred-yard stare. Shit, I had that before losing Amanda. My stare had gone infinite.

It was like I was trying to see between things and beyond things: part of me trained to be aware of everything at once, part of me desperate to retreat to nothingness and give it all up. A conflict of will I carried burden-like on my shoulders and in my hard gaze.

But I digress, don't I?

It's so easy for me to get lost in the past. My memories are like some intricate, horrible maze. Let me get back to the bust.

His name was Dr. Fozie L. West. Late sixties, white-haired, bone thin. In the hours before the raid, sipping coffee with the DEA at the Sheriff's Office, we'd each been given a printout with his picture and a brief description. He looked like someone from a different time, a previous century. The 1920s maybe, with his tweed suit and long, grim face like H. P. Lovecraft or Albert Fish.

It was snowing when we converged on the clinic—a shabby building in a shitty part of town, surrounded by cheap motels, liquor stores and check-cashing joints. A crudely painted PAIN MANAGEMENT CENTER sign hung above the door. We quickly poured out, stomping across the fresh snow, and swarmed the place, the DEA barging in first, guns drawn, and us tailing behind.

We burst into a little anteroom where Christmas music was playing: Jingle Bell Rock. A startled secretary stared at us, stunned. A couple of dirty junkie-looking types sat in the corner by a small plastic Christmas tree, hooded sweatshirts and hooded eyes, obviously waiting for a fix. The place was filthy and reeked of cat shit and a swampy fetid odor coming from a huge fish tank, half-filled with green water and swarming with turtles. A DEA agent kicked open an office door and there was the doctor, trying to worm his way out of a small window, squirming, legs furiously kicking insect-like. An agent ordered him to freeze, and he slipped down to the ground and turned. There was a pistol in his hand.

Before anyone had a chance to even scream or holler a warning, he had the barrel of that gun up against his temple and was squeezing the trigger. The gunshot rang out like an explosion in that cramped office. He fell to the floor and the blood made an awful sluicing sound as it squirted up, out of his head, splashing the walls.

Pandemonium broke out. The secretary was screaming hysterically, the junkies running to the door. There were cries to call an ambulance, agents and sheriff's deputies racing about frantically. I was oddly calm, enveloped in an eerie sensation of detachment and curiosity, as if I was watching the chaotic scene from a distance. Time stretched and slowed, the hurried motions of the people around me playing out frame-by-frame as a high-pitched ringing filled my head, and I found myself wandering away from the madness of the front rooms and down a long corridor.

A rangy tabby cat mewled up at me as I slipped down the hall, an otherworldly push leading me into the depths of the clinic.

It was a confusing maze of passageways and rooms, medical waste bags strewn everywhere, flies swarming and buzzing over puddles of brown liquid on the floor, splatters on the wall, random boxes filled with cat shit and shredded paper. I came to a big industrial refrigerator, opened it and peered inside. More medical waste bags, an apple, yogurt containers, a half-eaten sandwich, and several tall glass jars filled with tiny white feet floating in a milky liquid.

Yes, feet. No bigger than the nub of your pinky, but perfectly formed: little ankles and toes. Dozens and dozens of them. All left. It was so surreal and disgusting. I gagged, but still felt this desire to keep moving and explore.

Onward I went, that crazy buzzing tone growing louder in my skull, past piles of trash and broken, discarded medical equipment, past a doorway where in a dark, tiny room a young girl lay on a gurney, groaning softly. She turned her head to me, a dazed-and-pleading look in her eyes. She held out a hand. But I kept walking.

Finally, I came to a black door adorned with a small, innocuous sign: BASEMENT.

I did *not* want to go down to that basement. The rational part of my brain was howling against it, but some strange force compelled me. Barely conscious of my own movements, in a foggy daze like a sleepwalker, that ringing in my ears rising a notch in tone, I pulled the door open and started down those dark steps and into the shadowy cavernous chamber.

The muffled cries of women moaning echoed from back rooms, and a new scent hit me, both antiseptic and sour, like cleaning products and death. Drawn forward, I passed stainless-steel tables where I saw unspeakable things in the pale-blue scintillating fluorescent light: piles of little body parts, fetuses like miniature, pale, discarded baby dolls, dismembered and sewn back together, some missing heads, some with their arms and legs switched and backwards. It was truly awful, beyond anything I'd ever seen in war.

And then . . . then I was before a small red door with an ornate brass handle.

I knew I shouldn't be down there. That I could potentially be polluting or even destroying evidence, that this was more than a crime scene, it was an abomination against nature and all that was good in the world. But a compulsion I couldn't name or control drove me to try and open the door, to twist and tug on the strange knob.

It was locked.

The door wouldn't budge, and I actually breathed a sigh of relief. For I didn't really want to go back there at all. In fact, I wanted out of that terrible dungeon of a place and my mind was screaming, "Get out! Get out! Get out now!"

But just as I stepped back from the door there was a creak, and I gasped, nearly choking on my own breath, as the door cracked open.

Out of no volition of my own, I reached out, opened the door, and found myself staring into the vastness of deep space: planets and stars, galaxies spiraling throughout luminous nebulas of purple and orange.

I wavered under the enormity of it, remembering myself as a child beneath the gaping maw of the planetarium, staggered by the vastness, and later as a soldier staring at the infinite desert sky, the constellations scintillating and glimmering, melting together.

But blinking, I realized it was just hundreds of candles. Yes, hundreds of candles in a dark room with black-painted walls. I took in a deep breath of air, let it slowly out through clenched teeth, jarred by that ringing which seemed to fill my entire body now, curling my toes and straightening the tiny hairs on the back of my neck.

My eyes adjusting to the dim amber light, I saw there was a star-shaped pattern painted on the floor in red, with strange writing and symbols around it, and before it an altar of sorts rose up, draped in black cloth, lit with elaborate steel candelabras.

I stumbled forward, the terrible feeling of being a living-marionette percolating inside me, and there, up on that black alter, lying deathly still in a pan of oily liquid, was a tiny pale fetus. Yeah, a little human baby fetus, all curled up in that iconic way, like the space baby in *2001 A Space Odyssey.*

Some sick fuck had tattooed the little thing. Weird markings, triangles and crescent moons, writing in a bizarre alphabet. I was filled with a terrible sympathy for it: Such an innocent, cute thing, misused, tortured, left dead here in this strange chamber. It was beyond sick. I thought of Amanda and the child that had swam in her. My child. And suddenly I was choked with tears.

Sobbing, I stared down at it, and to my amazement, it stretched its arms—tiny hands curled into perfect fists—then yawned, as if awakening from a nap! It turned and looked up at me. It was alive! A fucking miracle.

Impulsively, I reached in and scooped it up. Once in my hands it appeared bigger than it had in the pan. More like an infant than a fetus. There was a weight to it, a heftiness and heartiness. It nuzzled against my palm and let out a soft coo. My heart throbbed with heat. It was a girl. A little girl. And, yes, she was much bigger than she had looked, filling both my hands.

A craziness filled my head. I don't know how else to describe it. A strange insanity. For I took her.

God help me, I took her

At the time it seemed I was guided by empathy, by love. That it was my desire for a family that drove me to try and save her from the media and scientists and cops and Feds.

But I know better now.

Then, it felt like destiny: How I was so easily able to slip up the stairs, through those godforsaken halls and out that open door, with her cradled against my chest, hidden behind my thick Sheriff's coat.

No one even glanced at me.

But it wasn't destiny. That thing was controlling them, just as surely as it was guiding me.

By the time I made it to my patrol car the infant had tripled in size. More. I took off my parka and lay it on the passenger seat, nestled her there, wrapping her in the folds. Purple veins crisscrossed the tiny pale body, and I could see dark fluid pulsing within them, and those weird tattoos gave off an unworldly glow. I noticed then, for the first time, that its eyes were yellow, with rectangular pupils, like a goat, its lips glistening and black.

How had I not seen that before?

Suddenly I didn't feel too good about this whole situation.

What the fuck had I done?

There was an old-fashioned basinet in the garage, a hand-me-down from Amanda's parents. A heavy, wooden thing from the sixties when they built things to last, covered in white frills and lace. I hauled it out, Daisy at my side, panting, her kind eyes curious, and put it in the spare room that was meant to be a nursery.

Placing the creature in it, it looked blasphemous there. Obscene, that tiny, ugly thing, skin like a green-and-yellow bruise, in that cute frilly bed made for a human baby.

Daisy approached, ever curious in that canine way of hers, sniffed at it, then whined and backed away, ears flat against her head, tail curled between her legs, and again I wondered, *just what have I done?*

A feeling of loathing settled over me, a sense of doom, the creature just staring at me blankly, its black lips sullen, yellow eyes cold as the depths of space. For the briefest moment I was actually filled with the urge to kill it, but then something inexplicable happened: it batted its huge eyes, and smiled warmly at me, cooing with laughter.

My heart lifted as the infectious giggles filled me and before

I knew it, I was laughing too, bending down to stroke its cheek with the pad of my finger. It gave a soft, contented sigh, turned its head, and grasped my finger, kicking its pudgy little feet.

It's like a drug goes off in my brain and I'm awash in some kind of opiate high. I think, I have to name this thing, this glorious creature. It's like I am pierced with a radiant light, like a spear from a different dimension, and there's a name in my head. It just comes to me. Later I will learn what it means, but then I was ignorant. Alnilam: the brightest star in Orion's belt.

The next day I called in sick to work. My uncle answered the phone.

"What happened to you yesterday?" he asked in his gruff voice. "You just disappeared."

I told him that the clinic, the whole scene, just brought back so many memories of Amanda being pregnant that I had to leave. Just couldn't bear to be there. I apologized, said, "My anxiety is at maximum and my therapist says I should take some time off to try to work through this." Truth was, I hadn't seen my therapist in months. Hated her smugness and condescending attitude. It made me feel weak.

"Take as much time as you need," he told me.

She won't eat.

I've tried formula and milk. Warmed it and tried to feed her with a bottle. She just turns her little face away. Tried spooning baby food of all types into her mouth: vegetables, fruit, meat, from jars, tubes, little pouches, homemade recipes I researched and put in a blender. She just spits it out and clamps her lips shut. In desperation I tried bits of hamburger, doughnuts and cake. Even pizza. Nothing's worked. Not even a nibble. I don't know what to do.

But she's plump and healthy-looking. And keeps growing. No longer the size of a newborn, she's now a hefty infant. She's able to sit up, hold her head high and look around. She even squirms on her belly as if any day she'll begin to crawl. She even smells healthy, that fresh, clean, intoxicating baby smell.

I keep her in diaper. Though there's really no need, she hasn't once peed or had a bowel movement. Which also worries me.

Christmas.

I think she may be feeding on me somehow. Draining me. I feel weak and listless. My hair has begun to fall out, clumps coming loose from my head in the shower and clogging the drain. My gums ache and bleed.

This morning I lost a tooth. A canine on the upper right side. I could feel with my tongue that it was loose. When I jiggled it with my finger it slipped right out of my skull, long and slender, slightly yellow and dotted in blood. I was turning it before my eyes, studying it, a weariness deep in the center of my bones, when I heard a thudding crash followed by a high-pitched yelp.

How to explain the horror I saw after racing to the nursery? I don't know how. Alnilam, the baby, *that thing*, was out of her crib and on the floor, spilled out on her belly like a white puddle, gripping Daisy's snout in her fat little hands, pudgy legs kicking.

Daisy was still but trembling slightly. She had gone completely white, unnaturally white, as if bleached, and a strange purple mist sluiced out her mouth and nostrils and into Alnilam's gently parted lips. The strange markings that adorned her body, *those weird tattoos*, glowed with a pulsating green light as she slurped the mist up, lifting her unearthly eyes to mine and grinning.

I screamed, pressing my palms against the sides of my head, as if my skull might crack apart if not held fast by my hands.

Alnilam burped and a giggle escaped her as she tossed the dog aside. I dropped to my knees, tears welling up, and took Daisy's head in my hands. Her lips were shriveled and dry, mummified, her eyes hollow and blank. She was stiff, and incredibly light, as if devoid of substance. I pulled her into my arms, rocking back and forth, clutching her to me and weeping.

Alnilam lifted herself up, cocked her head, and pointed a fat finger at me. "Da da. Da," she said, her voice a sweet singsong. Those words hit my heart like a wrecking ball, and everything seemed to change.

Da da. Those elemental and ancient sounds. She saw me as her father. And when I looked at her, Christ, it was *so* easy to look beyond the preternaturally pale shade of skin, the black lips, goat's eyes and glowing markings, to see a sweet, fat-faced baby girl. A cute little thing grinning innocently, clapping her chubby hands.

And how could I be upset? How could I be angry?

But later, digging Daisy's grave, wearily cracking open the cold earth with a mattock, beyond the strange influence of that baby thing, I made a grim decision: I'm going to kill it.

She was an abomination. Evil. She had to die.

Daisy was the last connection to my old world. To Amanda. To normality. Slipping her into that dark pit, spilling soil over her emaciated and bleached form, I realized why I was chosen. It was that empty part of my heart. That place Amanda had emptied with her death. That hollowness that yearned to be a father, a husband, to have a family.

That's why Alnilam had chosen me.

She needed someone wounded. Someone vulnerable to be her keeper. Someone desperate enough for a sense of family that they'd accept a demon into their life. She was using my hurt, my festering inner-wounds.

Yes, she had to die.

I approached the nursery slowly, my service revolver clutched in a trembling, sweaty fist, finger on the trigger. I had to be swift, without hesitation. I stepped into the room and raised the revolver, centering the sights on her.

She turned her strange goat eyes to me, those black lips yawning upward into a terrible grin, and my finger froze, locked, unable to squeeze the trigger. My hand quaked as she tilted her head, commanding me. I was helpless, under her complete control, as she demanded I lift my arm and put the barrel of the revolver to my head, pressing the cold metal to my temple.

And, yes, I admit, I found some peace in the thought of death. Welcomed it. I shut my eyes, took a breath, and gave in to her.

But she wouldn't even give me that condolence. She needed me and wouldn't let me die. Worse yet, it was then she let me know what she wanted. What she needed. What she feeds on. She had no need for flesh and blood as sustenance, no. She wanted souls. That's why she didn't want formula or baby food, dead stuff, pieces of meat and vegetable, fruit and milk. She needed something living, something with a consciousness and self-awareness. She craved to devour spiritual essence and had taken mine to the brink.

And Daisy had a soul. That glint of love and empathy you see in a dog's eye, that's what Alnilam fed on, leaving nothing but a shriveled white shell, a worn-out body drained of life.

But what was the innocence and affection of a mere dog compared to that of a human child?

I found the first one standing just outside the park, staring forlornly towards the playground swings, a dripping ice-cream cone in her chubby hand.

She was a fat little thing in a pink sundress, with bushy-blonde ponytails bobbing on either side of her head, lapping sullenly on that vanilla cone. She couldn't have been more than four, her mother yapping away to a group of other young women in a gossip circle. Didn't even notice me take her by the hand and lead her away.

We've had to stay on the move. From California to Arizona to New Mexico and now Colorado. Looking for places where tourists come with their children. Living in cheap hotels beside third-rate amusement parks. I'm weary of the road, but constantly moving is the key to remaining undiscovered. Jurisdiction to jurisdiction, leaving no links, nothing for law enforcement to put together.

She's sick! My poor little Alnilam. I'm in an utter panic.

She's fevered, burning up. She just lies there moaning and there's something terribly wrong with her back. Her little shoulder blades have these nasty boils on them. They started as tiny welts, but have been growing and swelling, weeping a foul-smelling green puss. And I can see a weird movement in them, the swollen skin fluttering, as if there's something living inside them.

Can I take her to a hospital? Call a doctor?

Are these options even possible given our predicament?

I feel so helpless. She's all I have now. The thought of losing her is beyond soul crushing.

WINGS!!! SHE HAS WINGS!!!

This morning those nasty blisters on her back split open and out unfurled slick, slimy, beautiful black wings! All leathery and bat-like. Her fever was instantly gone and she was immediately back to her old happy self, laughing and giggling, flapping those wonderful new wings.

Oh, what a relief. My soul feels as if a terrible weight has been lifted from it. Thank God. Thank God my little Alnilam is all right.

She can fly. Actually fly. It's so amazing. Such an incredible sight.

I brought her back a toddler I found wandering around by the fountain at a shopping mall. A chubby little boy in OshKosh overalls with big blue eyes and a double chin. I led him into the room, and as soon as I shut the door behind us, she spied him from the bed, lifting her head, those beautiful yellow goat eyes studying him as he plodded around clumsily.

Her pupils narrowed and those black wings fluttered to life and rose, beating softly, lifting her gracefully upwards. The little boy saw her and grinned, pointed a fat finger, mumbling nonsense, a bit of drool dripping off his bottom lip as she circled, as predatory and beautiful as the most American of bald eagles.

Then, in one swift and calculated motion, with the precision of a striking snake, she swooped down, catching his surprised face in her hands. He staggered back, nearly falling, but she held him fast, pulling him towards her, sucking his spirit from out his nose and mouth in a stream of purple mist. The little boy's ruddy complexion went pale, his rolls of fat shriveling and drying up, his wide eyes going blank and empty.

Then she released her grip and he toppled gently, nothing but a little husk of a child now. Alnilam laughed and swept across the room as I clapped my hands and whooped for joy, tears of happiness swelling in my eyes.

She's so amazing. The greatest daughter I could ever have asked for. An answer to my prayers. A Christmas miracle. And I know within my heart, we have nothing but wonderful, wonderful days ahead of us. I'm just sure of it.

And now, right now, I'm the happiest man in the world.

AUTHOR'S STORY NOTE

Inspired by an incredibly disturbing true story, "The Happiest Man in the World" is more than just a Lovecraftian abortion clinic story. It's a tale of hope, new beginnings, and the magic of Christmas.

SYNAESTHETE

MELANIE HARDING-SHAW

From *Black Dogs, Black Tales*
Editors: Tabatha Wood & Cassie Hart
Things in the Well Publishing

The first time I remember noticing a flash in someone's eyes was the day I started preschool. The shadow of black and red in the teacher's eyes matched the feathers lining the korowai cloak of the girl sitting next to her who was leaving that day to start school. I thought that was clever. The flashes had always been there, of course. In the eyes of my parents and the adults who came to visit. When I was old enough to wonder, I thought they must be spirit animals. Guardians, perhaps. I was oblivious in the way that many children are. Or maybe I just didn't want to see.

I can remember the first time I looked in the mirror to search my own out. Staring into the depths of my eyes and feeling a moment of panic that there was nothing there before I saw the shadowed outline, the hint of movement from the rise and fall of its breath. I shouted at the mirror to try and wake it, but it did not stir. I sometimes wonder what would have happened if I had succeeded in waking it that day. It was only when I closed my eyes and saw the afterimage on my eyelids that I could make out the shape. A hound as black as my pupils curled in sleep. It wasn't until puberty hit that I started to realise the truth.

Scotty was the first boy I thought I wanted to kiss. I didn't tell anyone because all the girls wanted to kiss him and it was ridiculous to think he might pick me. I just stared at the back of his head in class. Admired the casual swagger that somehow came across even when he was sitting still.

And then the party. Those first gulps of cheap and burning vodka. Stumbling into a bedroom, and there he was. His casual swagger, now a stagger. His hands pulling me closer. The sudden sickening realisation that I did not want *this*.

I pushed him away in panic. "No!"

"I've seen the way you look at me," he slurred.

I shook my head and stepped back.

"Freak."

My stomach churned with dread and my frantic eyes met his, searching for a sign that this would not make my life "over." That I would be able to show my face at school on Monday. The thing is, I didn't usually meet people's eyes. Somewhere between kindergarten and that party, I had realised no-one else saw the flashes and I had decided I would not see them either. I watched their mouths instead: the twitch of hidden amusement at one corner or the downturned edges of lost patience. Maybe I would have been prepared if I had been watching eyes all those years. If I had let myself become accustomed to my changing sight.

I stared into Scotty's eyes and I saw the rabid peacock tearing at his brain. Clawed feet scratching gouges down his amygdala as its sharp beak wrenched at optic nerves stretched so tight his eyes might pop out the back of their sockets. The bird's majestic iridescent wings spread wide, bloodstained and razor sharp as they beat within his skull, slicing the soft tissues like the cutty grasses that used to catch our unwary arms as we walked to the beach.

I stood in that room and I screamed and I did not stop screaming until the ambulance came. I could not show my face at school that Monday or any Monday after.

It was weeks before I could even step foot outside my room. Weeks before I could bring myself to cry on my mother's shoulder. I watched her mouth as I crept out into the lounge. I saw her fear for me in the tightness of her lips. I heard the tentative tremor in her voice, the uncertainty that she might say the wrong thing and make it worse. I kept my eyes down, scared of the coloured flashes lurking higher.

I sat beside her and leaned my head on her shoulder. I felt the comforting weight of her arm around me. I couldn't see her face from there. I was safe.

"I love you," she whispered.

I didn't say anything. I could feel a tendril creeping down my face, caressing me. Each time it pulled away, I felt pinpoints of my cheek stretch outwards one by one. Tiny circles of pain. Not a tendril, but a tentacle. I jerked upright to stare at her, despite knowing better. I didn't notice the metallic reflections of the octopus's eyes within hers at first. I was too distracted by its tentacles tearing off the features of her face to shove them into its beak. I could see glimpses of her flesh further in. Pieces of her nose and ears being ground down by a tongue covered in rows of teeth.

I tore myself away and ran back to my room, the sound of her voice calling after me muffled by the squelching of those tentacles rending her faceless.

I could feel a sickening movement in my eyes, the first stirrings of a slumbering animal. I broke every mirror in the house.

My therapist thought that writing might give me an outlet, and it did. I chatted to other writers online. I could communicate, be supportive, and have value; and I did not have to see their faces. As I grew more confident, I could even meet them sometimes. I would sit and stare down at my paper, focusing only on the letters I was forming on the page. I would laugh at their jokes, offer solace for their trials. But it is a hard thing to look away from the pain in a friend's voice.

There came a day when I lost focus. I glanced up for a moment as I spoke.

"You are doing it! You are a writer already!" I tried to say.

My words were cut short by a missile smashing into my nose. I covered my face in my hands, but not before I saw my friend's eyes bulging outwards with the pressure of a thousand cuckoo's eggs. The mother bird invisible inside their skull but for the sound of her beak clacking in sinister pleasure. I staggered to my feet as a stream of projectiles flew at me, beating me backwards. I caught a glimpse of my friend as I ran away. Unimaginable pressure sending eggs erupting from their scalp like pumice flying from flesh volcanoes. Their red blood lava oozing from the open wounds.

The squeaking sound of hound's teeth worrying at my synapses, not unlike the noise of biting into haloumi, echoed in my mind and drove me running home.

So, I locked myself away from the world once more, reaching out only through my keyboard and the screen. Groceries delivered to my door. Feet dragging, shoulders hunched, and the smell of loneliness permeating every space. The ache of claws and teeth inside my skull never left me and I wondered if there was anything left there and what that hound would feast on once it was stripped bare. There was a single mirror in my subsidised apartment. I had covered it with rainbow lines of duct tape. The colours made me feel like it was a choice; an interior design quirk that I could remove any time I wanted. I never did.

You can't stay inside forever, though. The day I met Sid, I was walking to the letterbox. She was walking her dog, a golden terrier. Even with my eyes cast down, I noticed her nails reflecting in the sun. They were the most beautiful nails I'd ever seen; works of art with rainbow chrome colours shifting as she walked. I didn't know it then, but people often stared at Sid. She didn't match what they expected to see. She didn't match who they expected her to be.

I stared at Sid, too, and maybe she saw the horror in my eyes because she looked away. Her shoulders hunched slightly against the blow she thought might come, just like mine. Everyone I met had something eating away at them. Sid was different, though. The thing consuming her was not inside her skull like mine. Its human mouth was latched onto her legs gnawing on an Achilles tendon while the weight of its body dragged behind her each step she took. As I watched, its jaws loosened but only so that its rooster talons could tear chunks from her calves. It was the cruel alpha, driving her away. A monster denying her the right to live.

Somehow, she strode on despite the creature hanging off her that was part human, part beast and all the cruelty of the world. I watched her pained footsteps almost pass my gate and I couldn't take it anymore.

"Hi," I cried out, and she turned around, uncertain.

I could feel the gnawing in my own brain pause.

"Hi," she said.

I stood and stared at this beautiful woman, the horror of her parasite now hidden behind her legs. I tried to imagine how to convey to her that I was different, too. I didn't have the words. I reached up and buried my face in my hands. My dank, unwashed hair fell forward to hide my face as sobs shook my body.

She didn't see my dirty nails clawing into my eyes, tearing out the creature I could feel inside. And I am certain she did not see the black hound that I threw to the ground between us. Its teeth were bared in a snarl and its muscles were poised to leap back up; to savage my face before digging a hole back into my brain as if my frontal lobe was freshly mown grass begging for its claws.

She saw the red scratches down my cheeks, though. She saw the tears. She reached out to me, a stranger, and she hugged me in the street.

"Do you want to come for a walk?" she asked.

I nodded.

There is a forest at the end of my street where I had never ventured. At the entrance was a sign: "Dogs must be kept on a leash."

Sid saw me reading it. "It's to protect the birds, our taonga. We can't let dogs roam free or they will destroy them," she said.

Sid set off towards the trees. I looked at the black hound stalking beside me. I could still see the vestiges of my brain tissues on his snout, my blood colouring his whiskers. Then I looked at the almost human creature ahead of me, clinging to Sid's shoes. It had lost its grip when I started walking beside her, shrunk back a little. It was still horrifying, but now it was no bigger than the playful terrier trotting by her side.

I glared at the black dog, looked deep into his eyes. We can't let dogs roam free or they will destroy what is precious to us. I bared my teeth and planted both feet firmly on the track. His snarl faltered, his ears pressed down to his skull, and his tail twitched downwards until it was pressed tightly up under his belly.

I pointed at Sid's creature and he streaked towards it, slamming his head into its side and sending it careening into the shadows of the undergrowth where it peered at us cowering. When he returned to me, I reached down to touch him with a trembling hand, to finally feel that coarse black fur. He tried to snap at my fingers, to crunch the tiny bones in his powerful jaws. I slapped his nose and grabbed the leash lying across his back. I had never even noticed it was there.

"Are you coming?" Sid asked from up ahead, her steps now gloriously unconstrained.

"Yes."

She smiled at me. I could tell because of the tiny creases forming by her eyes. In their glossy depths, I could just make out the reflection of the silver fronds of a young ponga fern beside the track.

FULL MOON SHINDIG

PATRICK C. HARRISON III

From *Visceral: Collected Flesh*
Death's Head Press

Chandler's house is like a dream—something familiar, yet foreign and odd. I went there almost every weekend through high school. Hell, it was like a second home, really. But now it's different. I guess nine weeks of basic training and another twelve of AIT will do that to you.

As Franco pulls his Maserati into the long driveway, he's telling me about some girl he supposedly laid in Dallas last weekend after a concert by a band I've never heard of, and I'm looking past the house and trees and the line of cars, at the lake, the setting sun shimmering off its waters like rippling fire. Silhouetted in the orange is a small bass boat and, in it, a man with a pole. It must be cold out there; it's January and cold and the wind is blowing. I wish I was him, alone with the lake and the fish and the dying sun. Do fish bite this time of year?

"You should have seen her, Travis," Franco is saying, like I give a damn about his sexual exploits, real or not. "She was wearing this little pink thong and had these huge fake tits. She kept telling me we had to keep it down cuz her kid was asleep, that was the only sucky thing. I would be tearing into her pussy and she would be moaning and I would be moaning and the goddamn bed would be squeaking, and just as I'm about to blow, she wants to tell me to keep it down. You believe that shit, man?"

"I don't know," I say, watching the fisherman in the distance as we draw closer to Chandler's house, "I guess she didn't want to wake her kid."

"Yeah," Franco says, shaking his head and pulling the car behind a Ford truck that could probably fit a Maserati and a half in its bed. Ice has already crystalized on its taillights. Fuck, it's cold. "I can't believe you joined the army," he adds. "Who does that?"

I don't answer, even though he is looking at me. Getting out of the Maserati, I zip-up my leather jacket and light a Marlboro Red. I started smoking in AIT. It's nice. Franco gets out and throws a pill into his mouth and dry swallows, then lights a Newport. I don't ask what the pill is, though I'm curious. I start walking towards Chandler's, but Franco stops to take a piss behind the Ford, so I stop too and watch my breath on the cold air and the fisherman on the lake and the ritzy cars in the driveway—two BMWs, a Mercedes, an old Corvette Stingray, and a couple of large trucks with mud-grip tires, which probably rarely get muddy. Closer to the house, I see a red Cadillac that I recognize as Gwen's, and I groan. We dated off and on in high school and she gave me my first blowjob. I hear her and Chandler are a thing now.

"Let's go, army man," Franco says, zipping his fly and walking up the driveway puffing on his cigarette. Music is thumping from inside the house—some hip-hop song I don't recognize. As we approach the house, I look once more at the fisherman, and I think he's watching us, perhaps wishing he was about to walk into the warmth of Chandler's house, or perhaps feeling sorry for us. I kind of want to wave at him, like I would have done as a kid, and ask him if he has caught anything and if he is cold, but that would be stupid and he is too far out to hear me over the wind anyway.

Franco rings the doorbell. I ask if we can smoke inside since Chandler's parents are away for the weekend, and Franco shrugs. The door opens—it's Gwen. Of course, it's Gwen. She is wearing a skin-tight, lowcut pink shirt that matches the shade of her lipstick. Her blonde hair is pulled back to show off the diamonds in her ears. I think her breasts have grown since the last time I saw her. In fact, I know they have.

"Hey, Franco," Gwen says, then turns to me and says with a kind smile, "Welcome back, Travis."

I'm about to tell her thank you when Franco cuts me off: "Let us in, it's fucking freezing out here. Can't you tell? Your nipples are about to shred that fucking shirt." Gwen rolls her eyes and tells us to toss the cigarettes, so we do, then follow her inside, and

I'm pretty sure her ass has gotten a little rounder in the last few months, too. She is looking good, and I'm wondering what the chances are that I can fuck her at some point in the next couple of weeks, before I head back to the army. Probably not very good, but she's been known to slut around at times.

We walk through the foyer with the crystal chandelier and into the living room where there is a porno movie playing on the massive flat screen, showing a chick with one dick in her pussy, another in her ass, and another in her mouth. Sitting on the couch is Stan Hedley, and he's masturbating, and clearly stoned out of his mind. At the other end of the living room, three guys are laughing hysterically at Stan, and one of them is filming the spectacle on his iPhone. Gwen walks past this scene as if it's nothing, and I follow, staring at the floor. Franco is snickering behind me.

We enter the kitchen where Sofia and Britney are making margaritas in a blender. Lance Higgins snorts something off of the counter and when he turns around to see us, he has some of the white substance on the tip of his nose. Franco inquires if Lance has any more of that and Lance tells him that was the last line and Franco calls him a 'fuck nut.' Sofia is wearing a tank-top and nothing else. No pants or shorts or panties. She pours a glass of margarita from the blender and turns around to look at us as she sips. She has no hair between her legs and her labia is long and hanging. I want to suck on it, but I see someone's sticky cum clinging to her right thigh and decide I won't be putting my mouth down there tonight. By contrast, Britney is wearing jeans, boots, a turtleneck sweater, and a wool vest.

"Y'all want a margarita?" Britney asks. Gwen and I say sure and she pours us each a glass.

"Where is Chandler?" Franco asks.

"In the game room with the others," says Britney, pointing to the hallway that leads to the den, the library, a spare bedroom, and the game room.

Sofia sticks her finger in her pussy, then pulls it out and licks it.

"Does he have any Norco?" Franco asks.

"I don't know," says Britney, "but he has some Fentanyl patches, I think."

"Cool." Franco leaves for the game room. I can hear a lot of hooting and hollering and laughing from that direction, and I suddenly wish more than ever that I was that fisherman on the boat, all alone with the lake and the fish. So what if it's cold. I take a sip of my margarita; it has way too much tequila.

"Where have you been, Travis?" Britney asks. Her eyes are dilated, so are Sofia's.

"He joined the army, remember?" Gwen says.

"The army?"

"Did we have a threesome last spring?" Sofia says to me, sticking her finger back in her pussy, then back in her mouth.

"Not that I recall," I say, raising an eyebrow.

"No, that was Kyle," Gwen says, and I'm suddenly sure she was the third party to this threesome. We were still together last spring. I wonder who Kyle is. Surely not Kyle Davis; he's poor and skinny and ugly.

"So, how you been?" Lance says, still with that white powder on his nose.

"Yeah, how have you been?" Gwen says.

"Yeah, how have you been?" Sofia says. I wonder if she plans on donning pants at some point.

I shrug and say, "Pretty good, I guess. Just been training."

"Are you getting muscled up?" Gwen says. "You were getting kinda thin before you left."

This statement hurts me more than it should, more than her having a threesome while we dated. She never told me I looked thin. "I guess," I say and take a long drink of my margarita.

"I fucked a marine one time," Sofia says. "He had muscles.

Looked good. He came too quick, though."

I nod as if this is interesting. Gwen finishes her margarita and asks Britney to pour her another, which she does. Lance takes a Corona from the fridge and pops the lid off on the counter. Sofia finally notices the glob of cum on her leg and wipes it off with her finger and shoves it in her mouth, then chases it with a drink of margarita. From the living room, I hear more laughter and one of the guys is saying Stan is going to rub his dick raw. From the game room, I hear more cheering and laughing. Franco comes running into the kitchen holding Chandler's dog, a pug named Pugs, in arms.

"Travis, you gotta see this shit," Franco says excitedly, a cigarette teetering on his bottom lip.

"Franco, get rid of the cancer stick," Gwen says.

"Chandler said I could smoke in here, you cunt."

"Don't call me a cunt, you prick."

"Whatever, bitch. Travis, watch this." He sets Pugs on the floor, then kneels down beside him. "Watch this shit," he repeats. Franco reaches beneath the dog and grabs its penis, then starts jerking on it.

"What the fuck are you doing?" I say rather loudly, cause, honestly, I want to know what the fuck he is doing and why he is doing it.

"Watch," Franco says, continuing to jerk the dog's dick. Sofia says something about Franco being crazy. Britney has her phone out and is videoing this. Lance and Gwen are laughing. Pugs suddenly starts thrusting forward, and Franco releases the dog's now erect red rocket, but the dog keeps thrusting. He—Pugs—is standing there fucking the air with its little doggie dick. He just keeps going, pumping away like some puppy pussy is lying beneath him. Meanwhile, Franco is now rolling on the floor laughing. Gwen chokes on her margarita she is laughing so hard. Britney is still filming and saying 'oh my god' repeatedly.

"Dude, you're fucked up," I say.

"Get it, doggie, get it," Sofia says, then finishes off her drink.

Pugs finally stops fucking the air, then walks slowly towards the living room, looking back over his shoulder multiple times as if he is ashamed or afraid we may chase him down. Franco is still on the floor laughing.

"Is that what y'all are doing back there, jerking off dogs?" I say.

Franco, still on the floor, finally tempers his laughter and says, "No, we're doing a lot more than that. You need to come back to the game room, Travis."

"You joined the army?" Lance says, as if he just now grasped the conversation from moments ago.

I nod.

"Are you, like, going over to . . . uh . . . you know, one of those countries to fight ragheads?"

"Fort Benning, Georgia." I say.

"Where is that?" Lance says.

"In Georgia."

"Who gives a fuck," Franco says, and for once I agree with him. Who does give a fuck? "Come on, Travis, come to the game room. You gotta see this shit"

"No more jerking off dogs?"

"No, goddamnit!"

"Promise?"

"Travis, come on!"

I finish my margarita and set the glass on the counter, then grab a Corona from the fridge. I don't much like Corona, but that's the only beer they have, apparently. I pop the top on the edge of the counter and follow Franco down the hall. Gwen, Britney, and Sofia follow me. I wonder who fucked Sofia. And was it just one guy, or two or three or more? If I asked, she would probably happily tell me, then maybe offer sloppy-fifteenths to me. Maybe later.

The hallway is gloomy, and the entrance to the game room at the end is like a brilliant light at the end of a tunnel. We pass the library (or is it a study?), and the mellow scent of cigars and pipe tobacco wafts from within. I've always enjoyed that smell. We pass the spare bedroom where I'd walked in one day to crash after popping two Ativans in algebra class (Chandler always let me crash when I needed it) and caught Chandler's father banging the housekeeper. He'd had her bent over the bed and his belt around her neck. Her face was beet red—almost purple—and when her eyes opened and she saw me, she winked. Chandler's dad didn't even break his motion to shoo me out of the room; he just kept pounding and pulling on that belt. I stepped back out and closed the door. I never said anything about it to Chandler, and certainly not to his dad or mom. The housekeeper turned up pregnant a month or two later, then overdosed on Ambien a week after that. She sure seemed to be enjoying herself, though. We pass the den (Chandler's mom calls it the second living room) where I drank my first beer as a freshman while we watched college football, and where I smoked my first joint while watching some stupid horror movie with Gwen and Chandler and Becca, with Gwen's hand in my pants the whole time.

Franco looks over his shoulder at me, his cigarette poking from his smiling mouth, and nods at me as we enter the game room. The game room is usually where all of Chandler's parties end up. Not only does it have a pool table, a shuffleboard table, a large flat screen, and every game console and game that you can think of, but it also has a liquor cabinet with every kind of top shelf whiskey, gin, and rum there is. The game room does not, however, typically have a naked girl bound to the pool table.

The room is packed with people—the Brantley twins (Jill and Jan), Steven Douglas with his overly tight shirt and jeans, Gavin Cross wearing sunglasses and puffing an e-cig, Gerri James with her watermelons bursting out of her skimpy shirt, Andrea

"No Tits" Smith with her short, dyke-like haircut (maybe she is a dyke; I don't know), and a dozen others, some I know and some I don't. And, of course, there is Chandler who is wearing his typical bright polo shirt and sporting a spiked hairdo. He's laughing about something and drinking a Corona. Everyone seems to be drinking Corona. Except Jose Sanchez who is drinking a Modelo Negra like any Mexican with even a hint of self-respect does. But my eyes are on the girl; I can't look away. She is slender and pale and her nipples are pink and her pussy lips are pink too with a few days' worth of short pubic hair around them, and her eyes are brilliant blue and her hair is a soft, light brown with streaks of blonde. She is tied to the legs of the pool table with ropes around her wrists and ankles, and she looks scared. And, my god, she is young.

"I told you, you had to see this shit," Franco says.

"Travis, 'bout fuckin' time you got here," Chandler says, moving through the crowd to meet me, his hand held out in a fist before him.

"What's with the girl?" I ask, knocking knuckles with Chandler. The girl has tears streaming down the side of her face. The green felt of the pool table is darkened from tears. Her bottom lip is trembling.

"What girl?" Chandler says, laughing. He takes a swig of Corona. "How's the fuckin' army?"

"It's fine," I say.

Sofia walks to the pool table, sticking her finger in her pussy again, then plunges the wet finger into the restrained girl's mouth. The girl gags and Sofia removes her hand, saying "You like that, slut?" The girl spits and a glob of saliva sticks to the edge of her mouth. Fresh tears fall. Everyone is laughing. Franco has walked to her and blows cigarette smoke in her face. Gavin Cross blows his vape in her face. Gerri pours half of her beer on the girl's chest, and the girl tries to shrink away but has nowhere to go.

"What's with the girl?" I say again.

"She's just some chick," says Chandler, shrugging and looking over his shoulder at her. "Hot little body, though."

"She's not *some chick*," Gwen says. "Her name is Sara Hamilton and she thinks she's the fucking homecoming queen."

"Homecoming queen?" I say. "Like at the junior college?"

"She does have a hot body," Franco says.

"Yeah, I'll fuck her here in a little bit," says Chandler.

"Excuse me," Gwen says, "I haven't given you permission to fuck her."

"I don't need your permission, bitch."

"The hell you don't!"

"You let that cunt tell you what to do?" Franco says.

"Fuck you, Franco," Chandler and Gwen both say.

Meanwhile, Jose Sanchez hangs his bare ass over the edge of the pool table and farts in the direction of the girl, Sara's, face. Everyone finds this extremely funny. Sofia slaps Jose's rear and tells him he is disgusting and needs to shave the hair off his ass.

"She was homecoming queen at KJC?" I ask, pulling gently on Gwen's arm. She is watching the scene with delight.

"What? No, this tramp beat out Stephanie for homecoming queen. Can you believe that?"

"Stephanie?" I say, but I know who she means—Stephanie is Gwen's sister, a sophomore in high school. "This girl is in high school?"

"What?" she says again. She keeps getting distracted by things. Now, No Tits Smith is twisting Sara's nipples with her fingers, and the girl is screaming and pleading for her to stop. Sofia slaps her face. Steven Douglas flicks her ear. Britney is tickling her feet, but the girl doesn't seem to notice.

"How many days are you here?" Chandler asks.

"Huh? Oh, uh, couple weeks."

"Then back to the army?"

"Yeah."

"Throwing a party on the barge next weekend. We'll get out to the middle of the lake and have that fucker rocking. It'll be cold as shit, but we'll have plenty of Patron and dope to warm you up."

I nod. I used to love the barge parties, but it sounds agonizing to me now. Just thinking about going gives me a sense of dread. I would rather be the fisherman on the boat, all alone. Why do I feel this way? What has changed?

Chandler continues: "I've been fucking this nurse that works at a nursing home, and she got me a shit ton of Fentanyl patches and this cream that has Ativan or Xanax or something in it that you rub on your wrists. It's good shit. She gave me sixty Ultrams, so I slapped the fuck out of her. Like anybody wants that weak-ass shit. Ultram ain't too bad though—it keeps you from cumming too fast when you're fucking."

I'm nodding at Chandler, but not really listening, although I notice Gwen's silence when he mentions fucking the nurse. I just want out. I want to run from the room and out of the house, sprinting into the winter air, not stopping until my lungs and thighs are burning, not stopping until I'm miles away, until I'm alone and surrounded by leafless trees and the only conversation is between me and the moon.

Franco retrieves the cue ball from one of the pool table's pockets and centers it on the felt between Sara's ankles. He then grabs a cue stick, bends down to line up his shot, and says, "Center pocket!" The cue tip collides with the ball and the ball thumps hard against Sara's pussy.

"Please stop!" Sara cries. "Why are you doing this to me? Why!"

"Shut up, slut," Sofia says, slapping her across the face again.

"Somebody gag her," Chandler says.

"I'll gag her with my cock," Franco says, grabbing his crotch.

"Your cock isn't big enough to gag her," says Britney.

"Fuck you!"

Gavin pulls a white cloth from his pocket, blows his nose in it, and stuffs it into the girl's mouth. "I may need that back in a minute," he says. "My nose has been running like a motherfucker."

"Somebody spread her pussy lips apart," Franco says. "I wanna see if I can get this cue ball to stick." He lines the ball up again and bends down to aim as Jill and Jan Brantley spread Sara's pussy. It's pink, and the flesh around her pubis is red from being hit with the ball. She is crying and making muffled sounds around the rag. Franco strikes the ball, but it isn't straight this time and instead hits the fingers of one of the twins (I never could tell them apart).

"Damn it, Franco!" Jill or Jan yells, jerking her hand back and sticking the ring and middle fingers in her mouth.

"Well, get your fucking fat fingers out of the way!" Franco yells, retrieving the ball and lining it up again. "Pull her pussy apart." Reluctantly, the twins do as they're told. But this time, after he strikes the cue ball, they both let go and the ball slams into her closed cunt and bounces back to him. "Goddamnit! I said hold her!"

"Chandler, is this really necessary?" I say. "I mean, what did this girl do?"

"Huh?" Chandler says, finishing off his beer and tossing it into the trashcan beneath the game room window, where I see ice collecting on the window seal. "She didn't do anything, Travis. She's just a stupid cunt." He laughs after saying this and shakes his head, like I'm being ridiculous, then he shouts for Britney to go get him another Corona, which she does.

"She's in high school," I say, but Chandler is walking away. He slaps Gwen on the ass, then slaps Sofia's still bare ass. Shaking my head, I light a cigarette. Britney puts a fresh beer in my hand, even though I didn't ask for one, and takes my empty bottle. I look out the window, ignoring that now Chandler is taking shots at the girl's pussy with the cue ball; Franco and Jose are holding her open. Sara is screaming through Gavin's snot rag. Through the window, I see mainly darkness, but perhaps I see the occasional ripple of lake water, and I think maybe it's snowing or sleeting, probably sleeting. Is the fisherman still out there? Even with the sleet and wind, would he stay out there on the frigid lake? I would. Fuck yes, I would.

"Her pussy is too small," says Jose. "The cue ball won't fit."

"It'll fit," Franco says.

"Yeah, it'll fit," Chandler agrees. "Spread her cunt, I'm just going to shove it in there."

My eyes jerk away from the window and look at Sara and everyone around her. Her entire pelvic region is red and turning purple—already bruising from the trauma. Franco and Jose are spreading her apart, their fingers digging into the flesh in that area, Jose's long fingernails actually pealing back skin and drawing blood in two spots. Chandler has the cue ball in his hand is leaning over the table.

"Chandler, wait," I say, but not very loud. No one hears me; no one wants to.

He presses the ball against Sara's pussy and applies pressure. She's screaming, her arms and legs thrashing about but unable to do much. Whoever tied her down did a decent job of it. "Hold still, bitch," Chandler says, pushing harder. Only a portion of the ball has crossed beyond her lips and when Chandler pulls his hand back, it falls back to the felt tabletop. "Fuck," Chandler says. He angrily blows air out his nostrils and, picking up the ball, holding it in his palm, he thrusts his arm forward with more force than could possibly be needed. The cue ball disappears inside Sara and blood spits out around it, splattering the green felt with red droplets. "Yes!" Chandler says, holding his arms up in 'touchdown' fashion. "Fuck yes!"

Everyone is cheering and laughing. Gwen has a hand over her mouth, her eyes wide. At first, I think she is shocked and disgusted, but then she removes her hand and I see the big smile it was hiding. I look to the window, then to the door of the game room. Can I leave without anyone noticing? Does it really matter if they do notice? Will they try to stop me? Franco probably would. Maybe Chandler too. But does that even matter, at this point?

"Put the eight ball in her ass," some guy I don't know says, and everyone cheers.

I wonder if this girl, Sara Hamilton, has family waiting up for her tonight. Maybe a father sitting on their front porch smoking a pipe and drinking a nightcap, thinking perhaps that his daughter is at the movies or cruising the streets with friends. Maybe she has a mother making her plate for dinner, putting foil over it to keep it warm. Maybe she has younger brothers or sisters already brushing their teeth and getting in their PJs, saying their prayers and asking God to watch over their sister while she is out. Who knows, maybe there is no one waiting for her. But what's that matter?

"Yeah, find the eight ball," Franco says.

The room is all cheers. I feel like I'm in some sort of auditorium that is designed to echo the sounds of cheering crowds. Wide, smiling faces everywhere. Tears of laughter on red faces. Beer being guzzled. Cigarettes. Steven Douglas applying a Fentanyl patch to one of the Brantley twins. Gavin with Sofia bent over the shuffleboard table and fucking her. The room is spinning. And cheering.

"Y'all get the eight ball," Chandler says, "I'm going to fuck her mouth."

Hyperventilating, my heart pounding, I stick my half-smoked cigarette into my half-drank Corona and toss it into the trash. I'm dizzy and convinced I'm going to pass out. What will be done to me if I'm suddenly unconscious on the floor? Will I wake up with the fucking two ball shoved up my ass and Jose ripping farts in my face? No, it will be worse. The night is still young. They've only just begun what they'll do to Sara Hamilton. The eight ball is coming. So is the rape. What then? How long before someone who doesn't want to make the trip to the restroom decides to take a piss on her? How long before someone puts out their cigarette on her face? How long before someone whips out their pocket knife and starts carving her up? How long before I dial those three fucking numbers and put an end to this shit?

Chandler has his erect penis out and is at Sara's head. Britney is pouring another beer over her. I can see her gooseflesh. Sara is fighting, pulling at the ropes, the skin beneath them red and bleeding. Franco has found the eight ball and has Jose and Steven holding her ass cheeks apart, as best they can. Jose says they may need some lube, so Franco hocks a loogy onto the ball and smears it around. Removing Gavin's snot rag from the girl's mouth and grabbing her hair, tilting her head towards him, Chandler shoves his dick in.

Suddenly, Sara's body goes rigid, her back arching, the veins in her arms and neck bulging, her hands and feet curling. Her muscles are quaking, shivering, and I wonder if the girl is having a seizure. Jose and Steven let go of her ass, noticing the change, their eyes looking at her in confusion. Franco, holding the dripping eight ball a few inches from Sara's asshole, cusses them for letting go, apparently oblivious. Chandler, too, thrusting in and out of her mouth, doesn't seem to notice anything, until she bites his dick off.

He screams and pulls away, blood spraying across Sara's face and pouring down Chandler's pants. Sara is snorting and grunting—no longer screaming or crying—and her mouth is chewing on the mangled meat that had been Chandler's pecker. She's chewing, and her body is thrashing and convulsing. Her eyes, smeared with Chandler's blood, open, and they're scowling and angry, her head whipping from side to side, looking at everyone.

"My dick!" Chandler is screaming. "She bit my dick off!"

But no one is listening to him; everyone is watching Sara Hamilton, who is now . . . changing. She screams—although, it's less a scream and more a roar—and spits out what's left of Chandler's dick. It tumbles off the pool table to the carpet. It looks like it's been thrown in the blender. Lance, who entered the game room at some point, apparently high as fuck, picks up Chandler's tattered cock and looks at it curiously, then tosses it in the trash with the beer bottles. Chandler continues to scream, as the crowd of partygoers grows silent, backing away from the pool table and Sara Hamilton—backing away, but unable or unwilling to pull their eyes from her. Her eyebrows look more pronounced, like they need a shave. Her limbs and fingers and toes suddenly appear longer, her knees and elbows bonier. Is any of this possible? It can't be, right? One thing is for sure, this isn't a fucking seizure. Sara's nose flares and widens, looking more like a snout, her mouth spreading open, revealing teeth that look absurdly large for her face, and—my god—they're growing longer and sharpening as I watch. And now there's no doubt, she's roaring not screaming. There is hair on her arms and legs now, and the hair on her pubis is growing longer and curling. Dear god, there is hair on her chest too, and around her nipples and under her arms. It's all sprouting from Sara's skin at an unbelievable rate, like grass on those nature shows where they speed up time to show a week's worth of growth in a matter of seconds. It's growing that damn fast, and in no time her entire body, face included, is covered in not hair, I realize, but fur.

The game room is silent, aside from Chandler, who is now crouched in the corner, whimpering. Faintly, I hear the porno still playing in the living room. Sara—or what was Sara—lifts her head off the end on the pool table, staring past her clawed, furry feet at Franco, who is still standing there with the eight ball in his hand, his eyes wide with terror, his mouth agape. There is a rumble coming from within Sara's chest and jowls, not unlike the subtle growl of warning that may emanate from a tiger or lion. She's a werewolf, I realize, without much thought to the probability of such things being factual. What else could she be? Is there a full moon tonight? I have no idea.

With a sound like water being slapped with an open hand, the cue ball is expelled from the werewolf's loins, bouncing across the felt and coming to rest between its feet. Franco looks down at it, then back up at the werewolf and says "Jesus Christ" in almost a whisper. And then the werewolf erupts in violence.

The ropes that had bound Sara to the table are ripped to shreds by the creature that has taken her place. It bounds to its feet atop the pool table, looking around at everyone, its teeth bared. At last, some of the crowd is fleeing out the game room's door. I'm not one of them, however, and I stare at the werewolf dumbly, petrified by fear. Nor is Franco fleeing, and, being the closest to the beast, he is the first to meet his fate: with a quickness that blurs in my vision, the werewolf's clawed hand tears Franco's face from his head in one swipe, his nose, lips, and skin disappearing like a mask. One of his eyeballs hangs from the socket and its jelly drips from its lacerated side. He is screaming and still standing, but the wolf's other hand swings and tears his throat out, slinging blood and flesh all over the place. Franco collapses. Ragged remnants of his face and neck hang from the wolf's claws.

I realize there is screaming now, and running and shoving. And still I stand. The wolf leaps from the table, catching one of the Brantley twins by the shoulder and ripping her arm out of its socket. The other twin doesn't fare much better, getting her bowels torn out and slung across the shuffleboard table. The werewolf formerly known as Sara Hamilton is moving with lightning quickness, turning the gathering of young people into a heap of lifeless bodies. It decapitates Gavin (he had stopped screwing Sofia at some point during this ordeal) and throws his head through the window, ushering in a gust of frosty air. Sofia has her tits torn off by the wolf's jaws. Jose Sanchez has his heart ripped from his chest. Lance, standing motionless like me, has his jaw removed from his skull and his eyes clawed out.

Then the wolf, noticing the still sobbing Chandler sitting in the corner staring at the place where his dick used to be, pounces on him, mauling him, shredding him, cleaving his flesh from his bones. Blood and organs are being flung from this corner of the room, and something hits me in the chest and falls to my feet. It's a chunk of brain. Lying between my shoes in a puddle of blood, is a chunk of grey matter the size of my fist. For whatever reason, this is the thing that gets my feet moving.

I turn and sprint for the door. Amazingly, I'm not the only living person left in the game room, and I hear the monster attacking those that are left as I flee. I hear screaming and roaring and the sound of bodies being torn to pieces. Britney is stumbling down the hallway in front of me, drunk and crying hysterically. Shoving on her back, I try to get her moving, but she trips on her own feet and we both go down, me on top of her. Scrambling, I try to get off her, at the same time eyeing over my shoulder where the carnage continues. Britney is wailing beneath me and not even attempting to get up, not moving at all aside from her sniffling nose and trembling mouth. Perhaps that isn't a bad idea—just playing dead. But I can't do that. Tripping again as I stand, my knee jabs Britney's back, but then I'm up and running. And it's a good thing. As I make my way through the kitchen, I glance over my shoulder again and see the werewolf mount Britney, ripping the flesh off her back with its jaws. I'm out the kitchen and sprinting through the living room, where, unbelievably, Stan is still jerking off on the couch, his eyes rolled back.

"Stan, get the fuck out of here!" I scream, passing by him. "There is some bad shit going down!" And then I'm through the foyer and out the front door, where cold air and sleet hits me in the face. A BMW is skidding out the end of the driveway. Not far behind it, a large Chevy truck is picking up speed with several people in the bed. "Wait!" I scream, sprinting down the steps to the driveway waving my arms. "WAIT!" But they aren't waiting. The five faces in the bed of the truck are looking at me as it pulls out of the driveway and speeds away. One of those faces is Gwen's.

After trotting halfway up the driveway, I stop. The cold already has my lungs burning, and my eyes are wet and stinging in the wind. I'm surrounded by cars that I don't have the keys to. Unless someone left their keys in the vehicle. I try the door of Gwen's Cadillac: locked. I try the other BMW: locked. I try the Mercedes and a Ford and Dodge Ram: all locked. Pulling my cell phone from my pocket, I tap 9-1-1 on the keypad and look back towards Chandler's house, where the werewolf is standing in the doorway.

"Oh fuck," I say as the 911 operator picks up and asks what my emergency is.

The beast—the werewolf—Sara Hamilton is red with gore, its fur matted with blood, and shredded skin and guts hang from its claws and jaws.

"Sir?" the female operator says.

"I need help," I whisper.

"What's your location and what is your emergency?"

The werewolf bounds from the house, running at me on all fours, ice and blood kicking up from its claws.

"Fuck!" I scream and turn for the woods. The phone is forgotten in my hand. It's too late to call for help. My only hope is escape. Despite the frigid air and sleet, I'm sweating. I can feel it on my face and soaking through my shirt. The woods are dark and somehow colder, and limbs grab at my clothing as I run. I see myself getting stuck amongst the branches or running straight into a tree, knocking me out, and turning me into an easy meal for the wolf. And a branch does hit me in the face and blood pours from my nose and mouth, but I keep going. Because I can hear it. The beast isn't zigzagging around trees and bushes like me; it's running straight through them like they're nothing but brittle fucking twigs.

But I can see the ripples of the lake now. And on the lake, less than a hundred feet out, I see the bass boat and the fisherman. He has a lantern hanging on a hook above his boat, and the man is lifting a fish out of the water, and even in my duress I am thinking how nice and relaxing it must be to be alone with the lake.

"Help!" I scream. "Help me!" I'm out of the woods and running along the icy bank, my feet slipping briefly, nearly sending to my doom. I regain my footing and scream for the fisherman again. But he doesn't look up. He's removing the hook from the fish's mouth and smiling. It's a small catfish and the fisherman's hand fits around it easily. He kisses the fish on the nose and tosses it back to the lake. I scream again, "Help me!" The wolf is nearly upon me.

I run into the water, it's stinging my ankles and then my shins, and then my thighs. The freezing water is piercing my flesh like needles of ice. It's to my groin, then waist, then my stomach. I scream for help. I scream for my savior as the werewolf reaches the water and soars through it like a torpedo. I scream as the fisherman rebaits his hook, and I scream as the wolf's arms close around me and the fisherman casts his line into the water. And I scream my last scream as the wolf pulls me under, and I want to see the boat one more time before I die, but it isn't there—it was never there—and instead I see the moon, bright and full between the broken clouds.

AUTHOR'S STORY NOTE

In 2019 I was invited to write a story for an anthology that never happened. The project was a collaboration between Jarod Barbee and Kevin J. Kennedy, and the basic idea involved authors writing stories inspired by *their* favorite authors. There were some great writers attached to this project, including Ryan Harding, Chris Miller, Christine Morgan (as I recall, Christine was going to pen a tale inspired by Dr. Seuss; that would've been awesome), and several others.

I immediately knew I wanted to write a story inspired by Bret Easton Ellis. In two days' time I'd written a tale in BEE's nihilistic style, with PC3's monstrous, blood-soaked bite. "Full Moon Shindig" was born. Ultimately, the anthology was not to be. Instead, Christine and I conspired to bring the world a collection of body horror titled *Visceral: Collected Flesh*. My twisted tale had a perfect home!

A little sidenote about the story itself: The part about the dog actually happened to some poor pooch somewhere. I once worked with a guy who told me about a friend of his doing it at a party, and the dog reacting just the way I described. Just to be clear, I don't condone such behavior, but how could I not put it in a story?

THE DRINKING-HORN

CHRISTINE MORGAN

From *Brewtality*
Editor: K. Trap Jones
The Evil Cookie Publishing

Ullvik the Bottomless, they called him, his capacity for ale and for wine and for honey-sweet mead the stuff nearly of legend.

Men of many lands far and wide, he'd drunk under the tables, ever the last one still standing as they wallowed insensate, awash in their own vomit and piss. Men, and, it was said, those not-men as well . . . dwarfs and trolls, dark aelfs, even giants . . . had fallen before him in contest.

Matters of battle and bloodshed, he oft left to others. For them, the war-lust, the violence, the carnage. For them, the wild love of sword, spear, and axe. He could and did fight; he was no coward, no peaceable monk. When he took to the field, he dealt brutal savagery unhesitating. He split skulls, hewed limbs, spilled entrails rank and steaming, and brought on the slaughter well as any warrior. But he did so only with a grim taskman's purpose, a job to be done.

Far did he prefer the riotous revelry of the mead-hall, the laughing and singing, the plucked harp-strings, to the discordant clangor of blades upon steel or limewood . . . to the wet, meaty cracking of bone . . . the agonized screaming. Far did he prefer the scents of hearth-smoke and hearty fare to those of blood, shit, and death.

If he were to ache head and body next day, better it be from stumbling and good-natured brawling among the benches than crushed shoulder to shoulder in the shield-wall. If he were to wake naked and bleary with scant recollection, better to find himself abed beside some buxom whore than stripped of his mailcoat and left for dead in the mud.

This, then, yes, this was the life of Ullvik the Bottomless. This was his fame. His renowned thirst struck dread in the hearts of tavern-keepers and brewstresses alike, jarls' stewards, and quartermasters of war. Should they run dry, keg, cask, or barrel, who knew what might result?

He paid in fair sum, of course, good silver; what-so-ever plunder he took or with what gifts was rewarded soon enough made its way into their ready hands. Ullvik held no ambition for title or land, had no plans to marry, cared little for fathering sons. So long as he kept himself horsed and housed, kept his arms and armor in decent repair, and fell into no debt, he saw no need to hoard dragon's-wealth.

Not when there was drink to be had! If he could, through betting and challenge, get others to pay, then so much the better . . . but he was like as not to buy pots of ale for a dozen strangers, for who wanted to drink alone?

If he did harbor one ambition, it was one hardly uncommon. That he would, that he *must*, die well in glorious battle. That he would earn his way to Valhalla, there to make merry with mead-horns until the great final battle at the end of all days.

He took scant part in politics. Noble kings or rebel chieftains, to Ullvik it mattered not. Nor did it matter whether friends became enemies; in the end, when they were all joined together under Odin's banner, all old loyalties would fall away.

This, yes, was Ullvik. A big man, broad of chest, stout but solid of belly, brawny of arm and bushy-bearded of jaw. A man whose favorite of any skald's tale or sagas was that of Thor and Utgardr, in which the giant-king put the bold thunderer to test in a feat of drinking, for of course it was!

Ullvik loved that tale, could never hear enough of it. How the giants had presented Thor with an immense drinking-horn and bade him drain it in only three swallows . . . yet however mightily he guzzled from it, the level within barely sank . . . until even Mjölnir's mighty bearer had to admit defeat.

"Let *me* have a go at that drinking-horn," Ullvik was wont to say. "I'll do them one better, and why not? Haven't I out-drunk trolls, giants, and dwarfs? Give me a turn, then!"

"It was a *trick*," the skalds would, in exasperation, explain.

"It was *magic*! The horn's other end met the vast ocean! There's no way anyone, even a god, could drain it down!"

"I know *that*," he'd reply with a scoff. "I know, also, how even so, the giants, who had been set to shame and to mock him, dared not, for he still *did* lower the level within the horn! Which none, not even Utgardr, thought possible!"

"And which," they'd tell him, "from that day forth, caused the rising and falling of the tides—"

But, by then, Ullvik's attention had most likely strayed elsewhere. To the sad state of his own emptying vessel, perhaps, or the approach of a tavern-girl laden with full and generous jugs. Or men who'd heard of his reputation and wanted to see for themselves if the legends were true. Or a spirited tune struck up, or a brawl broke out.

Still and all, the thought of that fabled drinking-horn never far left his mind. How, he wondered, had its contents tasted? Not like seawater, obviously; whatever magic connected them must have also transformed it or masked its flavor, else surely Thor would have spat forth the first briny gulp in disgust. It must have been suitable to be served in a giant-king's hall. Strong ale? Rich wine? Mead to rival Valhalla's own?

Enough to fill even him, Ullvik the Bottomless? Enough to sate him, glut him, quench for a time his powerful thirst? Suppose he *could* do them one better, those giants and gods? Suppose he could, if not drain the horn, sink its level more than Thor himself had done? Change the very tides, and the pale course of the moon bound to them?

A deep winter came, in which jarls made truce so no armies went to battle. Longships lay idle at their moorings as thick ice choked the fjords and the bays. Women bent to their weaving, craftsmen to their tools. Artisans carved tafl-pieces from whalebone ivory. Weapons were tended and spring raids were planned. Days held dark, nights held darker. Husbands and wives bickered and fucked. Babes were born. Hounds nosed for scraps in the floor-rushes. Tales were told, songs were sung.

And Ullvik? Ullvik drank. He drank in the great hall until he'd worn out the lord's welcome. He drank at the taverns until he'd run out his silver. He drank with friends and with strangers. But all too soon, the mead-stores were depleted. All too soon, wine was nowhere to be found and ale had grown scarce. Only barley beer, and even that watered thin, stood between Ullvik's thirst and his utter ruin. His spirits sank into a glum despair, so that he found himself slumped wretchedly in the filth of a pig byre, listening to the boar sows snuffling at their trough.

A girl found him there, a swineherd's girl, bare-footed and shabby. Hardly his sort, not so much slender but scrawny, dark of eye and sharp of feature. Grime streaked her limbs. She wore a ragged tunic and carried a slop-pail. But, when she paused and asked him if he needed a scrap of bread or mug of ale, she might have been glorious golden-garbed Freya herself.

He accepted her offer, venturing into a shed both lit and warmed by only a single tallow-fat candle. The bread was hard as a whetstone and stale as dust. The mug, though, held good ale . . . while not the best, indeed far from the worst . . . and Ullvik guzzled its contents in a gulping series of swallows. A resonant, yeasty belch rumbled forth, followed by a sigh of relief wrung up from his very toes.

"Again?" asked the swineherd's girl.

"Oh, I could marry you," he said fervently, and she laughed as she refilled the mug from a small, weathered keg.

Ullvik eyed it, wondering how much it might hold. The girl caught his look. Her laughter became a wry smile.

"Not enough, I'm afraid." She rocked it, letting him hear the meagre sloshing. "Hardly Utgardr's drinking-horn, is it?"

"You know that saga?" Already feeling the ale's blessed balm suffusing his innards, Ullvik plopped onto a rickety bench that creaked beneath his weight.

"Of course I do." Refilling his mug yet again, the girl perched upon a spindly stool by the table. She'd found a few shriveled apples and began to pare off wedges to go with the bread.

As good as a feast, it was, in Ullvik's eyes . . . this humble shed fine as any longhouse . . . a narrow cot tucked below slanted eaves a veritable marriage-bed for this goddess who gave him ale and knew of Utgardr! Perhaps he *should* marry her . . .

"I also know," she added, dark eyes glinting in the candle's light, "of another such horn."

"Another saga?" By Frygga, he *would*!

"No mere saga. An actual such drinking-horn, a magic one, which fills far faster than it can be emptied."

He scoffed. "If only!"

"It's true," she said. "I've seen it."

"You never!"

"I did!"

"Where? In the hall of the giant-king, I suppose?"

She shook her head. "In the hovel of a witch."

"Tell me!"

The dregs of the keg she poured into his mug, seeming to consider and weigh her words. "Where it came from, and how she came by it, I know not. Dwarf-made? God-given? Stolen from some wyrm's treasure-hoard? Who can say? But she, loathing above all else happiness and joy, cherishing above all else misery and sorrow, keeps it hidden away in the depths of a cave. As it fills and refills, its contents overflow, only to spill onto barren rock and trickle away into the dark hollows of the earth."

Ullvik gaped at the girl. "And . . . and you've seen this horn? How?"

"I was her slave-thrall for a time."

"Did you ever . . .?"

"Drink of it? I dared not! She threatened me with the most

terrible punishments, worlds of suffering if I took even a single sip! Finally, when I could endure no more of her cruelty, I escaped."

He raised the mug again to his lips but found it empty. The ale was gone, leaving his mouth dry, his thirst stronger than ever. "Is it far from here? The witch's hovel?"

Now the girl gaped at *him*. "You cannot be thinking . . ."

"Why not? Why should such treasure be hidden? Such bounty be wasted?"

"But the punishments! Worlds of suffering!"

"I fear no old crone!" Only somewhat staggering, he pushed himself to his full height. "Take me there! Show me!"

Despite her reluctance, he would not be dissuaded, and so it was they were soon riding into the cold, wild woods. Ullvik rode cloak bundled against the night's chill, his horse stamping and snorting and steaming. The girl, astride a donkey as scrawny as she was, still went bare footed in just her ragged tunic, but neither shivered nor complained. Now and again, it struck him peculiar, but the prospect of the drinking-horn drove him onward.

At last, they reached a place where the trees rose gnarled and twisted, bent boughs draped in black moss, roots hunched thick from the loamy earth. Stones loomed, rune-carved or hewn into monstrous shapes. A hollow wind dolefully sighed, and unseen shapes stirred in the shadows.

"There," the girl whispered, pointing ahead at the faint glow of a fire. She stopped her donkey. "I must go no further. If she sees me . . ."

"Fine, then. Wait here." Ullvik dismounted. He settled his helm secure, left his shield slung across his back, and drew the short *seax* blade good for stabbing in close quarters.

For, close quarters so it appeared . . . the witch's hovel was just that, a hovel indeed, a crude assemblage of sticks built against a rocky cliff face. A hide curtain hung in its crooked doorway. Thin, acrid smoke issued from its crooked smoke hole. A fence of bramble bushes girded a garden of scraggly, sinister growth.

A momentary caution gave Ullvik pause, and cause to wonder if this was the wisest of actions. He hesitated, glancing back at the girl who'd led him here, but her face was a pale, unreadable blur in the darkness.

Then, through a hush in the easing of the wind, he heard the trickling echo of liquid splashing onto stone. The acrid smoke was supplanted by an intoxicating, familiar scent. Mead! Honey-mead, sweet and golden, potent and strong!

The very thought of it cramped a pang in his gullet. And the thought of it simply spilling away, wasted . . .

He strode forward, sweeping aside the hide curtain with one hand while holding his blade ready in the other. Let any stand in his way, man or monster, warrior or witch, he would—

None stood in his way. The hovel sat unoccupied, not so much as a cat. Its little fire flickered untended. Shelves held pots and jars, cobwebbed, dust laden. He pressed on, pushed through, toward a gap in the rock face at the back of the hut. A draft wafted from it, the sweet scent of mead having given way to the heady richness of ale.

Had he ever, in all of his days, been so parched? So craving? When he reached his prize, he would drink 'til he sloshed!

Into the narrow cave-gap, Ullvik ventured, hearing the echoing trickle splash louder. Each lost drop tore at him like the claws of a beast, bringing agony not just of body but soul.

The way opened before him to reveal a chamber, his torchlight illuminating rocky formations shot with glittering crystalline veins. Treasures lay scattered all about, gems and silver, neck torcs and arm rings, jeweled brooches. But what seized his gaze, and held it, was the drinking-horn.

It rested upon a stone ledge, held in a plain wooden cradle. If he'd been expecting gold-work and intricate carved ivory, he would've been disappointed. All he saw, though, was how it brimmed overfull, how the liquid—smelling now of grape wine!—spilled in steady stream. How it puddled on the ledge in a shallow pool, from there only to flow in dribbling rivulets, flow along cracks and down crevices, vanishing wasted and untasted into the stony heart of the earth.

He rushed to it, having sheathed his *seax* blade without heeding, barely mindful of the rubble beneath his feet, or the clatter and roll of strewn bones. Even when he kicked aside skulls, their naked jaws yawned wide in death, he gave scarce notice.

All that mattered was reaching out with his trembling, trembling hands. All that mattered was lifting the horn from its cradle, feeling the heft of it, the fullness. Wine—or was it mead now?—slicked his palms.

Ullvik brought it to his lips. Oh, and yes, it was mead, the best mead he'd ever tasted, mead that did, surely *must*, rival Valhalla's own! He poured it into his own open and eager mouth, gulping, guzzling, throat working mightily. And *yes*! However much he swallowed, the level did not sink! It was mead, and then ale, and then wine, and then mead again!

He drank, how he drank, as if he might never get enough! He drank, and he would have laughed, would have roared and cheered, would have sung, but all he could do was tilt the horn higher and drink even more! He drank to the dead men whose skeletal corpses surrounded him, to his war brothers past, to foes fallen and women fucked, and he drank!

He drank as the taste changed, turning bitter. Turning hollow, and aching, and empty, and sad. He drank grief and lonesomeness, regret, pain, and loss. The weeping of widows. Orphans' tears. He drank as fathers mourned their only sons, as bereft lovers yearned.

He drank and could not *stop* drinking. Could not spit it out, could not take the horn from his lips, could not stop its contents pouring forth. His own arms and hands would not obey him.

On it came, this unending dark bitterness! Flooding his mouth, filling his throat, backwashing harshly into his sinuses so that he gasped and coughed. It breached his windpipe, stung his lungs.

Was he to drown of it? Ullvik fought to turn his head, but that too would not obey him. Some of the liquid did run down his cheeks and chin, sopping his beard, but most continued rushing into him unabated. He swallowed as fast as he could, trying to gain ahead of the torrent.

Drink 'til he sloshed, had he thought? Slosh he did, belly bloating overfull, his guts cramping. He gagged, but could spew none of it back up, only mingle it with bile within him into a thick, vomitous stew.

From the corner of one tearful, watering eye, he saw the girl who'd brought him here step into the chamber. The girl who was not a girl after all, nor a witch, but something far older.

"Utgardr's horn," she said to him, her voice ancient as the ages, "met to the deep oceans, so that Thor himself could only drink of it enough to cause the tides. This horn connects to a different sea . . . a sea eternal and forever-replenishing . . . the sea of human sorrows."

Ullvik tried to speak, but of course he could not. Tried to plead, tried to protest.

"The more men drink of it," she went on, with a gesture at the strewn bones around him, "the more there will be. The horn never empties. The sorrows never end."

He drank, and *he* wept. For the widows and orphans, the fathers and sons, the lovers, the lonely, the anguished and grief-stricken. For himself, and for all the wide world.

His body seemed to swell like a pig's bladder, so that his clothes strained at the seams. He felt he might, at any moment, simply burst all asunder in a splattering rain of wet, sodden gobbets of flesh.

How was it he kept breathing? How was it he did not choke,

drown, and die?

He wept harder, tears streaming, swallowing misery again and again. Yet it kept on coming, wretched and bitter and cold.

"I think," she said, smiling a terrible, dreadful smile, "you'll last a very long time. So, drink now, oh Ullvik the Bottomless. Go on. Drink your fill."

AUTHOR'S STORY NOTE

The moment I learned of the themed anthology [for *Brewtality*] call, I knew it was time to go a'viking again. How could I not? The Vikings were almost as much known for their love of booze as of battle, to the point the two make their very idea of heaven. To take something so iconic and turn it into a nightmare was impossible to resist. Poor Ullvik the Bottomless. Beware of what you wish for!

OTTO HAHN SPEAKS TO THE DEAD

OCTAVIA CADE

From *The Dark Magazine*
Editor: Sean Wallace
Prime Books

A garden is a beautiful place to die. It was the only beautiful thing about Clara's death, which otherwise was a bullet and a broken chest, blood spilling over everything, the red scent of iron.

Had he been there, he might have vomited. Only might, because the revulsion he felt for death had lessened a little in the immediacy of the war, and he'd done so much to increase that death that it didn't do to be squeamish just because the dead in front of him now was a woman. One connected with him, and her death was a repudiation not directed at him—Otto wasn't the one married to her—but he had some responsibility nonetheless. He'd helped in the work she'd felt such revulsion for; she had seen the choice he'd made and refused her coexistence.

"Of course, I did," she says after they took her body away. She'd been covered after it happened, the suicide kept from sight, but not all of the blood she'd shed had soaked into dress and dressings. The rest had soaked into earth, was scatter-droplets on petals, and in the moonlight no-one could see it anyway, or was even out searching. Some things were too terrible to look at and her husband was inside, avoiding mirrors. The ghost of her stayed in the garden, with the closed-up blossoms, so she wouldn't have to look at him. "No decent person would be part of this."

Chemical warfare, and Clara a chemist herself. "There are some things I will not stoop to," she says, and it disgusted her that Otto had. That her husband had—that he'd covered his hands with burning, with suffocated blood, and brought them home to her afterwards, as if she were expected to touch them, to kiss them and be grateful for their presence.

She couldn't bear to be touched by him ever again. Hence the bullets, the garden death, and the house still in a mess from the party Haber had held to celebrate chlorine gas in trenches, and how he'd done it first.

"Better than the alternative," Otto argues. It's not exactly heroic, coming up with ways to slaughter at scale, but he'd rather cause others to choke and suffocate than do so himself. "There's nothing wrong with self-preservation," he says, because war is a terrible thing, yes, but sometimes scruples do nothing but extend it. Best to get it over with as quickly as possible, and with as little damage as possible. The rest he doesn't look at too closely.

"You should have the decency to look at what you've done," says Clara. She slips her arms out of her dress, lets the fabric fall to her waist. He doesn't want to look. It feels disrespectful, somehow, with her bare breasts slick with her own blood, and that gaping ruin between them. "Look," she says. "Look at what I think of you."

He'll go to his own grave swearing that he never got hard at the sight of her.

She's there every time he goes to sleep. A nightmare come to life. "You traffic in nightmares, don't you?" Clara asks him. "Well then. This is what you invited in."

She's a monster.

No, she isn't.

That's one accusation Otto will never have the right to make again. Monstrosity comes in many forms, but Clara isn't it, and he thinks as long as he can hold to that then there's something in him human still, something the gas hasn't changed.

He has a gas mask of his own now. It was only a matter of time. There is argument out of Britain: "We cannot win this war unless we kill or incapacitate more of our enemies than they do of us, and if this can only be done by copying the enemy in his choice of weapons, we must not refuse to do so."

It is an escalation that was entirely foreseen.

His face in the mirror is masked and wheezing. Clara stands behind him, the front of her blood-red and dripping, but her face is innocent of canvas and charcoal. "It suits you," she says. "But it won't make a difference."

She comes to him at night. He wakes to her kneeling on his chest, the breath being pressed out of him. Blood runs from her shattered chest, drips into his mouth, pools in the back of his throat. It's copper and iron and choking, the warm sweet scent of it. When she smiles down at him her teeth are rimmed with red, like they were in the garden when she coughed up the last of her own life.

"Poor baby," she says. "Did you have a bad dream?"

Her hair smells of flowers. That's always what sets him to weeping. If it were grave dirt, trench dirt, the scent surrounding him as he lay in his bed, he thinks he'd be able to treat her as revenant. To push her off him, to let horror take the place of bitterness and grief. That would be protection, of a sort, because the gas mask never is. He wears it to bed, when she's come too often for sleeping and sanity, but it smothers him regardless. It's too warm, too close, and he comes to gasping consciousness, slick with sweat, that same taste of salt.

Flowers are better. At least with flowers he can tell himself that what's waking him is external, the product of a grief he'd never admit to having, because what would that make of his life? His involvement is not peripheral. The responsibility for chemical warfare falls on him as much as anyone. Edith tells him not to worry, tells him he is doing his duty, and thank God his wife is not as dramatic as Haber's was, he does not think he could bear it. Flinches now when she goes into the garden. Pastes a smile on his face for her, makes of his features a smooth clean warmth, because she's never woken to ghosts in the bed and he doesn't want her to fathom what his work has brought them.

There are masks for horses, too, and dogs. All the innocent, useful beasts. Otto is useful but not innocent, and when he sees himself in surfaces, the canvas shifting with every breath, he wonders if this is what he looked like all along.

He's so sick of seeing her. "Why don't you haunt your own husband?" he snarls, an angry whisper because Edith is asleep beside him and he'd never admit it, never, but this nighttime atonement is nothing to do with her. Edith was never a chemist, she could never know what it was to have elements at her fingers, to be able to manipulate the very stuff of matter.

Clara's face freezes at him. Her red mouth, her red chest. Her red breath, because whenever she speaks small droplets spray out and smear the sheets, and he has to tell Edith he had a bloody nose in the night. "It will make no difference," she says. "Not to him."

Fritz Haber had left the day after the garden party, left to go back to the front. Left the garden still sticky with protest, left his young son still trembling with the feel of dead mother in his arms. Otto knows about necessity and the price of power, he's excused a lot for it, but he's not sure that this betrayal is ever one which could be excused. "Would you leave your son after such a grief?" Clara hisses at him, sibilant, with liquid in her chest.

He doesn't have a son. Is newly married, and children have not yet been gifted to him. "I'd never hurt a child like you did," he says, knowing it will hurt. He is good at hurting, has developed a proficiency for it. The thought of that child, alone, having found his mother in the garden, a garden he'll now have to look out onto every day . . ."Perhaps you *are* a monster," he says.

It's always so easy to condemn others.

"Do I look monstrous to you?" says Clara. In the moonlight the blood shimmers and fades, seems to seep back into skin, and the whole broken chest of her knits itself together, pale and gleaming. She's perfect, so perfect, and close enough to touch, and the entire bedroom smells of flowers now instead of iron, and the stars behind her give enough of a shine for halos, and Edith is a pale thing in comparison, insipid, and part of him hates her for it because he's planning the murder of hundreds, of thousands, trying to make entire armies choke and suffocate and suffer, and this is something she can just skim over, like it's *nothing*. In their marriage bed, sleeping, peaceful, like it's nothing.

"Do you want her to open herself up for you?" says Clara, smirking, and this is revenge, he thinks, for the cruelty of her son, for the way that Otto used him as reminder. "Do you want her to open herself up *because* of you?"

What a thing it would be to be so powerful.

(What a thing it is.)

Verdun, Zone Rouge.

A hundred years after World War 1, the place is still uninhabitable. 1200 square kilometres, saturated with ordinance, and with chemicals. The soldiers hit with chlorine gas, with all the gases that came after chlorine, they lived, some of them. Or died. Either way their stories were short ones. Packed off in stretchers, packed off in ambulances, buried not far from where the gas got them.

Not all the gas got sucked into lungs. Not nearly all of it. Most floated down, a gentle sinking. Soaked itself into soil, got sucked up again by plants, got eaten through plants by birds and mammals and gentle creeping things. Chlorine. Arsenic.

In some places 99% of the plants are dead. A hundred years later, they are still dead. Nothing can survive the contamination those shells left.

Chlorine. Phosgene. Mustard. Nausea, vomiting, headache. Blindness, asphyxiation, blisters. Lungs filled with fluid. Suffocation. Drowning.

Otto dreams himself awake to skin full of pustules and streaming eyes, irritation in his mouth and throat. Watery eyes, wheezing. The fluid in his lungs reacting to chlorine, forming hydrochloric acid. A burning, choking, agonising death, membranes leaking blood.

Clara takes her ghost-self through the undergrowth of Verdun.

There are dead trees there, dead skeletons. Nothing smells of flowers, but when the blood spills down her front—a smooth, endless gushing—it drops upon the earth like poppies, and for a moment the dead ground blooms. Then the soil gets them, drags them down, bleaches the petals to nothing and leaves them curled up and brown. Withered.

A ghost has light footsteps. They don't disturb the bombs, all the unexploded pieces, but sometimes when an animal wanders passed, one too lost and mazed to be frightened by the dead, it sets off a small blast and dies, twitching, in soil that is anathema to it.

Little bones are everywhere. It's nothing like a garden, Clara thinks, but at the same time it's her own, left to go wild because no-one can stand to go out in it anymore.

It's walking in a wasteland. Otto will never come here, so she scrapes the dirt up into her mouth, the dead dirt, whole horrible sterile handfuls of it. She is dead herself, so there's no danger of it. But when she goes to him at night, this man she never knew that well but can still see some worth in, worth that by the end she could never see in her husband, she breaths the scent of Verdun over him. The dusty, empty scent of it, crammed in her teeth, between canines and clogging up the hole in her chest.

There will be no escape. Not for either of them.

How to survive a chlorine gas attack:

1) Leave before it starts. Be somewhere else entirely.

Otto spends much of his time scouting for appropriate places for slaughter. Gas is a finicky thing. Climate and geography can make it less effective. Less lethal. This is war, after all, and it is best to be efficient. He is at Flanders before the second battle of Ypres, but when men are being gassed there—with the prevailing wind—he is off looking at another site, and then another. Belgium, Poland, Italy . . . he gets to see them all. Clara is never with him, but whatever field he stands in smells of flowers.

2) Try not to run. Exercise exacerbates the effects of the gas.

He thinks the travel sees her off, that if Clara can't find his bed at night it's because she's no longer able. Hatred is a difficult thing to hold on to, perhaps. But he volunteers himself as human guinea-pig, standing with gas mask on—it's like a second skin, now—and waiting for the gas to take him. The one disadvantage to using chlorine on the other side is that it's harder to get hold of their bodies. He could get out of testing, if he wanted—there's not so many scientists of his calibre that they couldn't find someone as German and much more useless to take his place. But the responsibility nags at him, the sense of horror he feels at the sight of the gas clouds seeping towards him . . . this is what he has helped to inflict on others, and there is something in him that feels he must face the same. So, he reports for testing, wears his mask and locks his knees together, hopes the protection he has is protection enough. If not, perhaps that is justice. When he forces his eyes open, Clara is standing with him, her face pressed against his gas mark, staring in. He can feel the chill breath of her through canvas. When he sees her watching, feels the strain in the legs that are not running, he understands that hatred finds a way.

3) Get to a high place. Do not lie down, not in the trenches. Chlorine gas is heavier than air, and it sinks.

Otto feels he is justified. He feels it over and over. The fit of the gas mask, the stink of chemical, of charcoal and urine . . . he has done his part. Self-respect staggers on, but it is nowhere near as close a justification as necessity. "We must break this deadlock," he says. "Better for everyone the sooner it's over. I'd not do this if I had the choice. No-one would."

"Lots of people would," says Clara. "Don't tell me about choices." She made hers, in the garden, with her husband's service pistol, and everyone around her paid, is paying for it.

"Hard choices take strength," he says, but secretly, in himself, he wonders more and more if what made his choices for him is weakness.

Otto has a son. His only child, and when he wakes one night to screaming he decides to let his wife sleep, see to the boy himself. Clara is hanging over the crib, and cooing. Her breasts are leaking over him, a mixture of milk and blood, and the room smells of dead earth and dead flowers.

"Strange how their screaming affects you," she says. Little Hermann screamed when he found his mother, Otto is sure of it. He's spent more nights than he cares to collect picturing the young boy and the shot and the screaming, the small hands trying to stifle blood and flailing, frantic, as his mother dies in his arms.

"Even when they're old, you don't forget it," she says. Hermann must be nearly a man now, and later, much later, when Otto hears that he has killed himself, taken to suicide just as his mother did, he'll remember this conversation and wish . . . for what? That he'd been kinder, to the creature overhanging his life? That he'd had sympathy for the devastation she'd caused? That he'd reached out, somehow, to another family's horror, and one he wasn't quite innocent of?

He isn't, and doesn't, and never does. She can't expect kindness, hovering as she does, like a ghoul. A hag. "You leave my boy alone," he says, snatching the child out from under and wiping his face clean with fingers that are smeared with old blood. "He's got nothing to do with this. With us." If her visits have waned somewhat there's an *us*, still. A relationship closer in death than it ever was in life, when she was the wife of his colleague and not much else. Why she's latched on to him he'll never guess and refuses now to try.

Mostly he doesn't think of her at all. As time passes the

trenches get further away. The nearness of death recedes, and it's easier to think well of himself. Easier to think on other things. Different things.

"There's a lot you don't think about anymore," says Clara. "You made the world he'll live in. You think that's nothing to do with you?"

"He'll have a better world than Hermann," says Otto. A better mother. A better father.

"All those boys you killed had fathers too," Clara reminds him, and then she's gone, the nursery still as if she was never there, and the baby choking in his arms.

The little chest is heaving, the little cheeks red, at first, then redder and redder then paling down to blue, and if Otto's work has taught him anything it's taught him the signs of suffocation, of gasping for breath that won't come. Of lungs clogged up and drowning, of no strength left to cry and tears coming regardless.

It's croup, he tells himself, *only croup*, and the baby lives and it's a small alarm only, a common ailment or so the doctor tells him, but Otto could swear, he could *swear*, that with his head pressed closed to infant chest to detect the signs of life he could smell nothing but chlorine.

(Hanno Hahn does not die from croup. He does not die in World War Two, not from gas nor from bombs. He and his wife are killed in a car accident, leaving only a young son. The boy is the same age as Hermann was, when he found his mother dying in the garden and his father left him to go on alone while he arranged the murder of other men's sons.

Otto cries and cries where the boy cannot see and wonders to himself if this loss is justice come at last.)

The War, the Great War, and he thought it was over. "The world we create is *never* over," says Clara, because there's another war coming, one bigger and more gaseous than the last, and now the responsibility is even more his because Otto has found something more dangerous than chlorine, and its name is fission. He and Lise Meitner discovered it, working together, and war will make of their work a wasteland worse than that ever seen in Ypres, or Verdun.

Lise is Jewish, and Germany is no longer a safe place for her. Otto helps her escape, because he has seen enough of blood saturating through the women of his acquaintance, and he was too proud, too stupid, too pleased with himself ever to help Clara. If he even could have. The only thing that could have saved Lise from the taint of her blood was the willingness to work, but work can only buy so much freedom and he has no belief in her ability to push through.

He knows she will abstain. Clara shot herself rather than give the approval of her presence. Lise has removed herself as well, and she will not work on the bomb. Not ever. Not for the Germans and not for the Allies. Such things, she says, are too hideous.

Otto thinks he may have forgotten what hideous is.

He digs out his old gas mask, the first one. There are better ones since, he knows them and has them, but the first is impregnated with nightmares of suffocation, and when he wears it he can feel his throat closing. When he wears it to bed, he wakes to find Clara crouched on his chest, the way she used to in the war gone by. It's been over twenty years and she's still wet with blood, still warm with it, and this time he licks it out of her mouth so he can remember what death is, what consequences it has. What his responsibilities are.

"I don't want to be that man again," he says. He can't tell when science stopped being a wonder to him and started being a horror, but in the back of his mind now is a fear that the chemical death he brought on so many is a small thing. A small and burning thing, and what is coming is holocaust. "I don't want to be that man again."

"Then don't," says Clara.

He does not work on the bomb. It's that easy.

The war drags on and on.

He cannot forgive himself for it.

AUTHOR'S STORY NOTE

Otto Hahn Speaks to the Dead was originally published in the April 2020 issue of *The Dark*. It tells the story of a really unsavoury bit of science history: the invention of chlorine gas as a weapon in World War One. Hahn was part of the team that invented it. He wasn't the head of that team—that was a man called Fritz Haber. Haber was married to another chemist, Clara Immerwahr, who was so disgusted with what her husband had made of science that she killed herself. (Hell, I wouldn't have wanted to stay married to him either.) Hahn, bit player in this saga, has always interested me. I find it particularly notable that, when offered the chance to work on German research for the atomic bomb in the second World War of his lifetime, he refused. I like to think he'd learned better by then. Perhaps horror had touched him too closely . . .

ALL THE STARS IN HER EYES

DEBORAH SHELDON

From *Andromeda Spaceways #80*
Editor: Tom Dullemond
Andromeda Spaceways Publishing Co-Op

Janet and her daughter sing nursery rhymes at bath-time. The last nursery rhyme must always be *Twinkle, Twinkle, Little Star* because that is Aurora's favourite. Aurora is three years old. As she sings, she waggles her fingers to imitate her mother, unknowingly mimicking the shimmer of distant suns. Janet feels both a rush of love and the anxious sensation that time is fleeting. She grabs her phone from the pocket of her dress and takes a photograph. Aurora, used to posing, widens her eyes and purses her lips.

The flash goes off.

Janet inspects the photograph. It is a good one. She will email it to her sister, Megan, who lives in Perth on the other side of Australia. Megan has not yet met Aurora. Neither sister can afford the airfare. They are both young, in their twenties. Megan is a waitress. Since becoming a single mother, Janet—the promising and talented graphic designer—has worked from home, freelance, designing book covers and selling them via her website because she can't afford childcare. She makes enough to pay the mortgage, put food on the table, clothes on their backs, petrol in the car. But not much else. She tries not to think about the future.

Janet is about to email the photograph when she notices something odd about it. She zooms in on Aurora's face. The child has brilliant blue eyes, like those of her father, which is unsettling because Janet's eyes are brown, and Janet remembers from high-school biology that blue is a recessive trait and brown is dominant. She reminds herself, frequently, that she must be mistaken, and while the truth is only a Google-search away, she will not investigate. Janet studies the picture. Aurora's pupils are sparkling as if filled with glitter. This must be a photographic glitch, similar to red-eye. Janet knows that red-eye is the flash reflecting on the retina. She puts the phone back in her pocket.

"Look at Mummy," she says.

"I am," Aurora says, and splashes the bath water. The rubber ducks toss in the surf.

"No," Janet says, and holds her daughter's chin. "Make your eyes big and look at me."

Aurora does so, giggling, as if they are playing. Janet's stomach tightens and falls.

There are tiny specks in Aurora's pupils. Hundreds of them. Thousands of them.

Each pupil resembles a snow globe, but the specks are suspended, unmoving. Fixed. Janet tries to remember if Aurora's eyes seemed unusual in any way prior to bath-time. She thinks back to dinner, just an hour ago. Wouldn't she have noticed? It doesn't seem possible that something so catastrophic could have happened to her daughter's eyes in so brief a time. Because this must be catastrophic. Aurora is going blind. Her retinas have come loose and are floating, disintegrating, shedding their light-sensitive cells.

"Let's go," Janet says, and hoists Aurora from the bath.

"Where?"

"Into town."

"No, Mummy, it's time for sleeps," Aurora says, with reproach. Janet recognises the tone as the same she uses herself when the occasion calls for discipline. Now she must keep the panic out of her voice or else frighten her daughter.

"It's a game," she says. "A bit of fun. Come on, let's get you dressed."

Janet's poky two-bedroom cottage is twenty minutes from the town centre, including long stretches of highway with a posted speed limit of 110 kilometres an hour. At first, the roads are gravel and there are no streetlights. It is a cloudless night in Melbourne's spring. The air smells of wild daisies; pungent and sickly sour. From her car seat in the back of the sedan, Aurora chats about the dark. Janet has never driven her daughter anywhere at night before. The unmade roads, lined with ditches and eucalyptus trees, are too treacherous. Aurora seems happy. Whatever is happening to her eyes must not hurt. Janet has to keep lifting her foot off the accelerator and reminding herself to breathe. The town hospital feels so far away.

She ignores the parking restrictions and cuts the engine directly out front of the casualty department. Running inside, the walls and floors beaming with harsh fluorescent lights, Aurora joggles against her chest. Janet holds the toddler against her instead of propped, as usual, on one hip. The urge to scream is powerful. Janet gulps it down.

Two nurses rush over. Their urgency spikes Janet's fear. Yet they must be reacting to Janet's demeanour, her body language. She must look pale. All the blood has left her skin and is pulsing red-hot in the core of her body.

"Help us," she says, as one of the nurses takes Aurora. "Her eyes. My daughter's eyes."

Aurora is crying. Howling. Panic is contagious.

*　*　*

They get home sometime after 3 a.m. Both sleep until mid-morning, deaf to the raucous squawks of wattlebirds, the mewling demands of baby magpies trailing after their mothers in the long grass. Aurora, cranky, eats toast while Janet talks on the phone to Megan.

"What's it called again?" Megan says. "Hang on, I'm writing it down."

"Asteroid hyalosis. No one knows why it happens." Janet consults the print-out sheet they gave her at the hospital on discharge. The consultants dragged the town's resident ophthalmologist out of bed to confirm Aurora's diagnosis. "It's caused by globules of calcium and fats in the vitreous humor."

"And what's the vitreous humor again?"

Janet scans the sheet. "The clear liquid that fills the eyeball."

"So, you're sure it's not serious?"

"Asteroid hyalosis doesn't affect eyesight, so they reckon. If it does, they can do an operation called a vitrectomy. They use a needle to drain off the vitreous humor—"

"Jesus, what the hell—?"

"—and replace it with salty water. Over time, the body replaces the water with fresh vitreous humor. Apparently, there's no damage from the condition or the treatment."

Megan remains silent. Janet suspects that she knows what her sister is thinking. Waiting, Janet listens to the line's hum and crackle. Her raw nerves move in concert with the random tide of noise. Through the open doorway, Aurora crumples a piece of toast in her hand and mashes it against her mouth. Aurora seems okay. After the initial fright, she drowsed through most of the examinations at the hospital, through the poking and prodding, the tests.

Asteroid hyalosis afflicts not just humans but dogs, cats, horses and some type of animal called a chinchilla. The condition affects one in 200 people, but Janet finds this hard to believe. She has never seen it before. Except for once. And, with help, she had long convinced herself that she either imagined or dreamed it.

"Are you still there?" Janet says.

"Yeah, I'm still here. I'm . . . oh shit, I dunno, I'm just . . . Do you need me to come over?"

Janet slumps against the kitchen bench. "Thanks, but it's too much money."

"I could borrow some. Pull some extra shifts. I can do it. Be there tomorrow."

Janet's eyes fill with tears. "No. Just having you to talk to is enough."

"Really?"

"Really." Janet bites at a thumbnail. Hesitates. If Megan won't bring it up, then she will. She says, "Look, I asked them if this asteroid hyalosis is hereditary."

She feels rather than hears the frosty silence.

"Oh, come on," Megan says. "Are you kidding me?"

"Please—"

"If you start this again," Megan says emphatically, "I'm hanging up."

Janet hangs up instead. She puts the phone in her pocket, hands shaking.

Later, she takes Aurora into the cottage's back yard. Aurora knows not to venture beyond the patio. Besides, the girl prefers to fossick in the blue-shell sandpit. The day is warm. Janet spreads a towel on the weeds and couch grass and lies down. Crooking an arm beneath her head, she closes her eyes.

When she opens them again, a dog has its muzzle near Aurora's face.

Janet sits up, heart seizing. She imagines toothy jaws clamping around her daughter's plump, perfect cheeks. Fear makes her freeze. The strange dog is sniffing, panting, tongue lolling, tail wagging. The dog is a black Labrador. Full-grown male. No collar. Aurora is smiling and patting the dog, crooning at it. The dog seems to like the attention.

After a few seconds, Janet finds her legs. The dog is a bomb with a mercury switch. Janet's every movement has to be careful, non-threatening, or else the dog is sure to bite. Gently, slowly, she picks up Aurora and takes her inside, sagging with relief when the screen door clicks shut. The dog stays put. Aurora remains by the screen door and babbles. The stray wags its tail, lips arranged as if smiling.

Hours later, at dinnertime, the stray has still not left. Janet considers calling the council, asking them to send a dogcatcher.

Aurora says, "Please feed him, Mummy. He's hungry."

"Good. If he's hungry, he'll go home."

"No! Give him something to eat!" Aurora's crystalline eyes

film with tears. "Feed him, Mummy. Feed him!"

Aurora won't stop crying and begging. Exhausted, Janet defrosts some beef mince and puts it on a plate. She turns on the outside lamp. The patio leaps into brightness and shadows. The dog, grinning, cocks its head. It seems friendly enough, but you can't be too sure.

"Hey there, mate," Janet says, wary of teeth. "You want something to eat? Here you go."

She puts the plate onto the ground.

The dog sits up straight. The illumination from the outdoor lamp catches the gleam in the dog's eyes. Catches the multiple gleams. Janet holds her breath and forgets her fear. She approaches the dog. It watches her. Janet's legs tremble. She squats down. The animal's eyes are filled with glitter. Each pupil brims with a thousand, glittering stars.

Janet falls back, gasping. The dog hurries over to her, licks her face.

"Let's keep him!" Aurora shouts through the screen door. "He's our dog, Mummy. Ours."

The coincidence is too great. Janet realises that Aurora's father has sent this dog.

*   *   *

She calls the dog "Comet". Comet settles into the household routine as if he has always lived there. He is a quiet, placid dog who doesn't bark. Janet likes having a dog. It makes her feel safer at night. Their neighbours are few and distant.

Aurora likes having a dog too. She and Comet are constant companions. Devoted to each other, in fact. Sometimes, Janet feels disquieted by the connection between them. Sometimes, they stare into each other's eyes, solemnly, silently, as if communicating telepathically, and it makes the sweat break out on Janet's palms.

Aurora's father had asteroid hyalosis.

The party was at a townhouse in a grotty inner-city suburb. Someone at work had invited Janet. She was twenty-two, slim and fit, and fresh from a break-up. She had worn a short skirt and thigh-high boots. "On the prowl," as she and her friends at the time had called it.

The townhouse was packed, stuffy with grass and cigarette smoke, the stink of countless perfumes and colognes. The old plaster walls vibrated from the thumping music. All the men were young, brash, cocky, loud, overly familiar with a hand on her shoulder, elbow or hip while they leaned in close and talked bullshit into her ear over the blare of music and the general cacophony of conversation, laughter, whooping. They bored her.

She met him in the laundry. Alone, he was leaning against a cabinet, drinking a beer.

The sight of him hooked her somewhere deep in the solar plexus.

Tall, tanned, lean to the point of skinny but with giant, callused hands that looked used to hard, physical labour. Boots, old denim jeans, faded t-shirt. Collar-length, curly brown hair. Square jaw with a dimple in his chin, three-day growth of beard. And big eyes. Big, sad, soulful eyes with long lashes, the irises a startling and brilliant blue. When he smiled at her, she felt it between her legs.

They talked. What about?

He told her his name. Or did he?

They soon tired of raising their voices over the hubbub and went out the back door. The yard was a scrubby square of grass with a few dead plants and a rusting barbecue. And overhead, through a clear sky, the turning wheel of the Milky Way. They talked some more. She could never recall their conversation. Yet she hadn't been drunk. Only three wines all night. Only three.

He kissed her and she kissed him back. His embrace jolted her nervous system, his fingertips leaving a tingle of electrical traces on her skin. When he pulled up her skirt to peel down her soaked underwear, she was already close to orgasm. He entered her. As she came, she kept her eyes open and they stared into each other. She realised that his pupils held a whirl of galaxies, contained myriad suns and orbiting planets, a slew of asteroids. The earth tipped away. She felt herself travelling through the heavens at the speed of light. And when he gripped her tightly and cried out, she saw the burst of a supernova and understood that her whole life hinged on this moment: forever bisected into *before* and *after*.

She never saw him again.

Didn't know his name. Couldn't recall what happened after their lovemaking.

Megan's take on the experience: The man had roofied Janet, and the drugs in her system had caused hallucinations and amnesia. Megan had urged Janet to have an abortion, but no, no. Janet knew in the deep, superstitious dark of her mind that she carried a star baby. *You're having another breakdown*, Megan had said. But no, no. Janet was clearheaded about the pregnancy. As the stranger's baby grew inside of her, Janet welcomed being part of the Bigger Plan. She only had to wait. Keep faith and wait.

For months after the party, Janet tried to track down the stranger. No one knew him. No one remembered him. It got so that Janet doubted her own memory of the event, but then all she had to do was run her hands over her belly. Privately, she called him Archer, the half-man and half-horse symbol for Sagittarius. One day, she would meet him again. He would return and they would be a family.

Megan grew to hate talking about Archer. *He took advantage of you*, she would say at first, back in the days when she would discuss him. *You were drunk and he took advantage.* Megan will no longer talk about him, even though he is Aurora's father. *Stop this bullshit about having a star baby*, she had said in the lead-up to the birth. *Give your daughter a regular name.* But Janet had known better.

And the arrival of the dog, just a few days ago, proved it. She has not told Megan about Comet. Megan wouldn't understand that Larger Forces are at play.

Janet is working on a series of inter-related book covers when she notices that the house is unusually quiet. On tiptoe, she moves throughout the rooms. She finds them in the lounge. Aurora and Comet are sitting opposite each other, motionless, staring, communing with their galaxy-filled eyes. Janet doesn't know what their behaviour means.

Hopefully, it means Archer is coming back.

* * *

Cognisance strikes Janet in the night, jolting her from sleep, as if the truth came to her in a dream. She lies awake until dawn, watching the clock. When she pads into Aurora's bedroom, the child is already sitting up in bed, smiling. Together, holding hands, they walk to the kitchen. Visible through the glass of the back door, Comet is standing on the patio, ears cocked. So, Aurora and Comet had the same prophetic dream and were waiting for her.

Nothing surprises Janet now.

Everything is in flow.

Aurora and Comet are patient, unblinking, while she photographs their eyes on her phone. Close ups. They follow her to the study. Watch as she switches on the computer. Neither of them fusses or hassles for breakfast. While the hard-drive boots, Janet inspects the photographs. She compares the glittering pattern of Aurora's pupils to Comet's. Their pupils look the same.

Simultaneously, she feels shocked and thrilled. She wonders why she is not hyperventilating, freaking out, as any normal person might. Instead, she taps at the keyboard, clicks the mouse, searching through star maps until she finds proof. And there it is. She sits back in her chair. The confirmation takes her breath. Causes the earth beneath her to stutter momentarily, tilt a little sideways.

Their eyes show the same patch of southern hemisphere sky.

It is unmistakable. Irrefutable. Here is the Southern Cross constellation with the blackest of black nebulae, the Coalsack, dropped within the scrim. There, the galaxies of Small and Large Magellanic Clouds, the globular cluster named 47 Tucanae, the blip of Omega Centauri. The pearly backdrop of opalescent stars. All of these spheres represented, dot for dot in their eyes, a snapshot of the firmament.

Vindication brings tears. *He's given me a star baby*, she had told Megan, yet Megan had scoffed, cajoled, bullied and gaslighted her.

Now, Aurora and Comet watch Janet weep. They say nothing. Janet stops crying, wipes her face, studies further the photographs and map. Wait. Each photograph of the pupils has something extra, something that doesn't feature in the star map. A white streak. Perhaps a shooting star? Piece of space junk? A satellite? Janet searches again.

And finds the answer.

Janet's heart thuds in the back of her throat.

She scans the newspaper article, stops, forces herself to read it again, slower this time. Her blood seems to cool and still. She has found what Archer was trying to tell her years ago at the party. Found his forewarning, his promise.

The headline proclaims: *SPACE ROCK ON COLLISION COURSE WITH EARTH.*

Janet leans closer to the monitor. The fast-moving asteroid called 327369 3117XI2, about the size of a skyscraper, is due to hurtle perilously close to Earth in about nine months. Unlike most asteroids, this one has a tail, probably of dust or gas. The hive-mind of the Internet has already dubbed the rock "Dino Killer". Memes abound. While NASA and most astronomers predict nothing more than an interesting nighttime spectacle as the asteroid passes, flaring its tail across the sky, a few other experts, including mathematicians, claim that the giant rock just . . . might . . . hit.

End of the World cults have jumped on board.

Repent or burn, some say. Or gather for the arrival of space-ships. For the return of Christ. Or let's kill ourselves before Armageddon and reach the afterlife together. Each cult has a different message. It is all nonsense. The blather of ignorant people who can only guess, panic, clutch at each other and pray, gibber. Only Janet knows. The only person in seven billion, which sounds impossible, except that it is the truth.

She dials her sister's mobile to explain, trying her best to sound reasonable.

"This is insane," Megan says.

Janet holds the phone tight and bites her lip. "I can send you the photos of their eyes."

"When was the last time you saw the doctor?"

"A couple of months ago. For my Pap smear."

Megan says, "I mean the psychiatrist."

"Oh, him." Janet sits at the kitchen table while Aurora and Comet watch her, unblinking. They are both unnaturally quiet. "I haven't seen him in a while."

"You ought to call. Today. Now. Make an appointment."

"God, Megan. Really? Look, I'll send you the photos—"

"Can't you see what's going on here? It's happening again. Can't you see the signs?"

"Stop it, Megan—"

"Your Messiah bullshit again? This is crazy—"

"Come on, I want to protect you. Save you. How could you even—?"

"—raped you wasn't a goddamned alien, he was a—"

"—never even tried to believe what I—"

"—for Christ's sake, Janet, listen—"

"—can't you just—"

"No, you *listen to me*!" Megan screams. "You've got a child, and in your state of mind—"

"Oh, fuck off, take my side for—"

"You might hurt her! You might hallucinate some awful, terrible stuff—"

Janet hangs up, breathless, shaking.

*   *   *

Despite its moniker, "Dino Killer" is not big enough to wipe out life on earth. Estimates suggest its impact would be similar to the Tunguska Event, which was when an asteroid hit Siberia in 1908. The Tunguska Event flattened 2000 square kilometres. Registered 5.0 on the Richter magnitude scale. Exploded with the power of 1000 atomic bombs. And killed just three people, since that particular area in Russia was all but uninhabited.

These facts do not comfort Janet because she understands that Dino Killer, or DK for short, will hit the city of Melbourne. She understands this at the subatomic level, within the molecular structure of her bone marrow. She understands it inside her dreams.

She has nine months to build an underground bunker. Plenty of time. And she has plenty of ground too; her cottage sits on half an acre of bushland. However, what she lacks is plenty of money. The cost turns out to be prohibitive, about the same again as her mortgage.

Which is why she is inspecting the cellar.

She has ignored it ever since moving in.

Because it is cold down here. Damp. The scent of earth is strong through the wooden panel walls. It reminds her of a grave. The floor is a poured slab of concrete, the ceiling low. Access is via a ladder through a trap door in the yard. The previous owners had used the cellar as storage space. Janet hasn't used it at all.

She kicks at the cobwebs. Roams her torchlight across the overhead beams. The cellar is small, about the size of the lounge room and kitchen combined, but it will have to do.

Besides, the shock wave from DK won't last long. She only needs to protect her family from the short-lived blast of hurricane winds that will fling uprooted forests, pulverised houses, airborne cars, and everything else in a single, titanic gust. Once the shock wave has passed, they can climb out. Rebuild the cottage. Start over.

And she will have Archer to help her.

He was a carpenter, wasn't he? Yes, she remembers that snippet from their conversation at the party. It explains his callused hands. All tradesmen have callused hands. Archer will construct a new weatherboard home for his woman, child and dog. His message in the townhouse's laundry: *Prepare for disaster and wait for me to come back.* She remembers. The knowledge surges to the surface from where it has lain dormant in her bone marrow.

Now to get ready. For starters, the cottage already has a rainwater tank. Good.

So, Janet's first purchase for her makeshift bunker is a food dehydrator.

The machine looks like a microwave but with six metal racks inside. To prepare food, she needs to slice the items thinly. She starts with fruit. Oranges and apples; Aurora's favourites. Who knows how long it will take Melbourne's food supply chain to resurrect itself? Janet is planning for at least three months.

"I wanna help," Aurora says.

"Not with the knife. Here, put the slices on the rack. Keep them spaced apart."

The machine is simple to operate with two buttons for temperature and time. It works as described. She stores the dehydrated fruit in labelled freezer bags. Next, she works on vegetables. She and Aurora are having fun, enjoying themselves. Janet hasn't told her about the asteroid. Comet lies near their feet, his head on his paws, twitching both eyebrows as he watches them. Periodically, Janet's phone rings but she lets it go to voicemail.

Next, she buys boxes of tinned goods from discount outlets. Packaged foods too. Giant bags of rice and dried pasta. The shelving units in the cellar are filling up with produce. She buys a camp stove and gas bottles. Doesn't bother with a refrigerator since the power stations will be out of commission. She hoards camp lanterns. Candles. Batteries, lots of batteries, and torches. Nightlights.

A compost toilet is the biggest expense, apart from paying a plumber to route a pipe from the water tank into the cellar and put a tap on it. Drainage for a shower is impractical and expensive. They will make do with a basin. Online, she discovers portable hand-cranked washing machines and buys one. Cot beds, board games, books, puzzles. Second-hand sofa and table. Rug.

The months go by. It starts to look like a home down there. A cluttered, crazy home.

One evening, she is bathing Aurora. Time is fleeting. DK is almost upon them. Janet raises both hands, as is their custom. "Ready to sing *Twinkle, Twinkle, Little Star*?"

Aurora shakes her head.

"What's the matter?" Janet says, dropping her hands.

"Are we really gonna live in the cellar?"

Janet hesitates. "Not for a little while yet, honey. And if so, only for a few weeks."

"I don't like it down there."

"Oh, why not? Don't you like cosy places?"

Aurora pouts her lip. The blip of DK, represented in her pupils, is larger. Has been growing steadily larger, in fact, with a longer and brighter tail every day. It is now the biggest object in Aurora's pupillary night sky. Janet is afraid but excited. Melbourne will be flattened, yes, but Archer is coming back. Some days, the tug-of-war of these contrary feelings overwhelms her, stymies her, whispers for the peace and release of sitting back in a warm bath with a sharp blade, the suggestion so intense that she has to shake herself out of its lure. Comet watches her these days. Watches her closely. As if he knows. Can read her mind.

Now, she tries to smile at Aurora, and says, "The cellar is okay. Come on, what's wrong, hon? There'll be lots of fun things to do. We'll spend all our days playing together."

"It's too dark."

That's true. It is autumn. By the time DK strikes, it will be winter. Janet imagines how cold it might be for them, buried under the house, buried deep inside the earth. And what if DK sparks bushfires? What if the cottage burns above them? Kills them with smoke? With falling, fiery debris? Her resolve falters.

But then she remembers Archer. She wishes she could tell Aurora that her father is coming back. They have never discussed him. Not once. Not ever.

"Comet doesn't want to live in the dirt either," Aurora says, pouting.

*   *   *

From dollar stores, Janet buys cutlery, plates, bowls, cups, glasses. Knives and serving spoons. More knives. First aid kits. She wants to buy an indoor gas heater but is scared of carbon monoxide poisoning despite the manufacturer's exhortations of safety stamped on the box. Yet the weather is cooling. The sun is withdrawing, rising later, setting sooner. In the night sky, Janet can see DK. It resembles a lit match-head with its blue halo.

Blankets, blankets, blankets. Janet purchases them by the armload from op shops.

She buys a small generator and stockpiles cans of petrol. She will need, at the very least, to keep her phone charged and there is no other way. Without her phone, she will be cut off.

She receives a text, an ultimatum, from Megan: I'M FLYING TO MELBOURNE.

Janet is compelled to call. It is the first conversation they have had since Megan expressed the fear that Janet might hurt Aurora.

"Are you okay?" Megan says, sounding out of breath. "Is Aurora okay?"

"We're both fine. There's no need for you to visit."

"Listen, have you heard the latest news about the asteroid?"

Janet sucks on her top lip. Finally, she says, "Yeah. I've heard."

"Oh my God. I mean . . . shit. Holy fuck."

Janet doesn't reply. Feels that she doesn't have to say anything. Not anymore. Not now.

"Did you hear?" Megan says. "NASA reckons it might hit after all."

"Uh-huh."

"And you knew," Megan says, her voice reedy. "Jesus, you *knew*. Months ago. Can you send the photos now? Of Aurora's eyes. And the dog's too. Do you still have the dog?"

Comet walks into the kitchen, his claws clicking on the linoleum. He stops. His expression seems to communicate something important. Janet tightens her grip on the mobile. "Don't come here, Megan. There's no room for you. I haven't allowed for an extra person."

"What? What do you mean?"

"If you come here, I won't let you in. That's all."

There is silence on the line. Eyes closed, Janet rides the waves of static and crackle, breathing, aware of the steady beat of her heart, fluxing, strumming, singing her blood.

"We're sisters," Megan says. "Remember?"

"But I'm the crazy one. Remember? Don't come here," Janet says and hangs up, shaking.

The last few days consist of ferrying belongings into the cellar. Aurora helps when she can. She has mastered the ladder; Janet no longer needs to help her. Comet is dexterous, bolting up and down whenever the trap door is open, acting more like a sure-footed cat.

"You see?" Janet says on one of the last days. "Comet likes it in here. You should too."

Aurora says nothing. She often stonewalls instead of talking. Such behaviour makes Janet uncomfortable. But what to do about it? She can't change her daughter's personality. Maybe Aurora gets this quirk from her father. Will Archer notice when he meets Aurora for the first time? Will he love the reflection of himself? Love his mirror image?

Janet keeps a variety of radios in the cellar, including a crystal set. She has thought of everything. They will be safe down here. Safe and sound. She dreams every night of Archer. He is streaking across the Milky Way without a spaceship or suit; a ghost, an alien, perhaps even a god. In a lockbox, she has cash. A few thousand. The DK asteroid will take out not just power stations but the Internet too. Electric cash registers, the tap-and-go facilities.

And she has knives.

In apocalyptic situations, the unprepared—those who assume that governments will take care of them—are caught short and turn on the preppers like Janet, stealing their food, their water. No, no. Janet can't get a gun because of restrictions and licences, but knives are freely available. Cleavers, chef's knives, a range of paring, bread, utility and steak knives. Stashed around the cellar. Taped to the underside of drawers, hidden beneath mattresses. At any point in the cellar, she could put her hand on a hidden knife. Just in case. Because people in crisis, desperate people, can lose their humanity as well as their sanity.

Janet is a good mother. Has made sure that Aurora can't find the knives by accident.

The days count down. The world comes together, apparently, with a plan called "Defending Earth," which is devised by the signatories to something called the *Planetary Defence Conference*. Janet doesn't bother checking the Internet anymore. It doesn't matter to her what the world governments plan to do. DK burns in the night sky. It resembles a spotlight. The brightest object apart from the moon. Soon, the moon will be outshone.

Aurora and Comet are agitated. Janet often sings nursery rhymes to them including *Twinkle, Twinkle Little Star*, but her forced jollity has no effect.

"It's okay, we'll be safe in the cellar," she urges on the Final Day, carrying Aurora against her body instead of propped on her hip. She can't bear to look into her daughter's eyes. She descends the ladder and puts Aurora down. Comet follows, padding around and around the cluttered room, whimpering. The furniture, the bookcases, the shelves. Barely space to move.

"No, I don't like it here," Aurora announces, hands over her eyes.

"It won't be for long," Janet says, as she reaches up, closes and bolts the trap door.

Comet stares at her. His blighted pupils are ablaze with twin flares.

*　*　*

DK bears down. The light show is grand, insistent. Its brightness burns through the chinks in the boards. Curiosity gets the better of her. Janet opens the trap door.

"Stay inside," she cautions.

Meekly, Aurora and Comet cower. Janet emerges.

It is after midnight. Yet the yard is alight. For a moment, Janet wonders if she has lost her mind. She steps out, shades her eyes with her hand. In the sky is a bright burn of fire, shimmering in shades of blue, yellow and orange. Janet blinks away the afterimages.

Melbourne will soon be obliterated. Buildings gone. Greenery erased. Yarra River choked with debris. Janet has never been a fan of the CBD: too noisy and busy, an assault on the senses.

But how many people will die? However, it is only one city after all, and the bulk of the world's population doesn't know, doesn't care, or makes jokes and creates memes.

DK is alluring, mesmeric. Janet smiles, despite herself.

She scans the sky. *Archer, where are you?* The recollection of his scintillating touch provokes tears. Not long now. Her mobile jangles. Baffled, she takes it from her pocket. She remembers how to touch a button, put the device to her ear. She hears the crackle of distance.

"We're safe," says Megan's joyful, trilling voice.

"What?"

"The asteroid. It's going to pass us by. Oh, wow. Oh, God. Can you *believe* it?"

In the glittering firmament, DK glows as red as a hot coal. Janet understands that Megan is scoffing, cajoling, bullying, gaslighting. Megan didn't believe that Archer existed, had wanted her to abort Aurora, has never taken Janet's side against the doctors and psychiatrists. Megan is evil, trying to make Janet expose herself and her daughter to Armageddon.

"You're lying," Janet says.

"I swear, it's passing right on by. Like, missing us by a million miles or something."

"Goodbye, Megan."

"Wait a minute! There's no crisis—"

Janet hangs up.

Comet is alongside. She didn't hear him on the ladder. His eyes are luminous.

There are sudden noises beyond the trees. The breaking of branches. Is that a scuffle of footfalls? *Interloper.* An unprepared neighbour wanting to steal Janet's stash. She realises she has knives on her person already and takes hold of them. The night sky is dazzling. The bushland glows. Where is Archer? Janet scans the heavens, murmuring in prayer to him.

"Mummy?" Aurora says, for she has emerged too.

What a naughty little girl. So wilful. So defiant all the time.

"Go back inside," Janet orders, nudging her towards the ladder. "Do as I tell you."

Aurora pouts her lip, stands her ground.

To pick her up, Janet must drop one of the knives. This is a difficult decision. Child or knife? Leaf litter crunches beneath the shoes of the unseen interloper. Janet must protect her family. On the other hand, it could be Archer out there. The footsteps cease. She waits. Nobody presents themselves. Nobody calls to her.

"Archer?" she cries.

DK has turned blood-red. Janet remembers the warm bath, the sharp blade.

Where is Archer? Is he coming or not? Or must she go to him instead?

Comet's eyes are communicating with her. Helping Janet to make a decision. The answer turns out to be simple once she realises that DK *is* the message from Archer. DK's purpose is to tell her exactly what Archer needs her to do. And Janet obeys, even though it's not what she anticipated. Not what she wanted. But the solution is neat, perfect, precise, and rises up from her molecules and bone marrow, from her dreams. Everything makes sense now.

"Come here, hon," she says. "Let's go and meet Daddy."

AUTHOR'S STORY NOTE

While rambling around the Internet, I discovered 'asteroid hyalosis', and was struck by how much an affected eye resembles the night sky. The title hit me in a flash. But it took some pondering to find the story behind the title; specifically, what this ophthalmological condition would signify to a character like Janet.

THE VILLAGE

MATIAS TRAVIESO-DIAZ

From *The Fantasy Library*
Tell-Tale Publishing

That was the first I ever heard of shadowed Innsmouth. Any reference to a town not shown on common map or listed in recent guidebooks would have interested me, and the agent's odd manner of allusion roused something like real curiosity. A town able to inspire such dislike in its neighbors, I thought, must be at least rather unusual, and worthy of a tourist's attention.
—H. P. Lovecraft, *"The Shadow Over Innsmouth"*

Near the end of 1928 I decided to take a short vacation in a remote island off the coast of Africa. After three days of touring all over the island and seeing every point of interest, I set my aim at a small village I could see atop a tall hill across the bay.

The nasty remarks by the people at the resort in response to my inquiries surprised and egged me on. I was irritated by the way the townsfolk made fun of a tourist for asking about the village. "That pimple on the butt of the world?" "Why are you asking about it?" "It's trash, just a bunch of lowlifes rutting in hovels like swine." "You shouldn't waste your time going to that dump, really."

A shopkeeper took me aside and whispered in my ear: "There are stories of people who went there and haven't been seen again."

Despite the taunting, as I looked from the balcony of my hotel room the village did not seem trashy at all—a cluster of whitewashed cottages with red tile roofs at the foot of a high hill, shimmering in the morning sunshine. The view of the bay from the top of that hill should be nice and would be worth a visit, as I had already taken enough pictures of every other corner of the island and still had two days left of my vacation. So, I decided to ignore the negative comments and go investigate.

Getting to Los Juanes (that was the name of the village) was not easy. There was apparently no bus service, so I decided to make it a day-long excursion and got on my rented bicycle, hoping to burn off some of the extra weight I had put on from too many cocktails. A dirt road spurted from the outskirts of town and seemed to meander aimlessly for miles before turning eastwardly and beginning to climb. After two hours of pedaling, I was exhausted, but I pressed on until I reached the foot of the hill that I had seen from across the bay. The hill was too steep for me to climb on the bicycle, so I leaned it against a centenary oak and proceeded on foot.

I was near the summit when two men emerged from the woods. They were dressed in outdoors clothes and wore plaid caps that covered their ears. Each carried what appeared to be an antique hunting rifle. Next to them circled three menacing-looking hounds.

I was startled by the sudden appearance of the men, but greeted them: "Good morning, gentlemen. Nice day, isn't it?"

"Hello" responded one of the men, curtly. "What brings you to these parts?"

"Oh, nothing much. I came to see the view of the bay from this hill and check out the town."

The man grimaced. "It may not be a good idea for you to go into Los Juanes."

"Why not?"

"We've come from town chasing a fox that was seen acting suspiciously and may be rabid. She's probably somewhere around here but may have doubled back and could be lurking anywhere."

"Will it be safe for me to go to the top of the hill and snap a few pictures?"

The second man replied with the same brusqueness: "You are safe if you stay around only a few minutes, but after that you should leave."

"Alright" I agreed, disappointed. I continued climbing the steep path, and after a few minutes I reached a ledge from which I could see the bay and the town from which I had come.

The view was outstanding. It was the afternoon of a partly

cloudy day, and the cottages and mansions were suffused in a golden light that rendered every feature a bit magical. Even my hotel, a utilitarian box of no architectural interest, resembled a wedding cake festooned with bright rectangles as the light bounced off closed windows. I took several pictures and would have gone for more, but I realized it was getting late and it would not have been wise to linger.

As I turned around to leave, I glanced back and, out of the corner of my eye, caught a glimpse of a figure that was too large to be a fox. It was erect and moved quickly, so I lost sight of it almost at once, but not before I was able to get the distinct impression that it was human, but not quite so. I became somewhat alarmed and accelerated my downhill progress.

I returned to the spot where I had left my bicycle and began making a quick return to town. As daylight faded, I accelerated my downhill pedaling, until suddenly I struck a deep pothole on the road and was thrown over the bicycle, which careened and collided with the trunk of a tree. I got several painful bruises, but the bicycle fared much worse: the front wheel was cracked and had collapsed.

After a bit of cursing, I stopped to consider my situation. Walking back to my hotel would be treacherous since, once it got dark, I would not be able to see the ground ahead of me and could trip on a hole or a stone and take another nasty fall. After pondering options for a while, I decided to brave the fox and give Los Juanes a try. I would look there for an inn or some other place to spend the night.

The village was a disappointment. The town's only street was unpaved; with every step I took, clouds of dust were released into the air. Most houses were one-floor stucco cottages in various stages of disrepair; some were missing roof tiles, others exhibited large wall cracks; the white paint covering the plaster was peeling off of many. I searched in vain for a tavern where I could make inquiries and perhaps grab some food; hotels, inns or other public accommodations were conspicuously absent. This was a town that made no provisions for visitors.

I had made a circuit around Los Juanes and was approaching a road that led away, towards the mountains farther to the east, when I noticed what appeared to be a small church tucked away at the end of an alley, hiding as if ashamed of the poverty of its parishioners. Unlike the rest of the town, the white stucco building was in reasonable shape, all its Spanish clay tiles firmly planted on the roof, no cracks or stains in evidence. There was no cross, but a small tower on top of the structure held an iron bell that presumably would ring to call the faithful to prayer.

I approached the building reluctantly, for I am not a religious person, but this seemed like the only possible way for me to get help. The door, made of dark wood, was covered with carvings whose nature I could not discern. I pressed on the door, and it creaked as it yielded. Without hesitation, I pushed it open all the way and walked in.

It was, and yet was not, a church. There was an empty altar, devoid of decorations, at the end of a long, narrow nave. Stained glass windows on opposite walls let in the failing afternoon light, imprinting it with a multitude of colors; there were no candles or artificial lights adding illumination to the scene. Pews had been removed and replaced by fourteen armchairs set in a circle around a large wooden table. No images of saints, pictures or other decorations were set on the walls or on the tiled floors.

As I was examining the strange arrangement, a side door opened behind the altar and from it emerged a very old man wearing an ankle-length cassock. He advanced haltingly, as if fighting pain; in his right hand he carried a lit taper resting in a bronze holder. The flame from the taper wavered, as the man's grip seemed unsteady.

The man stopped a few steps from me and waved me to

approach the table in the center of the room. He motioned me to sit on one of the armchairs and deposited himself gingerly on another, two seats away. "What can I do for you, son?" He inquired in a grating voice that resembled the rasping of branches in the autumn wind.

"Father, I found myself in this village by accident and need to get a place to spend the night before returning to my hotel across the bay. Can you help me find shelter?"

The old man was silent for a long moment. "That's a problem" he started. "This is a poor village which seldom sees visitors. We have no public accommodations, and the people here do not take well to strangers."

"What can I do, then? Sleep on the ground outdoors?"

The man must have noticed the rising panic on my voice. He replied: "No, that would not be advisable . . ." He then added, with obvious reluctance, "I suppose you could stay here until tomorrow . . . I could set up a cot in the sacristy . . ."

"Oh, thank you, thank you. I promise I'll be gone by dawn."

"You can stay, on one condition."

"Anything."

"You must remain in the sacristy all night and not come to this room, no matter what you hear."

I blanched at the strange request and the stern manner of its delivery but nodded in agreement.

The man rose with an effort from the armchair. "Have you eaten?"

"No. I couldn't find any restaurant or tavern."

"Follow me. I may have some food in the sacristy."

We went through the door behind the altar into a dark room, much of which was occupied by a cabinet with many drawers, presumably containing vestments and other liturgical objects. There were two long tapers lit on a candelabrum on top of the cabinet, casting random shadows on the room as they flickered in a slight breeze coming from somewhere up high. The rest of the room held a lavatory, a table holding a large missal, and a bell over the door that would alert the congregation of the advent of the clergy. A small window near the ceiling let in the light of the early stars.

The man opened a closet and pulled out a folding cot, which after opening occupied almost all the empty space in the room. "Here" he pronounced. "I'll bring you sheets and a blanket in a minute. In the meantime, have this." He opened the top drawer of the cabinet and took out a heel of stale bread, an ancient looking chunk of salami redolent of coriander, and a flask of red wine.

I was reluctant at first to partake of the dubious goods but, all of a sudden, I felt an acute flash of hunger and set aside my qualms. As I began devouring the food, the old man went out by another door and returned after a while with a cushion to serve as a pillow, two sheets, and a blanket. "Help yourself," he instructed. "Good night." Without giving me time to express my thanks for his hospitality, he turned around and left the same way he had come.

The food was barely edible, the wine tasted sour and, as I lay on the cot, its thin mattress provided no support for my aching back. No matter. All of a sudden, I was dead tired and, as night fell, I slipped into a deep slumber.

*   *   *

Much later, I woke up with a start. The tapers in the candelabrum were burning low, and the sacristy seemed much darker than when I fell asleep, but nothing seemed out of the ordinary. Then I heard it: the bell over the door was tinkling loudly, as if an invisible hand was beckoning the faithful to a ceremony.

I approached the rebellious bell with trepidation, my heart drumming a fast tattoo inside my chest. As I reached for it, the sound ceased. Deep silence returned and I took a deep breath, relieved. My pocket watch read three thirty a.m., so I turned back towards the cot to resume my rest.

No sooner had I lay down, indistinct noises began filtering through the closed door, coming from the nave. At first, I heard the shuffling of feet, then the scraping of furniture as it moved over the floor tiles. Finally, a murmur like voices began rising— initially at random, and then in unison as if reciting some prayer. Then there was the sound of the old man, rising sharply above the rest: "Let's come to order! I have grave news to share!" The hubbub ceased at once, and the voice of the old man continued for a bit, now too low to be heard in the sacristy.

Whatever the man said had a deep impact on the audience, for the moment he was finished there was a chorus of shouts, screeches and what sounded like animal wails. "Silence!!" bellowed the old man. "He is asleep next door and may hear us!!"

Instead of quieting down, the nave erupted in a cacophony of angry human and non-human screams. One voice then rose above the rest, in a raw baritone that I recognized as belonging to one of the men I had met on the hill: "We can't let him get out! He has seen a J'ork!"

I had heard enough. I ran to the back door from which the man had come and gone earlier. It was locked. The room's window appeared too narrow and too far up the wall to provide an escape route.

As escape was impossible, I met the danger head on. I grasped the only available weapon, the lit candelabrum, and ran into the nave. I was confronted by a mob scene: a crowd had gathered around the round table, where fourteen figures sat in various states of agitation. Two of them were the hunters I had encountered in the afternoon.

Half of those present seemed more or less human, but the rest were strange creatures, with low skulls and prominent brow ridges above their eyes. They were hairy, stocky, and dressed in rags that barely covered their privates. The central part of their faces protruded forward and were dominated by very big, wide noses. They were as ugly as anything I had seen outside a zoo.

I tried to get past them, moving purposefully towards the front door, but I was seized at once by a couple of the quasi-apes and forced back to the center of the room. I soon realized that any efforts at resistance would be unsuccessful.

I was shoved at the round table. The old man that I had taken for a priest got up, made room for me to be seated, and stood behind me, holding me in position by pressing down on my shoulders. Despite his age and apparent infirmity, his grip was strong.

He addressed me, but his words were meant for the entire congregation. "Your coming to the Los Juanes area has been unfortunate. We keep patrols on the town's perimeter and the first hill to keep strangers out. The business we conduct with the rest of the island takes place during the day, in the center of town, and we try to minimize outside contacts by sending carts to other villages to trade and buy necessities. We do our best to be unwelcoming, and for the most part succeed in keeping visitors away. Somehow you managed to elude our guards and saw one of our friends. I thought that by confining you to the back room we would be able to keep you until it was safe to release you, but it was not to be." He paused, as if reluctant to proceed.

"Now you have met what I would call some unusual members of our community. What you have seen cannot be unseen. The question is what to do with you now to protect their privacy."

At these words, there were shouts of "Kill him," "He has to die," "Like we did to the Italians," and other threats and grunts. The old man pounded on the table and demanded: "Silence! We are not animals. We'll give due consideration to the situation and all the risks involved, and then decide what course of action is the best!"

He turned to me again: "I'm afraid that we will need to put

you under guard for the time being. You will be back in the room where you slept."

*　　*　　*

I lost track of time and could not remember exactly how long I had been confined in the room. In a drawer in the cabinet there was a thin stack of prayer books and I started writing notes in the margins with a stubby pencil I found. Judging by the number of books I filled, at least a couple of weeks went by; my unkempt beard was also an indicator of the duration of my ordeal. If the townspeople in the resort where I stayed could have seen my condition, their smirks would have turned to derisive laughs.

I was visited daily by someone from the village who came to bring me food, clean the bathroom and sweep the floor. They were always dour women who resisted my attempts to draw them into conversation. I had not seen the old man again, nor any of the male inhabitants of Los Juanes. They kept me in complete ignorance of what was going on in this village or what they intended to do with me, but the reference to "the Italians" was unnerving.

A few days after the start of my confinement, a fresh face showed up with my dismal dinner. It was a middle-aged woman that appeared distraught as she paced around the room. "You look sad," I commented, expecting silence in return. "My husband died yesterday." She broke down into tears.

I walked up to her and circled my arm around her shoulders. "I'm sorry to hear that," I instinctively responded. Her body heaved under my touch. Then, unexpectedly, she went on: "Those brutes killed him."

I held my breath. "Which brutes?" I asked, as softly as I could. "The J'ork" she replied. "I hate'em!"

That was the opening I needed. "Who are they?"

Between crying fits, she told an astonishing story.

"The first settlers of the village, over two centuries ago, were a knot of immigrants from the mainland led by two cousins, Juan Francisco Meléndez and Juan José de Armas, who named the settlement 'Los Juanes' after themselves. A few weeks after the initial efforts to establish a town, one of the colonists came upon a young child roaming the hill. It was a creature that looked more like a hairy ape than a human. The captive fought fiercely, but was subdued, brought to the village, and placed in a cage. All efforts to communicate with him were answered with snarls and guttural cries.

"That night, as the colonists sat around the fire near their half-finished huts, four adult creatures appeared from the darkness. They were armed with rudimentary clubs and advanced towards the villagers, making threatening gestures and swinging their weapons. Juan Meléndez got up and calmly approached them, waving his arm in salutation.

"The leader of the creatures raised a club and aimed for his head. Everything seemed lost, but Meléndez started a pantomime in which he imitated a crying child, pointed to the visitors, and inquired, in words and gestures, 'Is he one of yours?'

"The creature lowered his club and nodded. Meléndez asked his cousin in a low voice, 'Fetch the little monster and bring him here.' A few moments later, Juan de Armas returned, holding the child. No sooner had he and the visitors seen each other, they rushed to meet, and one of the creatures seized him and held him closely in its arms.

"Meléndez turned to the group's leader and pointing to the meat roasting on a spit on the fire, made signs of hunger and invited the visitors to join them in supper. All partook of the food, and Meléndez passed around a leather bota bag full of red wine. At first, the visitors looked at the wineskin suspiciously, but their leader put it to his mouth, took a swig, and opened his eyes wide with surprise and pleasure. He immediately handed it to one of his companions.

"The colonists and the strange visitors had a convivial meal together and Meléndez started conducting a sign language conversation with them. An hour later, when the visitors had become tipsy and sated, they returned to the woods. Colonists and creatures motioned goodbye to each other amiably.

"When they were gone, Meléndez turned to his companions. 'I think we have made an amazing discovery. Whatever we do, let's keep the existence of these creatures to ourselves. I'll write to my uncle the priest and see if he knows anything about them and can recommend what we should do. He is a wise and learned man.'

"While letters were exchanged back and forth with the Continent, the colonists got to see the creatures many times. They seemed to understand the rudiments of human language but were unable to speak. They referred to themselves as the J'ork and lived in caves in the hills around Los Juanes. They used wood and made sharpened stone tools, knew fire, and survived by hunting small animals, digging roots and eating berries. Despite their bestial appearance, they appeared somewhat intelligent.

"After a very long wait, Meléndez heard back from his uncle. 'All I have been able to find out is rumor, legend and conjecture. Old wives' tales claim that once men shared the earth with other, more primitive beings that were similar to them but less advanced. Over time, men overcame and extinguished those beings. Their existence is not mentioned in the Holy Books or any of the histories of the various peoples of the earth. So, I must conclude that the tales are just myths. On the other hand, it is possible that the creatures once existed, and a handful have survived in your isolated island. I caution you to keep your finding secret until you are ready to reveal it to the world.'

"Meléndez followed his uncle's admonition. When Los Juanes was finished and everyone moved in, they purposefully isolated themselves from the rest of the island to prevent discovery of their odd neighbors. A few months later, Meléndez died of a fever and de Armas became head of the colony. He retained the veil of secrecy instituted by his cousin, and little by little the two groups became closer to each other. Early the following year, a female J'ork gave birth to a child who partook of the traits of both her parents: she was taller and thinner than her mother and had humanlike features, marred by a pronounced brow and a wide nose. As the two races started interbreeding, thoughts of revealing the existence of the J'ork were abandoned.

"Things stayed peaceful until Father Manich arrived" continued the woman. "He had been sent from the Continent to establish new parishes on the island. But he is a rude and ill-tempered man, and other towns came to reject him and sought his recall. Instead of returning home, however, he came to Los Juanes and convinced the population here that there was a need for a proper religious center. Some wanted to lynch him, but a majority agreed to build him a church instead. When I was born, the church was already up and in use.

"Father Manich learned early of the existence of the J'ork and became convinced that it was his moral duty to evangelize them. His efforts always met indifference or actual resistance. Finally, he gave up trying to convert the savages and turned the church that had been built into a social center where members of both races could gather. That's where we are today."

"Why do you still hide the J'ork from the rest of the world?" I asked, incredulously.

"We are largely related to them by now. Also, the J'ork are at least equal in numbers to us humans and we fear there could be a bloody encounter if the J'ork learned we were going to betray them. The J'ork can be quite violent. Recently, there have been brawls over food between J'ork and humans. My husband was killed in one of those."

I took advantage of my new familiarity with the woman to make a request. "I am very thankful for the long story you have told me. Now, could you do me another big favor?"

Her eyes narrowed. "What?"

"Could you get me a table? I spend all day sitting on that chair but have no place to rest my arms or put a plate of food when it's brought to me."

"I'll see what I can do."

*   *   *

Every night, after the church quieted down, I climbed on the table and set to work on the plaster around the window frame using an iron crucifix whose head I had laboriously sharpened as my tool. I constantly feared that my efforts would be discovered, or that my captors would finally decide to do away with me, or that the enlarged opening of the window would still be too narrow to allow me to get through, or that I would break something when I jumped down to the courtyard, or that I would be captured and put to death. I was besieged by an army of worries.

Yet I was undeterred and continued to work away at the plaster, which was crumbly and broke off easily. And, one night, I finished removing a thumb's width of frame from all around the window. I carefully took the window down, slats and hinges and all, and set it on the table.

I left the prayer books with my story in the cabinet where I found them. If I made it out and was able to escape, I would be able to tell the story on my own and bring justice to this god-forsaken town. If I failed, someone might someday discover the narrative of my confinement and remember me with pity.

*   *   *

I barely squeezed through the window's hole, got lost as I went through Los Juanes in the dark, and stumbled and fell a couple of times as I fled madly away. I almost cleared the village, but as I reached its outskirts I was confronted by a small, non-human figure: a young J'ork, barely in his teens.

I never knew what the youth was doing out in the middle of the night; presumably it was his turn to patrol the village to spot strangers. Whatever his mission, he came at me blandishing a club and screaming in a shrill voice in an attempt to raise the alarm.

I panicked. I jumped at him to throttle his cries and we fought. He was strong for his age, but I was driven by desperation, so I overpowered him and, to my eternal shame, lost my self-control. The fear and resentment that had accumulated during my imprisonment exploded in a whirlwind of rage; I wrestled the club from his hands and started beating him over the head, on his arms and chest, wherever I could land a blow.

It was over in a minute. After the first couple of blows he stopped resisting and lay on the ground, unable to parry my attacks. But I did not let off. I kept beating his body to a bloody pulp, until I stopped, exhausted, and gazed at the immobile figure beneath me. I had killed him.

I then continued to run away until I was overcome by exhaustion. In the early morning, I was picked up not far from the resort by an oxen-driven cart laden with coal. I was barely conscious, battered and bleeding, so the cart driver took me to a dispensary where nuns cared for my wounds and let me rest for a couple of days before allowing the police constable to interrogate me.

As I lay waiting for the officer's visit, I was assaulted by doubt. Should I reveal what I had seen and experienced? Vindication would give me pleasure, but the boy's slaying would probably be revealed, and I would have to face justice for my actions.

When the officer arrived, I said that I had fallen in the hills, injured my head, and had been wandering aimlessly for many days, suffering from amnesia. I could tell he did not believe my story, but no crime had been exposed and I was left alone.

I tried to rationalize my silence on grounds other than trying to hide my culpability. The people of Los Juanes and the J'ork had lived in harmony for over a couple of centuries. Did I have the right to disturb their peace? Who knows what the "civilized" world would do to these lost ancestors of the human race? Put them in cages and display them in zoos? Turn them over to the scientists for their experiments? Men are cruel to anyone who is weaker or different.

I also told myself that I owed no debt of gratitude to the inhabitants of Los Juanes, human or J'ork, and the death of the youth was their own fault. I wanted to leave the island quietly and avoid further entanglements that might land me in prison or hold me there for a long time.

I returned home, but the memory of Los Juanes has travelled back with me. I was bedeviled by daytime fears and assaulted by nightmares. I suffered until, one day, I came to understand that all I felt was fear of retribution, not remorse. The villagers of Los Juanes and the J'ork were miserable creatures that deserved punishment. The slaying of one of their number was only scant retribution for the ills they had visited on me. I relived in my mind the bone-crushing blows I had inflicted on the young savage and the memory brought me only an odd satisfaction.

The discovery of the J'ork has yet to occur. I attribute this to the remoteness of the island, and the enforced isolation of the village on the hill. Yet, their existence coming to light is inevitable, and if civilization finds the J'ork while I am alive my misgivings may come to life. For that reason, it will be fine by me if the secrets of Los Juanes remain shrouded in mystery for a little bit longer.

In the meantime, I will continue to struggle with the pangs of my conscience. I am certainly not a better person than when I went on this fateful vacation; indeed, I am more callous and less respectful of human life than I was then. I made a great discovery but derived no benefit from it and will have to live with its consequences the rest of my days.

AUTHOR'S STORY NOTE

The Village was intended to examine the assumed superiority of modern man over its ancestors, and his ability to coexist with other creatures that inhabit our imperiled world.

THE SMELL OF NIGHT IN THE BASEMENT

WENDY N. WAGNER

From *Pseudopod* 730
Escape Artists Podcasts

looked up when Carlos came in with a girl, two Domino's pizzas, and a bag of marijuana gummies. It was a big basement, finished in places, dirt in others, a kind of half-assed bathroom in the corner with no walls or a door for privacy. You got used to smelling somebody drop a deuce or rinse blood out of their hair in the utility sink.

They said they were vampires. Sometimes I believed them and sometimes I didn't, but I didn't really care. I got enough to eat. There was always plenty of drugs and dancing and people to fuck. The screams bothered me sometimes, but not so much I wanted to leave the basement or Luca. Not that he would have let me leave.

Carlos brought her down the stairs, and she almost tripped on her sparkled flip-flops. Her ankles were all tiny and tendons, like deer ankles. A red patch of bug bites spread up the stick of her left shin. She blinked at me and stood real still when Carlos shoved her into the middle of the room.

"She was sleeping in the back of a car," he said. "Look how little and cute she is."

Alicia poked the side of the girl's neck with one of her long nails. The girl flinched away.

"Awfully skinny."

"And young," Carlos said. "She said she started high school last week."

I picked up my new nail polish, Electric Acid Orange, to show I was more interested in my manicure than a scrawny little mixed girl. "She's been on the streets a long time. She's probably a junkie." I rolled the bottle between my palms to warm the polish. I cut her a side-eye. She was super cute with her long black hair and her button nose. Even Luca would probably think she was cute. "Definitely a junkie."

"Fuck off," Carlos said. "If I want a pet, I can have one."

Gabriel emerged from the tunnel Carlos had started digging

on the other side of the bathroom. "Only if Luca gives you per-mission," they reminded Carlos. Then they shot me a look. They still resented Luca for keeping me around. They gave their spiked collar a twist as they stood there looking at the girl, running their tongue over their teeth.

Alicia opened the pizza box and took out a slice. Pepperoni and pineapple, because Carlos bought it. Alicia looked at the girl. "She right? You been working the streets?"

The girl nodded. She looked a little less scared, too, which I didn't like. You act like you're not scared, they might let you stick around. That's how it had worked for me.

I put down the nail polish and crawled over the stack of mat-tresses so I could see her better. Up close, she looked even younger than Carlos said she was. She'd been wearing pink lipstick earlier, and it had left a stain around her mouth like she'd been eating a Popsicle. My momma used to give me Popsicles after I blew her johns to get the taste out of my throat. No one in the basement eats Popsicles. That's one reason I like it here.

"What's your name?" I asked.

"Kendra." Her eyes went to my nails, still Sugar Poppin Pink because I hadn't had a chance to start my manicure. "I like your nails," she said, barely audibly.

"She's cute." Carlos took a bite of pizza. Grinned. "Like a puppy."

"Don't get too attached," Alicia warned. "You know Luca says we've got enough pets." She glanced at me when she said it.

I tried to look cuter as I reached for a piece of pizza.

"Pets?" Kendra asked. Her eyes looked impossibly big.

Carlos offered her a slice. "You just eat this, baby girl. Luca won't be home for a while yet."

I went back to my spot behind the mattresses and watched them eat. Carlos finished his slice of pizza, patted the girl on the head, and then returned to the tunnel. I could hear his shovel scraping in the darkness. Alicia had picked up last week's *New Yorker* again and was slowly nibbling crust while she turned the pages. Her roots showed brown against the white of her hair, because Luca said we didn't have the money for salon days. He'd still bought me my Electric Orange Acid polish, though. I was his pet, not the rest of them's.

The upstairs floor groaned, so I sat up straight. Marcie and Luca had gone out hunting hours ago. She doesn't usually take long. She's so pretty with her short red hair—men will follow her anyplace, no matter how dark and cold. But it could still be Luca up there. He's choosy, but he's lucky, too.

The door at the top of the stair swung open, and Luca slipped inside, all blond hair and club clothes. A dolled-up granny leaned on one arm. Her smile was so glassy I could see my reflection in it. Luca saw me looking and winked at me. Then he turned back to his cougar, and as she looked up for a kiss and a cuddle, he gave the small of her back a shove. She somersaulted down the stairs with a crunch and a crack and a whimper.

"Soup's on," Luca announced. He threw back his head and laughed.

Gabriel pounced on the woman, their pudgy hands closing around her throat and squeezing hard. Alicia grabbed the woman's feet and wrapped them tight in duct tape. Unconscious was best for storage. Semi-conscious was best for dinner. Awake was for play time.

Gabriel switched their grip to the woman's shoulders. They had some kind of sixth sense about how much life was left in a body. "Muscle up, Alicia."

She grunted as she hoisted the old woman higher. I saw the woman give a twitch and a jerk, but Alicia and Gabriel trucked her into the darkness too quickly to see if she had come awake or not. Carlos's voice carried low and rumbly out of the tunnel, probably making some kind of joke about Luca's catch, and they all laughed. They had a lot of good times in that tunnel. I stayed far, far away from it.

Luca dumped the contents of the woman's purse on the floor. He opened her wallet. "Fifty-five dollars in cash," he complained. "Hardly worth it." He picked a plastic shopping bag out of the mess. "At least she took me to Whole Foods on the way here." He began to spread a buffet of chocolate bars and snacks across the mattress heap.

Chocolate made him happy. Happy people like spending time with their pets.

I crawled across the floor to kneel beside him. "Looks like you landed a rich one."

A bit absently, he stroked my hair. I was glad Alicia had let me wash it this morning. "My favorite prey. Middle-aged women with plenty of money who don't look too closely at what they want to fuck."

I leaned into his hand, pushing his nails into my scalp. "You're so clever, Luca."

I could see Kendra watching me, her eyes unreadable. I hoped she wouldn't learn my tricks too quickly. I shifted so I blocked Luca's view of her stupid cute face and smiled my best smile.

He patted the top of my head. "Are you being sweet just to get a treat?"

I shook my head, wide-eyed. "You know how much I like you."

He put his hand in his pocket and then flipped a dime bag onto the ground. I snatched it up.

He laughed to see me like that. I should have hated him for making me crawl in the dirt, but for the moment, I could pretend he wasn't even there. It was just me and the little bag. White powder, probably Molly. Hopefully Molly. I fucking loved that shit.

I poured some on the back of my hand and took a good lick. It *was* Molly. I took a little sniff, just to get the party started faster.

Luca kicked me in the hip, hard. "What's that?"

I turned to look at him, and he pulled the bag out of my hand. He pointed with the other. "That."

Kendra huddled on the bathroom floor with the empty pizza box, scraping cheese off the lid. She looked smaller and scareder than she had before Luca brought out the drugs.

"Carlos found her."

Carlos appeared as if my voice summoned him, slinking down onto the mattresses and snaking his arms around Luca's waist. He tongued Luca's ear. "I thought she would be a cute little pet for the two of us."

Luca shook him off. "We're not an animal shelter."

Kendra hugged the pizza box closer to her chest. I couldn't help smiling at her. The Molly was already kicking in.

Carlos stroked the back of Luca's neck. "No skin off my nose, baby. I just want to have fun."

Luca turned into Carlos's warmth and nuzzled his neck. They kissed, their tongues long, thrashing lizards. Carlos was the only one Luca would fuck. That's why I made it a point to be his special pet.

The Molly began boiling inside me. I slid off the mattresses, watching Carlos and Luca twisting and moaning. I wished somebody would turn on some music. Now would be a good time to dance. I rolled from side to side, imagining it. The woman in the larder whimpered softly. I covered my ears. If she started screaming, it would really bring me down.

Kendra crept toward me, still holding the pizza box. My hands slid off my ears. My hair felt so soft under my fingers, like silk. Like nice things. I wished I could take Molly every second of every day. I wished life was just Molly, Molly, and sleep. If Luca didn't give me drugs, life wouldn't be worth living.

I smiled up at Kendra. I was crying a little, but it felt kind of good until a tear ran cold into my ear. Kendra looked from the men on the mattresses to me and back again. They had forgotten about us, all of them, Carlos and Luca caught up in the heat of their sex, Alicia and Gabriel in their own work. I heard the ripping of duct tape, and the granny's whimpering stopped. No screams yet.

Kendra patted my arm. "Are you okay?" she whispered. She had a nice voice. It reminded me of a girl I knew back at Rowe Junior High, a girl who had helped me on a math quiz once.

Little sparkles danced around her head. I couldn't help giggling. The basement stank of piss and old meat and no one had ever painted it, and the two lightbulbs set in the ceiling were white-blue fluorescent. There wasn't anything pretty in the whole space, and yet, here was Kendra, sparkling like a star or a field full of fireflies.

I wanted to hug her, but I knew that was just the drugs. "You should leave me alone," I warned her. I didn't want to get too attached, not the way Luca was acting.

The door at the top of the stair burst open, hitting the wall and ricocheting. A man laughed, and another shouted something about beer, and I realized Marcie had come home with a train of frat boys. For a moment the smell of beer was stronger than the other stinks, and my mouth watered. Only good thing Gabriel ever did was teach me to drink beer.

Gabriel went straight for the sixer that the biggest of the boys held. There were some blood sprinkles on the side of their face, but I don't think the frat boy noticed. Gabriel grabbed the boy's crotch and took a bottle of beer. The boy giggled. The sound echoed in my head, light and bubbly, as Gabriel downed the beer in one long, thirsty gulp. I didn't know how he could be so thirsty when they'd just drained an entire fifty-year-old woman, but when I saw them drink like that, I knew shit was about to get real. I reached for Kendra, but the Molly made it too hard to aim or speak or clap my hands over my burning hot ears.

With a gasp for air and a happy burp, Gabriel slammed the

bottle into the metal pipe of the stair rail. Glass crunched so loud I wanted to scream. The bottle slid through the air in a shining brightness that cut off the frat boy's scream in a long arc of blood.

The room went spinny-spin-spinning, and Kendra screamed, and Carlos pulled away from Luca. A frat boy's eyes went big as Carlos drove him into the ground with a laugh. Someone ran past me, and flesh went thud-squelch as the shovel from the larder connected with a boy's head. Alicia reared back and swung again, light and Molly-colors blurring her outline. Sparkles flashed off the shovel. Light traced everything, sparkling, flashing, dancing light, and I crawled away from the blood and the screams, my body going hotter, then colder, and I buried my icy head in a heap of old blankets, and there was silence.

I woke up when Luca ran a razor between my toes and began to lick the blood there. The razor hurt, but his tongue felt nice, slippery and friendly like I imagined the worm from Sesame Street if it passed between your toes on its way to Oscar's trash can. But then, my stomach bounced, queasy and weird, and when he squeezed my foot, his hand was impossibly cold.

"You slept through the fun, silly."

I opened and closed my mouth, but it was too dry to make words.

Off to my left, the sounds of mouths suckling. I cranked my neck so I could see what was happening on the mattress pile. Gabriel and Alicia crouched in the twisted blankets, and I hoped for a second they were leeching one of the college boys, but they were working Kendra's arms, one apiece, razoring little cuts on the softest places and lapping at them like kittens on their mother. Kendra just lay there, blinking once in a while, trying to fix her soul to the ceiling.

I smiled up at Luca. He hadn't picked her. That meant I needed to be extra-good to him.

I looked for words in my dry brain. "Is my blood sweet to-night?"

"Always, pet."

"You know I only take the drugs you give me, right, Luca?" I thought my voice sounded real sweet. "I don't mess with anything that would make me sour for you."

He flicked the tip of my toe. Blood flaked around the lines of his knuckles, crispy and brown. "The fuck you know about blood?"

I sat up real fast, checking his eyes for coldness. No one pissed off Luca. "Nothing, Luca. I just thought—"

"You don't think, pet."

I held my breath. Was this the day he stopped liking me? Was this the day he turned off the drugs or stuffed me in the larder like the others?

His blue eye-slits softened. "Of course, you didn't mean anything by what you said."

I shook my head. In the larder, someone groaned, and the shovel thudded. The groan became a shriek. Marcie and Carlos were juicing their catch.

"I just want to make you happy," I whispered. I trembled all over, and I hoped like hell he thought it was just the Molly coming out of my system.

He stroked my cheek. The powerful stink of sex and meat came off it, the smell of the basement, the smell of my mother's shabby old trailer, the smell of night. "You always do your best to amuse me." His smile reappeared. He was so much handsomer when he smiled. I could almost forget what he was when he looked like that. "In fact, I have a fun idea."

His arm shot out, fast as a pit bull biting a baby, and closed on Gabriel's arm. "Give me the girl."

Gabriel slapped Luca's hand. "You made me cut myself, bitch!"

"Shut up," Luca ordered.

Alicia slid across the mattress, wrapping her arms around Gabriel's middle. She kissed their cheek. "It's all right, sweetie," she crooned. A little of Kendra's blood dripped out the corner of her mouth. "Brother hasn't had a turn with our new little toy."

Luca's hand tangled in Kendra's silky black hair. "Soft." He began to wind it around his fist, pulling her closer to him, inch by inch. Her body slid to the edge of the mattress, her neck stretched awkwardly. I couldn't escape those brown eyes, fixed on my own, the corners filling with brightness.

I sat up so I didn't have to see the tears running into her eyebrows.

Luca loosened his grip on her hair and eased her arm out from under her. He held out his free hand. "Razor."

Alicia dropped a blade into his palm.

He dug the corner of it deep into Kendra's wrist. Blood welled up, thick and dark.

He smiled at me. "Drink up, pet. Be one of us."

I looked at her wrist, at the blood—a lot of it—running down her arm. I had seen so much blood since Gabriel brought to me the basement. The smell bothered me no more than the hot stink of a fast food restaurant. I had seen every last one of the gang lick or suck or smear my own blood out of every limb and orifice I possessed. But this was different, somehow.

She had patted my arm after Luca kicked me. She had used that very hand, I realized. I recognized the stains on her fingers.

"Drink," Luca ordered. There was ice in his voice.

I lowered my head. *It's just pizza sauce*, I told myself. *And if you eat your pizza, then you can stay out of the larder.* I put my lips over the hot mouth he had carved in her wrist, and the blood pressed up against my tongue, thicker than whole milk. I gagged on it, but I knew how to make myself swallow.

I looked up at him, feeling Kendra's blood running out the corners of my smile. "Did I do good?"

And then the blood hit my stomach, cold water on a hot skillet. My stomach bucked and heaved. I twisted sideways and spewed red and pizza.

"Don't you waste that!"

He slapped the back of my head so hard, I fell into the dirt beside my mess. The stink of it made me gag and choke. I pulled my knees up, clutching them over my burning belly. My head hurt, too.

Luca stood up and kicked my ribs. "Clean it up."

I crawled toward the bathroom, not trusting my legs. There was a pile of tee shirts with Greek letters on them, and I scooped up the puke as best I could. The utility sink was filled with clumps and bones, so it wasn't easy. Carlos stepped out of the larder and watched me work, shaking his head.

"I'm sorry," I whispered. I tried to catch Alicia's eye, but she wouldn't look at me. "I'm so sorry."

Luca shoved Kendra's body off the bed. She made a tiny sound when she fell, but she didn't move. Blood still oozed out of the cut on her wrist. "Go ahead and get rid of the trash."

"You mean, like, cut her up? Like the ones in the larder?"

He grunted. "Just take her out to the street. And take your shit, too."

I stared at him. "What?"

He jerked his head toward the stairs. "Go on now. Get."

Gabriel made to grab Luca's arm, but the look in Luca's eyes stopped them. "You're just letting her go? What if she tells someone about us?"

"Who'd listen to her?"

I sank down onto the floor beside Kendra's body. "Don't make me go. Please."

Luca's lip curled. "Get out."

My tears turned his face into crystal, all sparkle and shine, like vampires were supposed to be in those books Alicia had given me when I first woke up in the basement.

"Wasn't I a good girl? Didn't I do everything you asked?" I stretched my hands out to him. Begging, though I knew he hated begging. Weeping, though I knew he hated weeping. "Please, Luca! Who will take care of me out there?"

"Get out!"

The tendons stuck out from his neck, and his face had gone red. My legs shook. He could kill me, I realized. I wasn't his pet any longer, and any second, he could kill me like he'd killed my mama and her pimp.

"I'm going," I said. I took hold of Kendra's ankles. Her tiny little flip-flops had fallen off sometime. Someone would find them, twisted up in the blankets or under a shirt, and they'd throw them away just like us.

I hadn't seen Marcie come out of the larder, but she stood by the stairs, her face splattered and streaked with gore. She folded her bloody arms across her chest and watched me struggle up the stairs.

"Lock up after her," Luca ordered. "I don't want her coming back."

Kendra's head bump-thump-bumped up the stairs, one slow thud after another. I couldn't tell if she was alive or dead, but I hoped she was dead. I stared down at her pointed, freckled face and tried to imagine her soul flying up the stairs and then out the basement door as I opened it.

On the other side of the door, the side I hadn't seen since the day Gabriel carried me into the basement, I stepped on linoleum tile. Normal linoleum like you'd see in any regular house, beige but clean. I couldn't imagine any of them mopping it.

The light over the stove lit up the dark kitchen as I dragged Kendra's body, not so heavy, but getting heavier every step, past the fridge and down the hall, Marcie following slowly behind and sometimes stepping on Kendra's hair. I paused, breathing hard.

I wasn't used to carrying heavy things, and my body felt weird from all the Molly. I took a long breath of air. It was warmer than it was in the basement.

"Keep moving," Marcie said, her voice low and rumbling. "I ain't got all day."

I tried not to groan as I grabbed Kendra's ankles again and started dragging. Her tank top was riding up in the back, exposing her pale brown belly. It matched the carpet in the front room, even down to the gray undertones. I wished I could stop and fix her shirt, but Marcie growled at me when I slowed. She even growled as I fumbled with the deadbolt on the front door. Cheerful lace curtains let in the streetlight, sick yellow all over my tee shirt. I couldn't remember the last time I'd had seen light that wasn't fluorescent blue. A year? Two years?

"Go on," Marcie urged.

I opened the door, and even my fear of Marcie wouldn't let me keep moving. I stood on the porch for a second. Had anyone missed me in the time I'd been gone? Did Mrs. Hargrave, the homeroom teacher, ever wonder had happened to the girl who sat in the back and picked at her nails? Did anyone remember me, anyone at all?

My legs began to shake again. I looked into the darkness of the house, where Marcie's face made a vague pale spot.

"Don't make me go out there, Marcie. Please. I'll do anything."

She shoved Kendra's shoulder with her boot. "Get moving, or I'll bleed the both of you."

"I can't be alone, Marcie! Don't make me go!"

She reached for Kendra's hands and, with a grunt, hoisted up the girl's torso.

"I'll give you anything you want. My blood, my pussy, my nail polish—anything, Marcie." I pawed at her arms. "Please! I'll be good, just don't make me be alone!"

Marcie dropped Kendra onto the front stoop beside me. It

wasn't a big stoop, just a square of concrete and a green welcome mat with the word "HOME" half-covered by Kendra. "Get lost," Marcie hissed, and slammed the door.

I threw myself at the wood, scratching and pounding. "Please! Let me back in! Please!"

The deadbolt gave a final thud.

I crumpled to the ground. The rough fiber of the welcome mat bit into my knees. "Please," I whispered. "Please."

Beside me, Kendra groaned. I whipped around, staring at that stupid little face. She was so cute, so small, so perfect. Even Carlos had thought she'd make a better pet than me.

"Fuck you," I hissed. "I hate you. I hate you! You and your poison blood, you ruined everything. I'm alone out here because of you!"

She groaned again and pulled her knees up to her chest.

I scrubbed tears off my cheeks with my palms. "I hate you," I whispered.

Then I slapped the wood of the door. "I hate you all!" I shrieked.

No one answered. The house sat there, quiet and ordinary, its secrets sealed away from me and the yellow streetlight.

I wrapped my arms around my belly and crumpled forward. I had been a pet. I had been someone. I had had enough to eat and drink and someone to buy or steal me nail polish, and now I was out here. Alone. A-fucking-lone.

The tears came harder. I was alone. So alone. And now I wasn't even in the blue-fluorescent light of the basement, but back in the cold and the dark, and there weren't even any drugs to take me out of the darker cold that was my head.

Kendra gasped. I turned around, not sure if I'd really heard it. Sparkles outlined her head, like the lights I'd seen on Molly, only I was pretty sure I wasn't high.

"It's raining," Kendra whispered. "We're outside and it's

raining!" She pulled herself up using my shirt until she managed to grab onto my shoulders. "You saved me."

I just looked at her. The sparkle on her hair was just rain. The drizzle had turned her bangs to frizz.

She burrowed into my neck, her tears wetter than the rain. "Thank you," she said. "Thank you, thank you."

It took me a second to remember how to hug her back. It felt weird to touch someone so warm and soft.

"Thank you," she repeated, over and over. "Thank you."

My legs wobbled as I got us to our feet. Neither one of us had shoes. My feet were still bleeding from the cuts between my toes. If I had been a vampire, I could have smelled it, but instead I only smelled the faint stink of garbage and car exhaust. I wondered if I would miss the smell of blood, or if, like Popsicles, the memory of it would turn my stomach.

Broken glass winked in the yellow streetlight. I'd forgotten about dangers like glass down in the basement. I wondered what else I'd forgotten down there.

"You're shaking," Kendra said. "Are you all right?"

"Who's going to take care of us," I whispered. "Who's going to make sure we're okay?"

She didn't think for even a second. "You can do it. You *saved* me. You can take care of both of us."

I looked down at her, at her enormous, trusting brown eyes, at her pointed chin. So cute. And I was, too. We were two cute girls who knew how to act cuter.

I reached for her hand. "As long as we stick together, I'm sure we'll find somebody."

AUTHOR'S STORY NOTE

Sometimes a story begins from a single line that somehow just appears, quite inexplicably, floating around in the brain like glitter. This story started with someone saying: "They said they were vampires. Sometimes I believed them and sometimes I didn't, but I didn't really care," and I immediately fell in love with both the line and the speaker. Who doesn't care if somebody's a vampire? And what the hell is wrong with them???

THE SAINT

ALESSANDRO MANZETTI

From *The Radioactive Bride*
Necro Publications

Everybody in South Paris 5 talks about the Saint, the whore dismemberer. It is turning into a real business problem for Big Blue and his organization of jackals.

His stable of sluts and t-girls keeps thinning. Just yesterday, the Saint has torn apart two of his most sought-after whores: Patma—five-star altar of flesh, her third tit turning over as much as a small bone-grinding factory—was found in a flat on Rue Saint Colombe where castrated Catholic priests who survived the final purge panhandle. Her guts dangling from the dilitium chandelier, transformed into soft, dripping meat stalactites; her legs as organic support of a salon table, carefully affixed to the smooth plextek surface with pressure clamps grafted in the flesh; her cut head on the balcony, its skull top precisely carved, rubber geraniums sticking out among her hair. Her blue tongue jutted out of her mouth like a snail—porous as the giant antimony-rich syn-strawberries of the Rambuillet market—looking as though it were miming and nibbling at the words of her last thoughts, those you blow out when you pass on the other side, stuff like *holy shit, Hell smells worse than the sewers of this district*. And finally, the famous third tit: deftly removed, now listlessly lying in a dish, in its silicone-and-blood water. It looked like mozzarella soaked in its stuff. And then the usual ritual of the Saint: the whore's uterus, ripped away and plunged into an aluminum bucket, half full of water and synthetic ice cubes, where the bastard finishes the slaughter by pissing inside of it. On the bucket, as always, the motherfucker had written PARADIS in blue felt-tip.

The other thoroughbred of Big Blue's slut platoon, crippled the same night, was Crazy Clarisse: her specialty, the *Buddha Treatment*, evermore requested by rich fatties—the best customers in the district. Equipped with electronic Belier scalpels and the renowned Metzelder carvers—proudly made in Berlin-Brandenburg—she had gracefully engraved her passionate lovers' paunches for years, turning them into thin strips of fresh meat, like small stingrays garnished with New Scotland eggplants. She offered such delicacies to the donor themselves, as an appetizer to be licked directly between her thighs, as though they were living panties. Before lunging inside Clarisse—everybody knows—you needed to remove that coating and eat it; only then could you to reach her oyster, bordered in latex2 stimulators adjustable in hardness and temperature, looking like sharp transparent corals capable of wrapping and squeezing the customer-of-the-day's sexual organ. Clarisse's fakiric cunt and her living panties had stolen many hearts. They called her crazy because she kept her husband's cut-off head, well-preserved in probax inside a see-through container, a fancy display case over the bathroom fixtures of her brothel room. More than a few, the novice customers who pissed their pants, going to the john and finding that toothless grin staring at their cocks.

The Saint took care of Crazy Clarisse, too, right after working on three-tits Patma. "Tramp" Millander, one of Big Blue's most loyal Dobermans, was called last night by one of the eunuchs serving at the small whorehouse *Le Bouc Ennuyé.*

"She's dead, she's dead!"

The psycho whore was found in Situational Room 12: some-one had used her prized Germanic carvers to thoroughly flay her, removing her skin as only an expert Assyrian motherfucker could ever do. After entering the room with his Glock G2000 leveled, Millander found himself in front of a strange composite fresco. Clarisse's skin nailed to the wall like some fucked-up lion, her guts uncoiled and knotted on the floor to form a sort of square ring, and in its middle the usual bucket with Clarisse's uterus—smaller than Patma's—immersed in ice and piss. And the writing, PARADIS. The sign. The Saint.

After spitting on the ground and groaning something about butchering the eunuchs on shift—but later—Millander moved his crocodile shoes toward the bathroom, to find the mad woman's head inside the display case, together with her husband's. The usual toothless grin, and a new one—hers—choked by a penis. The rest of her body had vanished, as always; like that of the unlucky customer who had found himself in that mess and lost his dick, now rocking in that bath like a drunk eel between Clarisse's teeth. Some bad publicity for the new whorehouse. Customers are walking money.

Who the Saint is, what this is all about, is anyone's guess. What is sure is that the whole thing is pissing off Big Blue's gang for real; the demiurge of South Paris 5, by now, is having a hard time emptying his balls into his biomechanical dolls, all in a row like soldiers with strangled souls. His morning orgasms—when he activates that recreational hall with mouths, cunts and asses set in shells of neprom and flesh of still-thinking women—are thinning out. The abundance of demiurge-sperm flux is directly proportional to daily income, spinning on the room displays and slowing down more and more. "Fuck! *Fuck!*"

That Saint motherfucker is threatening the happiness of the Pope of South Paris 5 as he paces in circles dragging his slippers lined in female buttock-skin, his monogram BB engraved in gold on them; he gnashes his teeth, chews on bitterness and kills some lieutenant for showing up at his villa before 11 a.m. A shot in the forehead after receiving the proceeds of the day.

For the motherfuckers of South Paris 5—where morals are sucked on like mint-flavored candies and spat out when their taste is over—a brutal psycho like the Saint is simply a prick, primarily because he's damaging the goods of a big shot like Big Blue.

For them, the true psychos are those who snuff it slowly, forgoing illegal human meat and contenting themselves with swallowing three daily doses of Symprix, the green shit pouring out like glue from the taps of the Eat Stations, scattered everywhere, connected to underground pipelines parallel to the sewers. Sometimes, when pumps and exchangers tilt as they direct and split traffic of waste water and communal food, you may well happen to eat your neighbors' shit; only the color changes, the taste is almost the same.

Animal proteins are lethal, and crops are daily scourged by the many gifts of Uxor, which can turn harmless peppers into purple grenades and simple tomatoes into big Nazi cyanide pills: these days either you learn to bite into your fellow humans—risking the prion disease, a lottery offering you a generous 50% win-ratio—or you slowly wither, until it only takes a gust of wind stronger than usual, or a nice kick in your ass, to smash your tissue-paper molecules and suck you under the sidewalks by the aspirators, together with the junk of the day. If you snuff it at home, maybe in the comfort of your bed, your substance might even slowly fuse with the mattress, not a bad kind of death in South Paris 5. There are widows, here, the most desperate kind, who keep rubbing themselves against those soul-endowed mattresses, where their husbands and partners melted, to reach an orgasm and end it all like that. Joining them in fluids and humors.

Post-Uxor lovemaking.

*   *   *

The dismemberer has just retired two more of Millander's whores. The bulldogs let loose by the Tramp to go after the monster have missed their target, and they can only count the pieces, roll up meters of guts and report to their boss.

Therese—the slut specialized in dominating clergymen's purpled scrota—finished her career hanged on the steel2 grating of the Brasse convent. Therese's stiff and violated remains dangle and sway on the façade of the religious complex, wolf-lair of the sadistic New Order of the Malemites; she looks like a plaster doll, or a marble bust out of Ancient Greece. Her legs are cut off at knee height, her arms torn off their stringy roots, and her body—entirely shaven, including her long red mane and the rusty tufts between her legs—has been painted in translucent white.

Lifting her, they discover that she suffered a morblix enema: post-Uxor concrete—tough and cheap. The woman's ass, as well as all her *mercenary* ducts, has become an impregnable grave. Stuff for archaeologists aroused by underground crypts to sneak into, reaching out with sterile tweezers over macabre treasures and the insides of time; but it won't be an easy task, liquefying the hardened stuffing of the woman. In Therese's flat, in her baptized alcove, there is of course the bucket with the whore's uterus in ice and urine, and the PARADIS writing.

A Saint hitting in a convent, slaughtering and pissing? And, even more sacrilegious, writing "PARADIS" in that convent? Pure madness. Pure South Paris 5.

* * *

A few hours after the retrieval of Therese's petrified remains, the Tramp receives an anxious and stammering call from Ambroise, the manager of the small but high-class brothel *Le Diable Edentée*. Ambroise is the fattest man in Paris: 450 kilos of sins, forced to move around on a neuro-mechanical structure looking like spider legs grafted around his pelvis, with metal branches coming out from his sides, ass and navel, converging on a magnetic caterpillar platform. A permanent armed escort of seven men follows the Great Babà—so the fatso is called—to protect the whorehouse general against gluttons, connoisseurs, and all kinds of sharks. Despite the prudence, Ambroise sometimes shows bite signs.

Another thoroughbred has been crippled: this is, summing it up, the Great Babà's message to Millander. Isabeau, the favorite of Millander's own harem: a bronze-skinned, powerful t-girl, who would not have cut a poor figure among the first-line phalanxes of Spartan butchers at the Thermopiles bottleneck; she has been disintegrated. Literally. The smoothie of her, bronze-colored as well, but with a touch of green extracted from New Scotland cucumbers, was found in the Room 17 refrigerator, in small transparent plexis containers, piled up beside the bottles of synthetic Montrachet and Champagne, micro-pills of Cloud 5, and tubes of epidermal Hammer.

The usual cold stock of the high-class slut.

On the small table in front of the bed—a bad Boulle imitation looking like a micro-sepulcher with paws—a glass on display, half full with the Isabeau smoothie; apparently the Saint has drunk parts of his victim, maybe while toasting to the apocalypse. Who knows which parts the monster has tasted through the missing hundred milliliters of that centrifuged body, that random jam of lungs, long muscles, tongue, marrow, and all the rest.

Millander breaks into Room 17 more troubled than ever; he has leapt out of bed and, in his hurry, he has worn different shoes: one from his crocodile skin collection, with a kitschy red buckle; the other synthetic, blue with black stripes.

"Jesus goddamn Christ, how the hell did he fuck her up like that?"

The Great Babà reaches him, the deionic engine of his locomotion rig roaring and his seven goons at his tail—plastic faces, perfect idiots all the same.

"The bastard used *that,* but before, he must have hacked up the body . . . maybe with a Metzelder carver. It must have taken a while . . ." the Babà grumbles, pointing at the grinder set beside the fridge—a flexible water tank equipped with rotating blade systems and crumblers. The brothel whores use the machine to offer the customers a goblet of super-drug, *Cloud Gelée,* as a welcome aperitif; or aphrodisiac milkshakes with New Scotland cucumbers and maracuja2 pulp, from the reconstruction hangars of Sierra Vista, Mesoamerican Republic. Among the very few Edens on Earth that survived the whiplashes of Uxor, thanks to the technological support of the prestige-food corporations. At the current price of few kilos of certified environmental-control fruit, you could once buy yourself a Ferrari.

"And what about the cameras? We must have something!" Millander urges the Babà.

"We can't record inside the rooms, you know that, it's a matter of . . . customer privacy. We have the entry hall and all common areas. I've had those checked: nothing. This Saint must be a ghost or some fucking sort of spider crawling up the façade . . ." Ambroise stammers, scratching his head in confusion.

"Holy shit . . . Isabeau . . . *he drank her*," Millander whispers, then moves in front of the window. Late at night; South Paris 5 never sleeps. The blood of the district, made of lights, flows quickly on the streets without ever slowing down, ignoring murdered men and women littering the sidewalks. The mutated rats are already on the prowl; on the right, on the corner of Rue Mascat, they are dragging the corpse of a woman by her legs, toward their lair. They sink their teeth into her shriveled calves, those cold thighs so white that the moon seems to be aiming its spotlight right at them, to make them glow.

The Great Babà balances on his legs the bucket with Isabeau's uterus, floating in ice by now melted, and in the murky assassin's urine. He dips a finger and tastes the whore's broth, avoiding Millander's gaze, by now hypnotized by the night of South Paris 5 dancing inside his eyes and shaking her hips and swollen black breasts dangling on the pregnant belly of yet-to-be-born people.

*   *   *

The Saint's acts of bravado are by now on everyone's lips: some say he is a merciless Archangel, determined to clean up the apocalyptic district from vice, too long handled by that demon Big Blue. They picture him tall, blonde, beautiful, and androgynous, with his Paradise bucket in one hand and an electronic scalpel in the other. Others think he is even a Seraphim, six wings on his back and eyes everywhere, one of those dwelling in the Empyrean heavens, right under Jesus Christ's feet; maybe he is an irregular who wants to fix things his way, a carrier of slaughterhouse charity, a uterus cleaner, in the most literal way. A purifier, certainly not a monster, flaying sin directly from the flesh of Big Blue's army of sex, there where it lives and grows—foolish lust with its rapid-set glue—multiplying like black plague.

HER WOUNDED EYES

ROBERT GUFFEY

From *New Reader Magazine* #10
Editors: Kyla Estoya, Aira Calina, Neil Gabriel Nanta
& Keith Ayuman

"Which one should it be?"

Joel said this as he lined the bullets along the bed frame like the regiment of tiny toy soldiers Gordon's stepson used to play with on Saturday afternoons. Joel knew full well that those Saturday afternoons had always been oh so precious to them both. But that was before . . . before . . .

Joel sat on an end table at the foot of the bed, idly rearranging the half-dozen bullets as if he were about to play the shell game with Gordon. But neither of them was playing a game—at least not a child's game.

Gordon was tied to the bed. His mouth had been stuffed with rags, though Joel had been kind enough to take them out a few minutes before. No one would hear the screams anyway, not even in a sweet little gingerbread home in a quiet suburb of Los Angeles. No one ever heard anything, not in the middle of Los Angeles, not in the suburbs, not anywhere. Not if they could help it.

Joel wasn't worried. He doubted Gordon would scream anyway. It wasn't his style; he was too dignified. He might pray a lot, though. Yeah, he'd pray like a dumb son of a bitch to that nonexistent god of his just before the bullet entered his skull. Then again, perhaps he wouldn't. After all, people did strange things under pressure, didn't they? Joel decided to ask Gordon about this point-blank.

"What difference does it make?" Gordon replied in a dull monotone. "Either way I'll be dead."

"Maybe," Joel said. He could feel the sides of his growing smile twitching spastically. "On the other hand, maybe one of these bullets is an empty shell, and maybe if you pick the right one, I'll let you go free."

Gordon's eyes darted about nervously. "One of them is a blank?" The monotone had changed, replaced with a new sense of . . . hope.

Joel shrugged, teasing him. "It's worth a try, isn't it? What other chance do you have?"

Gordon glanced at the doorway leading into the hall. Scarlet pebbles still clung to the bare white plaster from the recent slaughter. No doubt, Gordon's mind was now filled with memories of Diana, Christopher, Tanya . . .

Joel laughed.

Gordon stared at him with hateful, tear-filled eyes. "Why, god damn it? What'd they ever do to you?"

"Nothing. What did *you* do to *them*, that's the question."

"What're you talking about? I'd never do anything to them. They were my family!"

"No!" Joel slammed the butt of his gun into Gordon's skull. Blood streamed down his forehead. "*Wanda* was your family. But you forgot about her, didn't you? You thought you could divorce her mom and start a whole new family and forget all about what you did to Wanda, as if it never happened. Well, Wanda hasn't forgotten. She knows what you would've done to Tanya if we'd let her stay here with you. Believe me, she's better off where she is, where you can't get your disgusting hands on her."

"What the fuck're you *talking* about?" Gordon said. Blood was now trickling into his eyes. "I never hurt Wanda in my life."

Joel slammed his fist into Gordon's solar plexus. "Liar!"

For the next few minutes Gordon could only gasp in pain. Despite his wheezing, he at last managed to whisper, "Wanda's the liar. That's why I disowned her. She burned her brains out on drugs a long time ago. She's totally unreliable, she makes up stories."

Joel laughed as he whipped out his penis and pissed in Gordon's face. "Fuck you, family man. I'm on drugs. Does it look like *I* burned my brains out? No, I didn't think so."

Gordon closed his mouth, winced in disgust. The urine intermingled with the blood on his forehead. Joel was able to piss for a long time. He'd consumed an entire 40-ouncer before working up the courage to come over here.

"You don't know how long I've waited to do this," Joel said. "Ever since that first night back in high school when I picked up Wanda to go to the movies. You looked at me in my ripped clothes and dirty jacket and actually *cringed*. You thought I was some kind of ignorant piece of white trash, I could see it all over your face. You made me feel like shit whenever I called to talk to Wanda. Remember when you got in my face that one time and accused me of giving Wanda drugs? What a laugh. She gave *me* drugs. Without her I never would've shot up for the first time. Not that I'm complaining. Wanda's the best thing that ever happened to me. She set my head straight, gave me direction. There's nothing I wouldn't do for her." He stuffed his penis back into his pants, zipped up. "How's it feel, huh? How's it feel to be treated like a piece of shit?" Joel slammed his boot into Gordon's left rib. Something cracked.

"You don't know what you're doing," Gordon gasped. "She's playing with your head."

Joel snorted. "Wanda couldn't play with anybody's head. She's too fragile, too eaten away with self-doubt. It's no surprise. Not after how you treated her." Before Gordon could respond Joel kicked him in the ribs once again. Jesus, he was getting such a rush off this. This combined with the speed Wanda had scored for him . . .

Joel was in Heaven.

Which was more than anyone would be able to say for Mr. Gordon Sovitch, church man, businessman, family man. So many "respectable" titles, so many masks, so many lies. Joel intended to destroy every single one of them within the next few seconds.

Unless Gordon agreed to play the game.

* * *

It happened to everybody once in a while: complete

disorientation. She wasn't sure how it happened, but sooner or later it always did.

Wanda had been hitchhiking down a darkened road in her old neighborhood at two in the morning, having just been kicked out of a truck by a fat man who didn't like girls who were tight with their favors. "Fucking whore!" he'd yelled (in truth meaning the exact opposite), screeching to an abrupt halt, propelling her out the door with a single shove. She'd flipped him off and called him a fag (in truth meaning the exact opposite) as he'd sped away into the midnight darkness. This incident hadn't surprised her. If she'd learned anything at all during her brief eighteen years, it was this: All men were insane.

What seemed like two hours later, tired, unaware of her surroundings—disorientated—she'd wandered from the main road and had found herself in a wooded area she'd seen many times before in her dreams. A forest.

A forest filled with impossible things: shadowy birds with glowing red eyes and transparent, black, X-ray bodies; men growing out of the ground like plants, reaching out for her ankles with long pale arms covered in mossy white fur; disembodied, bat-winged mouths with razor-sharp teeth soaring from tree to tree; things from a twisted storybook her mother had read to her once. (Only once. Her father had taken the book away, said it was a thing of hellfire, of the devilandtheimagination!)

But this scene, this forest, was not a phantasm plucked from her imagination, for she knew she didn't have any; it had been bled out of her by incessant threats of eternal damnation. Wicked strangeness like this could only happen to *her*. To delinquent Wanda. Whorewanda. Devilspawn wanda. Wanda with the wounded eyes.

Things crawled behind these eyes: shadows. Crippled shadows. Pinned to the inside of her skull. Writhing there. Wriggling to get free.

Her father had seen them on the day she was born. Ever since then he'd done his best to remind her of her "inherent evilness." For so long she'd tried to prevent his words from becoming a self-fulfilling prophecy. It had been no use. The seven deadly sins were ingrained in her very DNA. Other than undergoing a complete cellular and metaphysical make-over, there was little she could do to stave off destiny. It was as inevitable as death . . . something Wanda knew a great deal about.

Earlier that evening, Joel, the boyfriend she'd run away with, had tried to beat her in the park bathroom in which they'd taken refuge for the night. Life on the road had not measured up to his fanciful dreams. He'd begun to blame her, claimed *she'd* talked him into all of this. She'd tried to calm him down by the only means she knew well. She'd kissed him, whispering into his ear, tried to distract him with her body . . .

He'd socked her in the jaw. Called her a slut.

The pain of that word had branded itself in her brain, affecting her much more than the lingering traces of his fist. It was a familiar word to her. Her father had used it often. It was what she'd been running away from.

His assault had not ended with a single blow or a single word. The insults had come as fast as his fists. She'd been forced to protect herself. What else could she have done? Lie there and accept it? Wait for something magical to save her?

Like she'd done with her father.

No.

She'd lashed out. The broken pipe had been sitting in the corner of the bathroom for who knows how many years. Sitting there, waiting for a purpose. Waiting to be brought down on the skull of a raving maniac of a boyfriend. The resultant *crack* had been a sickening sound. He'd died instantly. She'd taken the bloody pipe with her, wiped her fingerprints off it, then stuck it in her backpack. She'd hidden it beneath the passenger seat in the fat man's truck while he'd been taking a piss on the side of the road. She'd hoped her present would be appreciated by Mr. Fat Man—maybe even by the cops when they found it, identified the blood, and dragged *him* in on the murder charge.

Standing in the weird forest, she recalled Joel's lifeless, glassy eyes: dull black tunnels leading down into nothingness. Her memory of them bore no resemblance to the brightness sparkling in the multiple, hazel pupils of the formless creatures who suddenly dropped from the overhead branches, ropy tentacles lashing out from their transparent, amorphous bodies. They were men: men reduced to their essential selves, dozens of stiff phalli erupting out of vaginal pockets in their protoplasmic bodies, phalli that were so long they tripped the creatures as they lumbered toward Wanda through the ankle-high grass. Their bodies blended in with the trees, rendering them almost invisible. She could only see them at certain angles, and then only as flat, two-dimensional beings. With scintillating, hypnotic eyes.

Eyes that prevented her from fleeing.

Eyes that abruptly lulled her into the deepest of sleeps . . .

First there were the vivid, vivid memories: memories of the bloody sac of flesh the doctors had sucked out of her womb, that formless blob she'd caught only a brief glimpse of during the operation. The nurse, after seeing Wanda's father in the lobby, had told her she should consider herself fortunate having such an "understanding father," one who would see past her mistake and make certain she received proper, professional care. Apparently to take her mind off the imminent operation, she'd asked Wanda if her boyfriend—by which she'd meant the "mistake's" father—had accompanied her to the clinic.

Wanda had almost laughed.

She'd almost laughed and said, "He's in the lobby. Awfully 'understanding' of him, isn't it?"

But no. Instead she'd shaken her head. *No.*

Her mother had never found out. It'd been a secret. Father had threatened her with Hell if she uttered a word about it. Which had seemed rather funny to her. After all, she'd been living there for fourteen years already, hadn't she?

Not long after the operation, she'd met Joel. Eventually they decided to flee. She from Hell, he from boredom. Joel had certainly completed his goal. After Wanda had gotten through with him there'd been no hint of tedium left in those empty, fetus-like eyes. Those dead joeleyes. Those wounded eyes . . . eyes like her father's . . . dull black tunnels leading down into nothingness . . . down into old, old memories better left forgotten . . .

Yes, first there were the memories followed by a painful haze, the gradual awakening. She lifted her face from the dirt and found herself lying on the side of a deserted road. No forest, no creatures, the visions gone like shadows in night. As always. Twenty yards away she could see the taillights of Mr. Fat Guy's truck as it receded into the darkness. Had no time passed? Behind her, far down the road, she could just barely see the dull white light glowing above a pay phone at a roadside rest. She knew she wanted to use the phone but didn't quite know why. Something about the police . . .?

She pulled herself up from the dirt and staggered toward the phone. She pressed 911. A woman with a gentle voice answered. She sounded like her mother. Wanda told her her name, then whispered through her tears, "I—I'd like to report a murder." The woman asked her where she was. "It doesn't matter," Wanda said. She gave the operator the address of her old house, the house where her father and that strange woman now lived. That strange woman and her awful children.

"Please tell me who's been murdered," the woman said.

Wanda thought about Joel. Joel was dead, wasn't he? Wasn't he?

"My . . . my baby," Wanda said at last. "My daughter."

"Please, Wanda, calm down. Tell me who killed her."

Father had threatened her with Hell if she uttered a word about it.

"Father," she said quietly, so quietly that even she couldn't hear it.

*   *   *

Gordon's eyelids fluttered open. Joel smiled. Though he hadn't passed out from the pain, he probably wished he had.

"Well?" Joel said, stroking Gordon's cheeks with his fingertips. Gordon winced at the touch. "Have you decided to play the game?"

Gordon's gaze alighted upon the bullets lined up on the bed-frame. He nodded slowly.

"Good thinking," Joel said. "It's really your only way out, isn't it?" He stood at the foot of the bed, waving his arms in the air like a sideshow barker. "I promise, old man, I'm good to my word. You've got a one in six chance. That's better than you gave Wanda. If you pick the right bullet, I'll leave. You'll have some explaining to do about the wife and kiddies." He jerked his thumb toward the blood-streaked hallway. "But that ain't nothin' to worry about. I'm sure they'll buy your story, particularly since it's coming from such a fine upstanding gentleman like yourself." These last five words dripped with sarcasm. "But by that time, me and Wanda will be long gone."

Gordon coughed, blood and phlegm rattling in his lungs. "Where is Wanda?"

"She's in a safe place. I left her back at the park, the same park you used to take her to when she was a little girl, before she was old enough to turn your head, eh? How old do they have to be? Twelve, thirteen? I hear Tanya would've been fourteen next month. Looks like I got to her just in the nick of time."

"Why didn't Wanda come with you?"

"Because she's too scared to see you again, she can't stand to look at your disgusting face."

"Or maybe she's playing you for a fool, just like she's done to everyone else, just like she did to me. She's crazy—"

"Shut up!" Joel was about to slap Gordon in the face once again, then pulled back. No need to go through that again. They had a game to play. He pointed at the bullets with the barrel of his empty gun. "Go ahead. Make your choice. You don't have all day. Neither do I."

"Wanda told these same lies to her mother, you know. That's why she divorced me. Even though there was no proof, she divorced me. All because she couldn't come to grips with the fact that her daughter is a habitual liar."

"Shut up," Joel whispered.

"She's insane. I saw it in her eyes the day she was born. She needs to be locked up. You're just reinforcing her delusions."

"Shut up!"

"Didn't you ever stop to think that *she* tried to seduce *me*, and not the other way around? I rejected her and she hated me for it. I tried to get help for her, but she refused. Instead, she ran away with you."

"God damn, you're one sick son of a bitch," Joel said. "Make the choice and let's get this over with."

Gordon sighed and closed his eyes. "The one on the far right."

Joel snatched the bullet up from the bedframe, tossed it into the air once as if it were a lucky penny, then jammed it into the chamber of the gun. He moved away from the double bed until his back was pressed up against the window. The window was half-open. A nice cool breeze blew into the room. He could feel it against the back of his neck. He aimed the gun at Gordon's head and fired.

Gordon's skull erupted, decorating the wall behind him with an abstract painting of white bone-shards and formless pieces of brain. It was pretty in a way, the final product of four years of utter frustration. Wanda's father wouldn't laugh or sneer at him anymore.

Joel swept the remaining bullets off the headboard and poured them into his palm like grains of sand. Each one was as heavy as the last.

"Oops," he said to the corpse, "I guess I forgot to empty one of them. Bummer deal."

It was at this point that he heard the sirens. At first, he ignored them, assuming they were headed somewhere else. Joel prided himself on his pessimism and would've bet his life on the complacency of the surrounding suburbanites. He knew deep down that none of them would ever lift a finger to help a neighbor in trouble, not even if it meant dialing 911. Clearly, then, the sirens were headed somewhere else.

But they weren't. The cars skidded to a halt in the driveway of Gordon Sovitch's two-story home. From the upstairs bedroom Joel peeked through the soft white curtains and saw four squad cars parked outside, their red and blue lights casting a hellish glow against the side of the house.

He could hear more sirens in the distance.

Everything's going to be okay, he told himself twelve times in a row as he slipped the five bullets into their chambers. More bullets lay in his pocket. Enough for a real party.

At least Wanda's safe, he said silently as he thrust the gun out the window and fired.

*   *   *

As the police converged on Joel's bullet-ridden corpse, Wanda stood on the side of a desolate road twenty miles outside the city. She stuck her thumb into the cool night air, hoping a nice gentleman in a truck would stop and agree to take her somewhere far away. She tried to ignore the forest and its strange inhabitants that were always there on either side of her, closing in.

Forever closing in.

AUTHOR BIOS

MATTHEW BROCKMEYER lives deep in the forest in Northern California. He is the author of the novel *Kind Nepenthe*. His short stories have been published worldwide in numerous anthologies, journals and magazines. When not writing, Matthew enjoys homesteading, reading, and bathing his fangs in human blood.

OCTAVIA CADE is a New Zealand writer with a PhD in science communication. She's sold close to 50 stories to markets like *Clarkesworld*, *Asimov's*, and *Shimmer*, and her work has appeared in *The Year's Best Science Fiction & Fantasy* as well as a previous volume of *The Year's Best Hardcore Horror*. She is the 2020 writer-in-residence at Massey University, and is an HWA member and Bram Stoker nominee.

ROBERT GUFFEY is a lecturer in the Department of English at California State University – Long Beach. His most recent book is *Bela Lugosi and the Monogram Nine*, coauthored with Gary D. Rhodes (BearManor Media, 2019). Forthcoming is a collection of four novellas entitled *Widow of the Amputation and Other Weird Crimes* (Eraserhead Press, 2021). 2017 marked the publication of *Until the Last Dog Dies* (Night Shade/Skyhorse), a darkly satirical novel about a young stand-up comedian who must adapt as best he can to an apocalyptic virus that destroys only the humor centers of the brain. Guffey's previous books include the journalistic memoir *Chameleo: A Strange but True Story of Invisible Spies, Heroin Addiction, and Homeland Security* (OR Books, 2015), which *Flavorwire* called, "By many miles, the weirdest and funniest book of 2015." A graduate of the famed Clarion Writers

Workshop in Seattle, he has also written a collection of novellas entitled *Spies & Saucers* (PS Publishing, 2014). His first book of nonfiction, *Cryptoscatology: Conspiracy Theory as Art Form*, was published in 2012. He's written stories and articles for numerous magazines and anthologies, among them *The Believer, Black Cat Mystery Magazine, Black Dandy, Catastrophia, The Chiron Review, Hypnos, The Los Angeles Review of Books, The Mailer Review, New Reader Magazine, Pearl, The Pedestal, Phantom Drift, Postscripts, Rosebud, Selene Quarterly Magazine, The Temz Review, The Third Alternative*, and *TOR.com*.

MELANIE HARDING-SHAW is a speculative fiction writer, policy geek, and mother-of-three from Wellington, New Zealand. Her stories have appeared in publications such as *Daily Science Fiction* and *The Best of British Fantasy 2019*. Her *Censored City* trilogy of novelettes is available on Amazon. She was awarded New Zealand's Sir Julius Vogel Award for Services to Science Fiction, Fantasy and Horror in 2020. You can find her on Twitter @melhardingshaw and at https://www.melaniehardingshaw.com/

PATRICK C. HARRISON III (PC3, if you prefer) is an author of horror, bizarro, and erotica. His current publications include *A Savage Breed, Inferno Bound and the Hell Hounds, 5 Tales That Will Land You In Hell, Visceral: Collected Flesh* with Christine Morgan, and *Cerberus Rising* with Chris Miller and M. Ennenbach, and his works can be found in numerous anthologies, including *And Hell Followed* and *Road Kill: Texas Horror by Texas Authors Vol. 4.*

PC3 is also the co-owner (with Jarod Barbee) and editor-in-chief of Death's Head Press, a Texas-based publisher of dark fiction. He and Mr. Barbee are the Splatterpunk Award-winning editors of *And Hell Followed*. Other books DHP has edited and published include *Breaking Bizarro, Dig Two Graves Vol. 1 & 2,* and *Obliquatur Voluptas: Deviant Stories for the Deviant Mind.* In 2020, Death's Head Press began publishing the Splatter Western series, which is taking the indie horror community by storm. The Splatter Western combines old west pulpiness with violent, bloody horror.

SEAN PATRICK HAZLETT is an Army veteran, speculative fiction writer and editor, and finance executive living in the San Francisco Bay area, where he considers writing fiction as therapy that pays for itself. Over forty of his short stories have appeared in publications such as *The Year's Best Military and Adventure SF*, *Year's Best Hardcore Horror*, *Terraform*, *Galaxy's Edge*, *Writers of the Future*, *Grimdark Magazine*, *Vastarien*, and *Abyss & Apex*, among others. He is an active member of the Horror Writers Association and Codex Writers' Group. His first anthology as an editor, *Weird World War III*, was published by Baen in October 2020.

ALICIA HILTON is an author, arbitrator, law professor, actor, and former FBI Special Agent. She believes in angels and demons, magic and monsters. Ever since she was a little girl and saw a ghost, she's been fascinated by the supernatural. Alicia's recent work has appeared or is forthcoming in *Akashic Books*, *Best Indie Speculative Fiction Volume 3*, *Daily Science Fiction*, *Demain Publishing UK*, *Departure Mirror*, *DreamForge*, *Litro*, *Vastarien*, *Year's Best Hardcore Horror Volumes 4 & 5*, and elsewhere.

Alicia has taught writing workshops through MWA and RWA, and has been a guest speaker at more than sixty law schools, including Harvard, the University of Chicago, the University of Pennsylvania, Northwestern University, and the University of Southern California. She received her BA in Sociology from the University of California, Berkeley, and her JD and MA from the University of Chicago.

As an FBI Special Agent, Alicia was a member of a foreign counterintelligence squad, and also worked undercover in two long-term criminal cases, posing as a drug dealer with ties to organized crime. Now, Alicia enjoys playing different personalities on the stage and screen. She's had acting roles with NBC's Chicago PD, Fox's Empire & Proven Innocent, Showtime's The Chi, Lyric Opera of Chicago, and the Joffrey Ballet.

RONALD KELLY has been writing horror tales set in the American South since the small-press days of the 1980s. A former Zebra Book author, his published works include *Fear, Undertaker's Moon, Blood Kin,*

Hell Hollow, The Dark'Un, Midnight Grinding & Other Twilight Terrors, After the Burn, Hindsight, The Buzzard Zone, The Essential Sick Stuff, The Halloween Store, Season's Creepings, and *Irish Gothic*. His audio collection of Southern-fried short stories, *Dark Dixie: Tales of Southern Horror*, was included on the nominating ballot of the 1992 Grammy Awards for Best Non-Musical or Spoken Album. He lives in a backwoods hollow in Brush Creek, Tennessee with his wife and young'uns.

AMANDA CECELIA LANG is a daydreamer from Denver, Colorado. She lives with her life partner, two cats, two birds, and an ongoing existential crisis. She writes weird novels and short fiction, tales of horror and sci-fi laced with whimsy and mayhem. Her short fiction has appeared on *The Other Stories*, *Dime Show Review*, and in the (upcoming) horror anthology *When the Sirens Have Faded*. You can stalk her at amandacecelialang.com, just don't be surprised if she leaps out at you from the shadows.

ERIC LAROCCA's fiction has appeared in various literary journals and anthologies published in the US and abroad such as, *Stiff Things* and *Year's Best Hardcore Horror, Volume 2*. He is also the author of several plays which have been developed and produced at theaters across the country including, Gadfly Theater Productions, Hartford Stage, La Petite Morgue, and Love Creek Productions. He currently resides in Cambridge, MA. Follow him on Twitter @ejlarocca.

ALESSANDRO MANZETTI (Rome, Italy) is a Two-time Bram Stoker Award-winning author (and 12 time nominated), editor, scriptwriter and essayst of horror fiction and dark poetry whose work has been published extensively (more than 40 books) in Italian and English, including novels, short and long fiction, poetry, essays, graphic novels and collections.

English publications include his novels *Shanti - The Sadist Heaven* (2019) and *Naraka - The Ultimate Human Breeding* (2018), the novella *The Keeper of Chernobyl* (2019), the collections *The Radioactive Bride* (2020), *The Garden of Delight* (2017), *The Monster, the Bad and the Ugly* (2016, with Paolo Di Orazio), and *The Massacre of the Mermaids* (2015), the poetry collections *Whitechapel Rhapsody* (2020), *The Place of Broken Things* (2019, with Linda D. Addison), *War* (2018, with Marge Simon), *No Mercy* (2017), *Sacrificial Nights* (2016, with Bruce Boston) *Eden Underground* (2015), *Venus Intervention* (2014, with Corrine de Winter), and the graphic novels *Calcutta Horror* (2019) and *Her Life Matters* (2020) He edited the anthologies *The Beauty of Death* (2016), *The Beauty of Death Vol. 2 - Death by Water* (2017, with Jodi Renee Lester) and *Monsters of Any Kind* (2018, with Daniele Bonfanti).

His stories and poems have appeared in Italian, USA, UK, Australian, Canadian and Polish magazines, such as *Dark Moon Digest, Splatterpunk Zine, The Best Horror of the Year Vol. 13, Disturbed Digest, Space and Time, Weird Tales Magazine, The Horror Zine, Illumen, Devolution Z, Hinnom, Recompose, Polu Texni, Nothing's Sacred, Okolica Strachu,* and anthologies such as *Splatterpunk Forever, Best Hardcore Horror of the Year Vol. 2, 4, 5, 6, The Big Book of Blasphemy, Midnight Under the Big Top, Bones III, Rhysling Anthology* (2015, 2016, 2017, 2018, 2019, 2020, 2021), *HWA Poetry Showcase Vol. 3 and 4, The Beauty of Death Vol. 1 and Vol. 2, Mar Dulce, I Sogni del Diavolo, Danze Eretiche Vol. 2, Il Buio Dentro, Sorrow, Pandemonium.*

He is the CEO & Founder of Independent Legions Publishing, editor of Molotov Magazine and Illégale Magazine (in Italian), HWA Active member and a former HWA Board of Trustees member. In 2021 he served the Science Fiction Poetry Association as the Rhysling Award Chair.

CHRISTINE MORGAN divides her writing time among many genres, from horror to historical, from superheroes to smut, anything in between and combinations thereof. She's a future crazy-cat-lady and a longtime gamer, who enjoys British television, cheesy action/disaster movies, cooking and crafts. Which latter two led a recent podcast to refer to her as "The Martha Stewart of extreme horror," so, make of that what you will!

Her short stories have appeared in dozens of anthologies, as well as the collections *The Raven's Table* (Viking-themed horror, with a companion volume due out in late 2020 or early 2021) and *Dawn of the Living-Impaired And Other Messed Up Zombie Stories* (zombies, obviously).

Her novels include the historical pioneer blizzard snow monstery *White Death*, the Edward Lee sequel *Lakehouse Infernal*, the totally trashy *Spermjackers From Hell*, the soon-to-be-rereleased *Murder Girls*, and others.

She also takes on editing and proofreading gigs, is a regular contributor to The Horror Fiction Review, has twice earned an Honorable Mention from Ellen Datlow in the Year's Best series, and been nominated in various categories of the Splatterpunk Awards. Christine currently lives in Portland, Oregon, where she works the overnight shift in a residential psychiatric facility. She is always glad to hear from readers, as well as other authors (and hey, agents, publishers, movie people, it's all good!)

RACHEL NUSSBAUM is a fiction writer and poet from the Big Island of Hawaii. Her short stories and poems have been featured in multiple horror and science fiction anthologies, including Blood Bound Books' *Night Terrors III* and *Crash Code*. Rachel recently graduated college and moved to California where she hopes to grow her creative career and one day to write and illustrate her own novels and comic books.

HAILEY PIPER is the author of *Unfortunate Elements of My Anatomy*, *The Worm and His Kings*, *Benny Rose, the Cannibal King*, and more. She is a member of the HWA, and her short fiction appears in Daily Science Fiction, Flash Fiction Online, *Dark Matter Magazine*, *Year's Best Hardcore Horror, Volume 5*, and elsewhere. A trans woman from New York, she now lives with her wife in Maryland. Find her at www.haileypiper. com or on Twitter via @HaileyPiperSays.

DEBORAH SHELDON is an award-winning author from Melbourne, Australia. She writes short stories, novellas and novels across the darker spectrum of horror, crime and noir. Her award-nominated titles include the novels *Body Farm Z*, *Contrition* and *Devil Dragon*; the novella *Thylacines*; and collection *Figments and Fragments: Dark Stories*. She won the Australian Shadows 'Best Collected Work' Award for *Perfect Little Stitches and Other Stories*, which was also long-listed for a Bram Stoker. As editor of *Midnight Echo 14*, she won the Austra-lian Shadows 'Best Edited Work' Award. Her short fiction has been nominated for various Australian Shadows and Aurealis Awards, and included in 'best of' anthologies including *Year's Best Hardcore Horror*. Other credits include feature articles, non-fiction books, TV scripts and award-winning medical writing.

MATIAS TRAVIESO-DIAZ Matias Travieso-Diaz was born in Cuba and migrated to the United States as a young man, escaping political persecution by the Castro regime. He became an engineer and lawyer and practiced for nearly fifty years. He retired, turned his attention to creative writing, and authored many short stories of various genres. His stories have been published or accepted for publication in forty paying short story anthologies, magazines, audio books and pod-casts. A collection of some of his stories has also been accepted for publication.

WENDY N. WAGNER is the author of the horror novel *The Deer Kings* (forthcoming 2021, Journalstone), the SF thriller *An Oath of Dogs*, and two tie-in novels for the Pathfinder role-playing game. Her short fiction has appeared in nearly fifty venues, including *PseudoPod*, *Beneath Skies*, and anthologies like *Cthulhu Fhtagn!*. She is also a Hugo award-winning editor. A lifetime resident of the Pacific Northwest, you can keep up with her at winniewoohoo.com.

ACKNOWLEDGEMENTS

"The Nipples in Dad's Tool Box" © Ronald Kelly, from *The Essential Sick Stuff* (September 2020) Editor: Ken McKinley

"Going Green" © Christine Morgan, from *Visceral: Collected Flesh* (July 2020)

"Whiskey to the Wound" © Rachel Nussbaum, from *Brewtality: Extreme Horror Anthology* (October 2020) Editor: K. Trap Jones

"/thestrangethingwebecome" © Eric LaRocca, from *34 Orchard* (April 2020) Editor: Kristi Petersen Schoonover

"Hey, Valentine" © Amanda Cecelia Lang, from *The Other Stories* Podcast Vol 39 (February 2020)

"In Subspace, No One Can Hear You Scream" © Hailey Piper, from *Mycelia* Issue IV (December 2020) Editors: Simone Hutchinson, Pamela Clarke, and Richard Taylor

"The Pogonip Fog" © Sean Patrick Hazlett, from *Galaxy's Edge,* Issue #42 (January 2020) Editor: Mike Resnick

"Gunfire and Brimstone" © Alicia Hilton, from *Vastarien: Volume 3, Issue 2* (December 2020) Editors: Matt Cardin, Jon Padgett and Michael Cisco

"The Happiest Man in the World" © Matthew V. Brockmeyer, from *Nest of Salt* (November 2020)

"Synaesthete" © Melanie Harding-Shaw, from *Black Dogs, Black Tales* (May 2020) Editors: Tabatha Wood and Cassie Hart

www.ingramcontent.com/pod-product-compliance
Lightning Source LLC
Chambersburg PA
CBHW070726280626
47159CB00023B/2774